THE LOST THUMB

By Orla Owen

2019
Lavender Publishing

LAVENDER PUBLISHING

The Lost Thumb
By Orla Owen

Produced and published in 2019
by Lavender Publishing

ISBN 978-1-9160366-0-4
eISBN 978-1-9160366-1-1

Typeset in Charter 11pt by Blot Publishing
www.blot.co.uk

www.orlaowen.com

For Jenny Owen.
We miss you.

The Thumb

Mother tells people Luella and I are identical twins but you can tell us apart. I'm missing the top of my left thumb.

I used to love sucking that thumb. Mother told me to stop, lectured me on the perils of thumb sucking: your teeth will stick out; your thumb will shrink; you'll need braces for the rest of your life; you will die, everyone knows thumb sucking gives people diseases meaning you young lady will one day prematurely die because you thought you knew better than to listen to me, your medically trained mother.

When I was six, after a particularly long and angry rant against my greatest comfort, I went to bed tearful and sad, slightly comforted by the hot chocolate she'd offered with a rare apology, "I might have gone on at you tonight. The ward was busy, and you exhaust me."

I woke up to beige plasters where the top of my thumb used to be, a spot of blood growing in circumference where I'd tried to suck it.

"Drink this. It'll ease the ache." She was standing by the bed, holding out another hot chocolate. "The pain'll soon go."

"But—"

"No need to cause a fuss now. Don't be a baby."

She left the room with the empty cup. Luella said my name but all I wanted to do was sleep. When I tried to tell her that, I couldn't make my lips open wide enough to reply.

~

Ten days after the awful awakening, Mother had a parcel for her sister that needed to be sent that very day. She decided I was in need of fresh air so was to walk with her and Luella to the post office, my first excursion since the accident.

As we trooped down the road I wondered what our aunt looked like. Mother said she was similar to a witch, likely to frighten young girls, with no time at all for children in her life and as she'd never wanted to meet us, we were better off not knowing her. I'd pieced together her picture: wild, black knotted hair, blood red lips, pale skin and an evil laugh that resonated through her house if she heard we were suffering from a fever or had fallen on gravel, grit painfully embedded in her nieces bloodied knees.

Marjorie, the storekeeper and postmistress, was stacking a shelf with tins of Del Monte canned sweet peas. When she stood up to serve us, her eyes locked on my hand.

"The door," snapped Mother. "She shut it in the front door, silly girl. There's a blood stain on the porch if you want to see it."

Marjorie laughed even though the twist in her lips made it look like she'd been about to cry.

"Oh you poor dear. That must have hurt so much. Have a candy cane to ease the pain."

I checked with Mother. She gave her approval with a quick flick of her chin then winced as I licked the yellow and red streaks all wrapped around each other. As I sucked, the sugar glazed my teeth and tongue. I licked and sucked, faster and harder, desperate for the flavours to spread through me. Luella watched, a blank stare hiding the envy I knew was behind her eyes; the thought of sharing it with her made me bite down so hard that the crack of the candy splitting made both adults turn to stare. A sharp edge scraped the roof of my mouth but I didn't mind, it was worth the pain. As I crunched the offending pieces, Mother's eyes narrowed, focusing on my mouth.

"You'd better give us some of that strong toothpaste to counter the effects of the sugar rotting the enamel far, far away." Marjorie sighed as she pushed the ladder down the rack and climbed up to reach the third from top shelf. "And some baking soda, mustn't forget to mix in baking soda."

Marjorie glided to the opposite end of the wall. The speed thrilled me and as the purchases were paid for I wished I could have a go, feeling the breeze in my hair. Mother motioned for us to leave the shop. As soon as my feet touched the pavement, she grabbed the remaining candy and threw it in the road.

"Bad enough having thumb ache without toothache too."

Marching home, her cotton dress began to cling to her damp back, the pale blue flowers turning sapphire on being watered. When we passed the pink cacti in Mrs Franklin's garden I imagined ripping them open to get at the water inside and when our house was in sight, I upped my pace at the thought of a glass of tap water. We climbed the steps to the porch. Mother stopped and stared at the spotless tiles.

"Wait here."

She came back tapping a sharp, jagged edged kitchen knife against her thigh, the one she used for gutting fish. Luella gripped my wrist.

"It's not for you, fool." And Mother sliced her own finger, squeezing the wound as she shook her hand so the blood sprinkled over the terracotta. "That should soak in nicely, our secret stain."

The Night

"I have to go away for the night, leaving you here, without me. I'm not happy about it but needs must."

Not happy.

Not out of love and worry like most mothers feel, more a distrust of what an evening's freedom might offer her two fifteen year old slowpokes.

Once her taxi to the bus station had passed out of sight, Luella and I ran back into the house and sat on separate sofas, unsure of what to do. We'd never been left alone with no barking reprimand from the kitchen, no need to monitor Mother's footsteps so we knew exactly where in the house she was. For ten whole minutes we sat in silence apart from the tick, ticking of the clock.

"This is nonsense."

"Shush," I whispered, thinking Mother would hear. We burst out laughing. We laughed loudly and freely. Luella stood on the sofa and whooped for joy.

"Not back until tomorrow. Can you believe it? We should be having fun," she hollered. "The most adventurous night of our lives!"

She jumped onto the floor and ran into the kitchen. As I plumped the two cushions she'd disturbed, a door slammed and Luella returned, carrying a dusty, green bottle.

"No," I said.

"Yes."

"But—"

"Father would have wanted us to live a little, like he did." She prised the cork out of the glass neck and drank from its cobweb coated mouth.

"This life is to be lived!" Luella raised the bottle, saluting the solitary photo on the mantelpiece. "Not as Mother does, not as Father did, but as *we* see fit. Two years from now we'll leave this house, you and I. We'll get jobs and pay rent on an apartment with two, three, or four rooms. Just think of all those rooms Lara. And tonight we're alone so come on, Mother's away which means we can play."

She poured some of the rosewood liquid into a glass and handed it to me. I tentatively sipped. It wasn't too bad, a slight burn on swallowing then warming on my throat and stomach, not as nice as cola, which we'd tasted once, at Sally Spelling's eighth birthday party. After a long walk to the stuffy hall Mother had left us at the door, preferring not to come inside and idly chit chat with the other mothers, and as we'd entered the room Mrs Spelling told us to help ourselves to drinks. Pretty cups covered in pink, purple and blue flowers lined the table, all with brown liquid inside them. We hesitated when we saw they weren't filled with water then our dry tongues got the better of us and we each picked one up. My cup was mainly purple, Luella's mainly pink. We held them like the most precious treasure, the prettiest thing we'd ever touched. The bubbles made us splutter and sneeze, the taste being so strong and unfamiliar.

"Enjoying those girls?" Sally's mother enquired, smiling whilst breezing past, waving to another mother, heels clicking on the wood.

"Yes thank you Mrs Spelling."

She didn't hear us, she'd already moved on. We didn't like the drink much but having been brought up not to be wasters, drained every last drop, then still thirsty we had another and another. And it turned out to be the most exciting day of our lives. All the mothers who stayed whispered they'd never heard us chatter so much, join in the games or laugh, yes laugh, did you see them they actually laughed! Until twenty minutes before the end of the party when we slumped in a corner feeling tired and fuzzy, brains still whizzing but mouths and limbs still. Mrs Spelling leant down, all concerned.

"Was it the sugar girls? In the cola? Are you intolerant to the cola?" The c word made our pupils enlarge and torsos shrink in.

"Oh Mrs Spelling," Luella whispered, "under no circumstances, under absolutely no circumstances are we allowed such a dangerous drink full of chemicals and nasty addictions. If Mother—"

Mrs Spelling laughed

"She mustn't find out," I blurted. "Please."

Straightening her face, she placed her head conspiratorially between ours.

"Don't worry. She won't. If you don't tell her and I don't tell her, well then she'll never know. Simple."

We considered her offer, having never told such a big lie to Mother before. She'd said if we ever did she'd know immediately and our punishment would be more severe than any we'd had so far.

"Deal," said Luella. "Consider us your lying mates."

The three of us nodded solemnly in agreement one second before Mother arrived.

Clouds had united making the walk home cooler. Mother questioned us on the food and behaviour of classmates, told us she disapproved of the colour of Mrs Spelling's hair, a rather wonderful array of golds and reds that shone in the sun. Whores gold, Mother called it. I liked that, a beautiful whores gold. Luella told her we drank water from a tap in the kitchen and that we had to help ourselves as Sally's mother was flitting here, there and everywhere, not the best host, not like Mother would be. Droplets of sweat formed on our brows as we waited for her to shriek, LIARS. Instead, she frowned in case we were sickening for something, perspiring in the cooler evening, and pushed us up the steps to the porch muttering, "too many fairy cakes no doubt, too many fancy flipping fairy cakes. That's the last party you go to. First and last. You're done."

~

Luella had finished three quarters of the wine. Laughing gleefully she put her hand down the front of her blue dress and plucked a piece of paper from her bosom.

"Look what I found," she chanted, waving round a ten dollar note. "Enough to take us dancing. Have you ever wanted to go dancing la la la la Lara?"

Christ.

"Where did you find that? Put it back wherever you got it. It's not ours. I—"

"What? Back in the gutter? Are you crazy? No way! A lady needs her spending money." She glowered at me when

I didn't laugh at her wink and when the doorbell chimed, gasped before proclaiming, "I wasn't sure they'd come." She smoothed her hair and licked her grinning lips.

"Who? Who weren't you sure would come?"

But Luella was already opening the door where in walked two boys from school. I vaguely recognised their faces. They were a bit pimply, a bit hairy above the lip. One was smiling broadly while the other looked round the room suspiciously.

"At last! The famous twinny twin twins. How wonderful it is to be here. Lara, let me introduce myself. I'm Georgey and this is Porgey.' He laughed uproariously. Luella joined in as she followed his footsteps. "Oh my, what am I like? I'm not on stage now. A pity perhaps; the night is young and I'm already on such fine form. Lara darling, I'm Sylvester and this is Daviid, with two 'I's hey Daviid? We mustn't forget the two 'I's, the irony being…" He paused to make sure we were all paying attention. "That in his head he only has one!" Luella looked flabbergasted before again joining in with his laughter. I stared at Daviid's face but he was looking at the floor so I turned away, ashamed at my rudeness.

"What's this? Started the fun without us?" He turned the dirty bottle in his hand with a mixture of pleasure and disgust.

"I'll get you a glass."

As Luella ran into the kitchen, Sylvester wiped the rim with one of Mother's good cushions and drank so fast that by the time Luella returned with the glasses, there was nothing to pour in them.

"Sorry darling. Now, where can I clean my hands?" And he wiped them on Luella, right down her front, feeling her body through the thin, navy cotton. She gasped. I waited for her to slap him and show him the door. "Don't tell me that's the only bottle?"

I glared harder at Luella.

"As if! We've got loads more," she boasted, strutting out of the room. I hurried after her but the boys slipped in front of me as hips wiggling, she led them to the basement door. When she started walking down the steps I pushed myself in front of Sylvester, and when she raised her hand to pick a bottle, I took hold of her wrist and squeezed it. She pursed her lips and clamped her fingers round the rim. I squeezed harder. Our eyes locked.

"Well hello treasure trove. Looky looky here. This night could be better than I thought Daviid." Without any hesitation he grabbed two bottles and disappeared up the stairs. Daviid smiled for the first time, grabbed another two and scurried after him. I loosened my grip on Luella's wrist as she loosened hers on the bottle. Before I could reason with her, she pushed past me and raced up the stairs shouting back, "Live a little Lara. Please. Up, up, up." The pitch of her voice getting higher as she leapt to the top.

I floundered, not understanding why she'd invited those boys. How she could think it was fun? When a scream escaped from the living room, I sprinted out of the basement to find Luella sprawled ridiculously on the sofa, laughing like she was having the time of her life. I would have slapped her if the boys weren't there; this wasn't how our first night alone was meant to be.

Sylvester smirked at me whilst Daviid kept looking down, drinking the wine so quickly he might as well have glued his lips to the bottle. Mouseling, I wanted to shout, take your cat away from here. But I didn't. Shouting was not in my nature; Mother had told me so. Instead, I clenched my fists and stood by the fireplace, my head in line with the picture of father. I wondered if he was watching with me, ashamed of his daughter, wishing he could avert his eyes from her crazed behaviour.

Luella and Sylvester were rapidly emptying the dark liquid into their mouths. Rivulets ran down their chins where their greed had made them miss. I felt ashamed watching Sylvester stroke Luella's thigh. I felt funny in my middle seeing his hand slip under her dress.

"Luella?"

She smiled at me before taking his hand and leading him into the kitchen. I remained standing whilst Daviid kept on drinking. From the kitchen I could hear moaning sounds. I hoped she was alright, not feeling sick, and I kept nearly going to check but when I moved my foot some invisible cowardice held me by the grate.

"Luella?" I whispered. The living room was too quiet. Daviid was staring mournfully into a now empty bottle. I tried to work out which eye was his good one and which the glass one when there was an almighty crashing sound like all the saucepans hitting the floor.

"Freak," screamed Sylvester.

Luella was laughing. She shouted back at him.

"Don't be so pathetic. What gives? Can't stand the sight of blood?"

I bolted.

"Hey twin," Luella slurred. "Look. We're the same again." She held up her right arm which was covered in dark, sticky blood.

I picked the frying pan off the floor, stepping threateningly towards Sylvester. "What have you done to her?"

"Me?" he cried "Me?! I should have listened. They were right. You're bloody crazy." He was hysterical, red in the face with bulging veins throbbing in his neck. Tears flowed down his flushed cheeks. "She did it to herself. How could you do that?" He tugged manically at his jeans zipper and his face filled with horror as he pulled something from his pocket and with a howl threw it on the floor and ran from the room.

"We're out of here Daviid, now!"

Stumbling down the front path, he tried to wipe his soiled hands on the grass. Daviid with two iis followed behind not quite running straight, not knowing what was going on, giggling nervously with a half full bottle of Father's wine in his hand. Luella remained on her side, on the floor. I carefully picked up her wounded arm; she was missing the top of her right thumb.

"What have you done you idiot?"

I knew I needed to stop the bleeding but didn't know how so ran to the bookshelves and pulled down Mother's medical dictionary. As I flicked through the pages none of the words made sense and when I got to thumb it told me how to prick an abscess or splint a broken bone but nothing about sewing a thumb back on, nothing about closing such a big wound, nothing about stopping the bleeding. I searched for stitches but as I reached that page I pulled too hard and the blood from my hands stuck to the paper, ripping through the text before I could read it. Mother would go mad at me destroying her property. I needed to call her but she hadn't left a number. We needed another nurse. We needed the hospital. I put the book back and ran into the kitchen. Luella was as grey as the linoleum floor.

"My hand hurts," she slurred.

"I know. Don't worry. It'll be fine, we'll get it fixed. It won't hurt for long." I ran back to the hall and picked up the telephone but I'd never made a call before. We weren't allowed, were not to be trusted. I'd seen other people do it though. I'd seen them look up numbers in the phone book in the booths on the street, so I opened the drawer of the table and pulled out ours. I found H for hospital but blood smeared over the thin paper so I tried dialing the numbers I could see but the voice of a lady kept saying, "Sorry. You have dialed an incorrect number. Please try again." So I did try again and I got it wrong again. I heard the doorbell. As I tried to control my anger it rang a second and a third time. When I opened it, Marjorie was there, her son Sean standing behind her, staring at the old blood stain on the porch.

"My God. What's happened?" She stormed in. "What's she—"

"It's Luella, she's hurt her hand."

"Where? Where is she?"

I pointed to the sleepy body.

"Have you called an ambulance?" I shook my head. "Sean, call an ambulance. Now. Luella, can you hear me? Wake up honey. Luella, look at me darling."

Sean grabbed the phone where I'd dropped it and dialed the number I hadn't known. As we waited for the ambulance, Marjorie stroked Luella's hair and Sean mopped up some of the blood.

"Shit." He pointed to the floor, by the fridge. Vomit went over my feet.

"Put it in ice. Wrap it up in a towel."

"But—"

"No arguing Sean. Please."

She seemed to know exactly what to do; I wondered if she'd ever trained to be a nurse, like Mother.

When the ambulance men arrived Marjorie whispered to one of them before they stretchered Luella out. The red of the blanket was brighter and more lurid than her blood. If they'd tried to make it match, they'd got it wrong; that much blood was a deep dark red, much heavier looking, thicker in texture than I thought it would be.

"Why don't you get cleaned up? I can go with your sister, and you follow on with Sean."

"No thank you. We stay together." I thought of Mother returning to the mess. "If you wouldn't mind starting to clean the kitchen?" I tried to smile sincerely with thanks.

"Where is your mother, honey?"

"At a friend's."

"You're sure? She's not here? You can tell me."

"She's at a friend's, due back tomorrow."

"What's the number? I'll call her."

"She didn't leave one."

"She must have."

"Why?"

"I— never mind."

The Hospital

"You should get some rest. She'll be asleep all night, maybe experiencing a bit of sickness but nothing serious. If you go home, you'll be of more use to her tomorrow."

The doctor put his fingers under his nose as he glanced at my stained legs. The hem of my dress was splattered with dried blood and regurgitated wine, hard to tell which was which.

"No thank you. I want to be here in case she wakes up."

I fell asleep in the gentle glow of the bedside lighting. And was woken by the harsh glare of the overhead, fluorescent tubing.

"Wake up. Now!"

"Moth–"

"We'll talk later."

A doctor was scuttling behind, trying to persuade her to let Luella stay.

"She should be watched for at least another night. As well as the anesthetic there's the blood loss and—"

"You think I don't know that?" She cut him short, the same way she did everyone she met. Then she put on her nice voice. "I've seventeen years' experience working as a senior nurse so can look after her just fine, and there's a much smaller chance of infection at home, don't you think?"

She drew breath to argue more but he gave in without trying.

"I'll write a prescription for her painkillers." And off he ran to his next emergency.

Mother exhaled slowly then busied herself with pulling tubes roughly from Luella's right hand. Little globules of blood popped up where each needle had been inserted; I wished the doctor was there to see his patient wince in her sleep.

"Should you be doing that? I–"

"Shut your mouth," she hissed. Tears welled up in my eyes, three words and I crumbled. I put my hand on Luella's good arm, pathetically trying to draw strength from the sickly sister. Her chin tilted to the right then left, her eyes opened and closed before staying open when Mother entered her line of vision. Luella showed no fear. She turned to me but when I smiled at her there was no joyous recognition, just a dull stare the same as she'd given Mother. The doctor came back in the room and handed Mother a piece of green paper. She made a show of putting it in her pocket. "Thank you so much, for every-thing. So efficient."

He took my hand from Luella's arm and gently removed her drip. "Now young lady, I'm going to be seeing you very soon. You come back in three days time and we'll see how well you're healing."

She half smiled and, following the pressure of Mother's hand on her shoulder, started to sit up.

"I'm sure you've sicker people to heal Doctor. Off you go, and don't you worry, I'll look after her now."

I willed him to stay and for one brief moment thought he'd sensed things weren't right but then a nurse called his name and he scarpered. As Luella leant forward she was sick all down herself.

"A reaction to the anesthetic, that's all. It's nothing to worry about."

Unfazed by the vomit, Mother cleaved off Luella's hospital gown. I tried to break the tension by asking after her night away, was it fun, how was her friend, did she have a nice supper.

"You'd better keep it zipped young lady, considering the trouble you're in."

~

When we reached home, Marjorie's car was parked outside and the front door was ajar.

"What the hell?" Mother kicked it open.

On the table in the hallway sat a silver vase that wasn't ours, full of yellow flowers, small petals, bright, strong, giving off a sweet perfume that failed to cover the smell of the blood that had seeped between the cracks where the kitchen cupboards met the flooring. Sunshine from the open door reflected on the vase throwing dots of light over the dark, wooden paneled walls, brightening the gloomy passageway. Marjorie held onto the yellow formica table in the kitchen as she rose from kneeling to standing.

"Out so soon? That's good. I thought they'd keep you—"

"I believe I'm supposed to be grateful for your help."

"You don't have to be."

She held Mother's eye contact. Sean stepped from behind the kitchen door and broke the silence with a nervous, "Does it hurt?"

Luella was staring at the dancing lights. When Mother pushed two fingers just below her shoulders she sloped towards the stairs, climbed them slowly and disappeared across the top landing. Redness seeped over my cheeks at the shame of our drama becoming common knowledge.

"We should go now. I can pop by tomorrow with—"

"There's no need to trouble yourself."

"It's no trouble at all. I'd be delighted to—"

"No. Thank you but really, you've done more than enough already," Mother cheerfully warned her unwanted helpers before shutting the door firmly behind them. As they walked down the path I saw Marjorie link her arm through her son's and felt a pang of something, I wasn't sure what. Was it nice to have that contact, to not back away from that touch?

Mother flicked her chin towards the stairs. She climbed them one step behind me and when we got to the landing stopped at the first door on her right and, taking a key from her skirt pocket, unlocked it. A vein on the left hand side of my neck began to spasm as we stepped inside.

When she pulled back the dark green velvet curtains, years of dust, grateful at being disturbed, waltzed frivolously in the sunlight. Silver and gold threads spun extravagantly through the bedspread gleamed and sparkled, calling the dust to them. And there was colour. Not various shades of brown like in the rest of the house but deep red cushions sitting on two forest green armchairs that sat facing each other, and silver fleur de lys feet beneath a white wardrobe that was resting on the pale wooden floor. Was this once their room? Did our parents sit in the armchairs, smile at each other and gaze at the leaves on the pepper tree?

"You'll be in here from now on." She tutted impatiently at my silence. "I can't have you sharing with your wayward sister; she needs special care. I always wondered if you were different and this has proved it, so time for a change."

"We're not different, we're the same. We—"

"Pah," she spat. "This is what's happening and I'll have no more moaning. We'll empty it and clean it and you'll sleep in here from this evening." Luella and I had been together since floating in the womb. Not a night had gone by where I hadn't heard her gentle breath, the whispered ramblings of her dreams. Mother was already bundling up the bedding.

~

Three hours later the room was scrubbed and virtually bare – just the bed and the wardrobe and one bedside cabinet remained. The green chairs with their comfortable cushions had been dragged away to the living room and the fancy bedding all boxed up.

"Please may I get a drink of water?"

She didn't look up from the spot by the window where she was kneeling, just leant further back on her heels, staring at the floor.

"Mother? Please—"

"Yes. I said yes already. Christ."

"And Luella?" I whispered, staying very still, not wanting movement to negate her decision.

"Alright then," she sighed, frown lines softer. I followed her to Luella's bedroom door where she took another key from her pocket. A quick twist pushed it open. Luella was lying in bed, staring at the ceiling. She didn't turn to look at us.

"Get up," Mother barked. I wanted to rush to my sister and hold her hand as she had mine, aged six, but the anger emanating from Mother stopped me. "Now," she hissed, pinching the bandaged hand.

Luella yelped. Her eyes met mine and I willed comfort to reach her. She summoned the strength to sit then stand, stepping slowly down the stairs and into the kitchen. Mother filled three glasses with water from the kitchen tap.

"Perhaps Luella could have a hot chocolate?" I asked.

"No. Nice try but no. A deviant deserves no release from their pain. Let her think on her mistakes. I know I shall. Luella, go back to your room and stay there until I say you can leave. I'll change your dressings when necessary and we'll speak no more of this debacle, I'm warning you, the both of you. No more, you hear me?"

She didn't mention the new sleeping arrangements. Would Luella be waiting for me to go to bed next to her, waiting for me to share her pain?

"You can fetch your things," she said.

Which wouldn't take long. We didn't own delicate trinkets like I imagined Sally Spelling did; no pretty pink boxes, no pale grey pearls, no brightly illustrated books to liven our minds.

Mother stood in the doorway as I gathered my clothes. I longed to lie with Luella, spoon myself around her so there was no air between us, my left arm over hers, gently holding her damaged hand, letting her know things would get better. But as Mother watched, Luella didn't move, showing only her back as if willing us to leave. Into the silence burst the ringing of the telephone; Mother hesitated before rushing to answer it. I took my chance, lying down on the bed.

"You'll be alright. We'll be alright. Two years from now we'll leave here and rent an apartment with two rooms." One of her fingers twitched and I leant over her to wipe away the tears. "We'll be alright, you and I." I kissed her hair. "You sleep well tonight, you hear? Enjoy the peace, no noisy tossing and turning from your annoying sister."

"Who's she talking to?" she whispered, but Mother's footsteps were now tapping up the stairs.

I sped out of the room and breezed past her before she had time to comment on what had taken me so long and as I hung the dresses in my new wardrobe, I could feel her eyes boring into my back but refused to turn round, no matter how much she was willing me to.

~

Students in school talked as if Sunday was their dull day. I tried to picture how it differed from their Saturday because ours didn't: same chores, same homework, same food, same company.

"You're not to disturb your sister. And you can do her chores today seeing as you're so worried about her."

I washed, dried, put away the dishes and went into the garden to weed beds two, four, six and seven. Six and seven were usually Luella's. Mother was in charge of one, three, five and eight. When we were younger, she'd tell us she had to work twice as hard to do twice as many beds but as we got older we cottoned on that hers were much smaller.

The sun shone on the back of my neck, soothing the taut muscles. As I dug, I planned. I'd distract Mother, tell her I saw a boy running across the front lawn and when she was searching for him I'd sneak in to see Luella and assure her that the minute we woke up on the morning of our eighteenth birthday, we'd break free. A mean scream broke my trance. My heart bumped over three beats as the sun disappeared behind a cloud, scared away by the furiousness in the air. I took the garden steps in two leaps, flying through the back door into a kitchen that was empty, a broken glass shattered in the sink. Shouts led me to Luella's room where limbs were so entangled it was hard to tell which foot belonged to whom. Luella's bandaged hand appeared; she wasn't fighting back. Mother was on top of her, slapping and punching. As I pulled her off she spat, "Fool. You stupid fool. No child of mine!"

When I let go she lunged back at Luella, aiming a kick at her stomach. I grabbed the hem of her brown dress and we both fell into the dresser. Warm blood trickled down my head; Mother had a gash across her eyebrow but that didn't stop her ranting.

"You think you're clever eh? All grown up now? What, he said you were pretty?"

She waved her hand in the air. Luella curled her knees to her chest, snot dripping onto her chin.

"What's happened?" Over here, look at me.

"What's happened? God, but you're ignorant. Your sister, your oh-so stupid sister, she— See?" She held out some material. "Stuffed behind the cooker as if I wouldn't find them."

She started laughing. Luella moved her hands over her ears. Mucus ran into her mouth as she opened and shut it, her lips like the fish that were trapped in the tank in the corridor at school.

"Humming won't help, damn you." I got between them. Mother and I fell to the floor. She clawed over me until her face was an inch from Luella's. "If you're pregnant, I'll pull that bastard from your womb in this very room and when I'm done I'll pickle it in a jar and it can stay on the mantelpiece as a reminder of what a mistake you are."

Luella's eyes shut as Mother threw the pants at her head before sneering at both of us and backing out of the room. My head hurt, the cut stung when I touched it. Luella winced as I approached her.

"Hey." I stroked her hair as I gently wiped her nose. I held her loosely, trying not to add to the pain where bruises were appearing on her arms and legs. I lay her on the bed and covered her with blankets right up to her chin. Her thumb dressing was seeping blood. I should call the doctor. Or Marjorie. Or no-one. It was all so shameful. I lay beside her. Her breathing steadied, and when dusk approached, the bedroom door slowly opened. Mother walked round to Luella's side.

"I was worried about what would become of you, what others would think. You make me so angry, you know that? Tomorrow, tomorrow we start again and tonight I'll see to your soreness. You're to go, Lara." Luella squirmed closer into me. Mother walked round to my side of the bed. "I said go. Your sister needs her rest." I crossed my ankles, the bones hurting where they pinged against each other. "She needs immediate rest. We all do." I tensed at her hardening tone and with a feeble squeeze of my hand Luella let me know I should leave. There was a sharp intake of breath behind me. Before Mother had time to say more I stood up and her exhalation wafted over my face as I passed her, warm considering the coldness of its creator.

The School

As I walked through the school gates I raised my chin higher, ready to defy any taunts. The gardener was pruning some bushes by the entrance, the skin on his knuckles as crinkled as the twigs by his feet. He nodded at me, not a sharp nod like Mother's, instead it was a slow, gentle one. Two girls whispered. Sideways glances and outright stares told me Sylvester and Daviid had spread their story. Luella and I were already sneered at, our clothes bleak compared to the bright fuchsias, emerald greens and canary yellow's the others paraded about in, strutting through the grounds like peacocks, all superior and confident, ever on show. We were meagre field mice in comparison, scampering from lesson to lesson then home again. And now it would be worse, and I was facing it alone.

"Hello twin." He blocked my route to the arched doors at the entrance of the red brick building. "Not going to ask how I am, if I'm recovered from your perverted madhouse?" There was a snigger from one of his flock that had gathered round us. I swallowed the nausea. "Speak to me freakoid," he commanded. "Don't you know it's rude not to reply? Tell us all how your mentalist sister is. Is she not coming to school today? What? Has she got a sore thumb?"

Bile rose and porridge spewed from my mouth over his chin and down his maroon blazer. Speckled dots stained his white leather loafers. A loud ooh sounded from the crowd. A collective urgh followed that. Time went slow-mo. Sylvester wiped his chin with the back of his hand, flicking the excess on the ground before spreading his arms out, palms towards the sky. He raised his head to the heavens then back at me as he aimed his fist at my face. I didn't flinch. If Luella could take a beating then so could I, but as the world sped up the wrist was grabbed and Sylvester stumbled backwards.

"Not on my grounds." The gardener kept hold of Sylvester's arm and squeezed. "Go home. Clean yourself up." I couldn't see Mr Jonas's eyes beneath his hat but next thing Sylvester shrugged his arm free and stormed off. "Everyone, shoo. Go on or you'll be late." He sounded younger than he looked and spoke with the authority of a teacher, making the crowd disperse. I closed my eyes, buttoning down my desire to scream.

"Are you alright?"

I opened them to a familiar voice; Mr Jonas's place had been taken by Sean.

"Fine," I replied, holding back the tears, making them run down my throat instead of my cheeks.

"Are you sure? I thought you'd be staying at home today. I—"

"I'm fine. Thank you." I held my books to my chest.

"What happened to your head?"

As I hurried past, I pretended not to have heard him.

~

English was usually my favourite subject but the teacher's

25

voice warbled over my ears as the eyes of the class bored into me from all sides. They couldn't hurt me; I wouldn't let them. And what they thought didn't matter because I didn't need them, just my family, not even family, just Luella. Not Mother. I didn't need her.

"Something to share?"

"Miss?"

"Did you want to say something Lara?"

"No Miss."

"You're bleeding." I frowned, touching the sterile strips on my forehead. They felt dry. "Your hand."

The front of my good thumb was stained with blood from where I'd gnawed at the sides of the nail. I tasted metal as I licked my lips and sucked the blood off the skin to *urgh* and *gross* and *freak*, the whole class voicing their disgust. I wouldn't accept being called that word again.

"Lara! Where do you think you're—"

"I'm not well."

"Whoop whoop," was shouted from the back of the room and more cat calls followed but I was already out of the door and halfway down the empty hall. The path through the main garden was empty. I breathed in the scent of the lavender and as it lined my lungs Mr Jonas appeared.

"Sorry, I didn't meant to startle you." He let go of the wheelbarrow he was pushing. I headed to the gates. "Are you—"

"I've got an appointment. Sorry. I need to go."

Even though I could feel him watching me, I didn't stop or turn around. My walk turned into a run. I sprinted. My lungs hurt but I kept running, no matter how unlady-like, how unnecessary, no matter what a fool Mother said it made me look. I ran recklessly over the road, one quick glance behind and in front then whoosh, over I went. At the corner, by the bank, a car hooted as it just missed hitting me. I screamed out of fright but ran on, away from home, out of town, towards the lake. We weren't allowed to go to the lake. It was where idiots congregated to waste their meaningless lives. Yet I'd seen a postcard in Marjorie's store and it looked beautiful, green water as smooth as glass with tall trees as a surround. My pace slowed as the hill steepened. My calves tightened. My lungs hurt. But I reached the top and it was worth it, the view below me was just like the photo.

Clouds parted, letting an intense heat hit my face. Come on the blue sky. An airplane flew over the lake, its trail like a pen that was colouring clouds into the picture. One day I would get on an airplane and fly a thousand miles away. When it was out of sight, I walked down to the water, sweat gathering on my face, back and belly. As I licked my lips I tasted blood and when I wiped at them with my hand, dried red flecks stuck to the palm. I rubbed them on my dress and they fluttered to the ground, becoming lost against the pale, brown dirt.

At the shore I untied my shoelaces, slipped off my shoes and placed them neatly under a tree. My feet were hot and sweaty and smelly. I unrolled my socks and tucked them into the right shoe then, dress still on, stepped into the lake.

The mud felt gooey and cold on my soles but the water was warmer than I'd thought it would be. I let it ensconce my bare feet, calves, thighs; it tingled and tickled my waist. My red dress floated up, material turned maroon by the water. When I pushed it down bits of the material rose around my hands and I tried unsuccessfully to push them down again. But no-one was there, no-one was watching, no need to be shy. I raised my arms and roared to let go of the *I'm fines* I'd stored over the years. I cried out again and again and again, spinning in the water, splashing it up in the air, cupping it over my head. I threw myself back into the lake, submerging my whole body, and when I couldn't hold my breath any longer I jumped up, gasping for air. I jumped and ducked, floated and sank until I was empty, then crouched down, still, simply letting my hands float on the water. The blood had gone, the thumb was clean. My right hand created five ripples, my left hand four. Luella was wrong. We weren't the same again, her pattern would be the opposite.

~

"I'm home," I called as I ran up the stairs.

Mother ran after me, knocking sharply on the bathroom door, twisting its pewter handle.

"Why's it locked?"

"I'm pissing."

"Don't be crude. And you're not to lock it. The minute you've finished, you're downstairs for water."

I sighed with relief as her footsteps went away and turned my attention to tidying myself up. The dress had dried on the walk but a fine beige dust was stuck to it and my skin. I rubbed off as much as I could, aware she'd be counting the seconds until I appeared. As I left the bathroom I checked Luella's door, locked. I mumbled her name but there was no answer.

"Lara!"

"Coming."

She watched my every move. I tried not to squirm even though it felt as if my guilt was breaking through any dust I'd missed, shouting out my badness. I sipped the water the same as I always did. She rubbed a finger down my left arm.

"I fell." The reply was too quick. She scraped her nails roughly down my other one.

"That's a lot of dust for a fall."

"Isn't it?"

She frowned as she examined my face then breathed out noisily, like a horse snorting at its annoying rider.

"I've enough to think about without you stumbling around like a simpleton. You're lucky you didn't tear your dress. Go and do your homework while I get dinner ready." I didn't move. "Well?"

"What about Luella?"

"She's resting."

"Can I—"

"Maybe later, if you don't annoy me."

Maybe was a positive; best not push it into a no with further questions. I left the room to pretend to do homework I hadn't brought back with me.

I had to make sure Mother didn't find out I'd skipped school, had to make sure they didn't get hold of her. I reckoned they'd write which meant I'd need to intercept the letter. Perhaps they'd send it home with me. No. They weren't stupid, no letter would ever get to a student's parents. It would come by post, which made the challenge much harder. A clatter from the kitchen disturbed my plotting. I looked at the empty table and hurriedly got out some books from my bag. History and Literacy were safe, ongoing topics to be handed in on Wednesday and already completed, but Maths was different. I'd missed the lesson that afternoon and Miss Simpson always gave homework to be handed in the next day. I moved my fingers to my mouth and started to rip off the skin from the smallest nail.

The doorbell rang.

Which was wrong.

We never had visitors.

I held my breath hoping they'd go away but the bell was stubbornly pushed again. Mother stormed into the hall, wiping her hands on her apron, and as she opened the door sunshine flew over the floor, desperately trying to push some light in the house. I heard a man's voice.

"Lara. Come here."

I stayed at the table. She frowned and clicked her fingers. I got up and walked towards her, unable to believe my bad luck, that the school was already there to tell on me when I hadn't worked out my story yet. My heart pummeled too hard trying to escape through my rib bones, same as I wished I could burst through the walls. Mother's lips twitched as I stood beside her.

"Your maths homework. You left it in class."

Sean's fake smile warned me not to question what he was doing. I looked at his feet, his pumps were whiter than my teeth. Mother grinned at my discomfort then turned her attention back to him.

"Thank you so much. It's good to see that someone uses their brain. We won't keep you. Have a lovely evening." She took the book from him and shut the door in his face. "Get on with it then you idiot." She pushed it into my hands and as I went back to the table, a tummy tickle pushed a smile onto my lips. That was nice of him, going out of his way, doing that for me.

We ate beef, carrot and potato with a little gravy for the meat. There was no dessert as that would rot our teeth. I chewed each mouthful ten times, tedious but necessary so as not to overwork the digestive system. And Luella wasn't mentioned. I missed her. I had to do her chores, had to wash, dry and put away while Mother sat in her chair embroidering a cushion cover with a picture of two cats, grey, proud, mean looking, ugly.

"My homework's finished." I counted to five. "Please may I see Luella?" The strength of Mother's silence pushed me into the wall. I felt like crying but couldn't let Luella down. "Just to say goodnight?" She lowered her tapestry. I wanted to run. "Please?"

"Shush would you." I waited, my shoulders pressed against the wood. "Two minutes. And don't say I'm not good to you." I started to climb the stairs. "The keys." She threw them on the floor near the sofa so I had to scramble to find them while she carried on with her sewing. Clutching them, I ran to Luella's room and fumbled with the lock before stumbling in. It was pitch black, the navy velvet curtains drawn even though it was still light out.

"Luella?" She didn't move. "Luella," I sat on the bed. "It's me." Her head twitched. I stroked her beautiful dark brown hair then leant over and saw she was crying. My tears were noisier, more out of control. Her hand reached up. "Sorry. That I haven't been here. I'm so sorry. I'll open the curtains."

"No," she whispered. "The light hurts. My head aches."

As my eyes adjusted I spotted new bruising on her hand that disappeared up and under her sleeve.

"Can I get you anything? Have you had dinner? What about some water? Is she giving you painkillers?"

"She says I need to feel the discomfort of my body's healing to appreciate its power."

"What? I—"

"Don't worry. I'm fine."

"You're not fine. I'm going to get us out of here. I—"

"Time's up," Mother barked. "Luella needs her rest."

The Fever

Miss Simpson raised an eyebrow as I handed in my homework.

"You weren't in class yesterday Lara."

"No Miss."

"Well?"

"I was poorly." She gestured impatiently for more details. I floundered. I'd never had a day off sick. Then Sara-Jane sauntered into the classroom laughing with Margaret and I remembered her favourite excuse.

"Ladies pains Miss," I said loudly. Guffawing erupted behind me and Miss Simpson blushed from the corners of her lips to the tip of her eyebrows. Shuffling the papers on her desk, she muttered 'fine' and motioned for me to sit down.

Sean smiled from the back of the room and I was about to smile back when Sara-Jane laughed and flicked her hair and winked at him. Of course the attention was for her not me. As Miss Simpson chalked some algebra on the board, I ran my fingers through my hair to try and look more like the other girls but it was no use, there was nothing to play with. I doodled furiously on my pad and when the lesson ended was the first out of the door.

At home time, on the way out of school, Sylvester leered at me, thrusting his hips so his groupies laughed and cheered as they anticipated my pain at the humiliation but they were fools because I didn't give a toss, until I saw Sean was watching them.

~

Mother had started stitching the cats' eyes with red thread.

"I've done my chores and homework. Please may I see Luella?" Pathetic tears sprang up; I blocked them from escaping by not blinking.

"Two minutes." I missed catching the keys so they slid under the table and I banged my head as I retrieved them, cursing my clumsiness as the key caught in the lock again, taking five seconds out of the one hundred and twenty I'd been given. I willed Luella to turn over, to recognise my smell, my footsteps, that I wasn't Mother, but she didn't even twitch. When I sat beside her she stayed still. As I placed my hand on her arm a murmur of pain slipped from her lips.

"Sorry. I'm so sorry. I've a plan, I promise. I'll follow the usual routine, keep Mother calm then—"

"What then?" She shook my hand off hers.

"Time's up," Mother snapped.

I wished she'd disappear, life would be so much easier.

~

"My chores are done."

"Good."

"Please may I see Luella?"

She carried on sewing. I stuck a finger nail into my hand so hard that the tip broke through the soft skin making a little blood ooze under the nail. I pressed my right foot on my left. It hurt but I kept on doing it, trying to stay focused on that pain rather than my fear. "Is she nearly better?"

"Speak up. I can't hear you."

"Is she nearly better?"

"See for yourself." She threw the keys hard and fast right at me. I winced as they hit my wrist then picked them off the floor.

The curtains were drawn, the light was off. I stroked her head.

"You're hot."

"It's warm."

"Not really. Do you want some water?"

"No."

"Are you eating? I—"

"Time's up!" There she was again, looming over us. "Go to bed Lara and don't you offer her water, the nurse in the house takes care of that."

As I undressed I wondered if other people my age felt so tired, so blue. They all seemed so full of energy and laughter compared to me, apart from Daviid, he'd been sad looking.

~

"Mother?"

"Damn it." She sucked the finger she'd pricked. I wished she'd fall into a deep forever sleep and she scowled at me as if sensing my hope. "God, you're so predictable; every evening the same. Do you not get bored?" She held out the keys. I hesitated. A pair of scissors was resting on the arm of the chair and she was holding a needle in her other hand. She smirked. "I thought you were in a hurry to see her?" I bit my lip not wanting to annoy her by giving an answer she already knew. She shook the keys impatiently. "For Christ's sake hurry up." She pushed them into my outstretched palm and returned to her needlework.

Luella was lying on her back, not her side, a good sign I reckoned.

"Good evening Missy and how are you today?"

"Sore."

"That's good. I mean, it's not good but that's the healing. It gets sorer as it gets better. Is the skin feeling tight? You'll be back at school before you know it, wishing you weren't." I couldn't see whether she believed me or not. "I'll open the curtains."

"No."

"It'll do you good," I cajoled. "A little light in the room."

"My head hurts."

"Have you eaten?"

"No."

"You've got to eat. It won't help your head if you've had no food. I'll sneak you some." As I spoke, I slyly pulled back a curtain letting sunlight flood in. "There we go. It's such a lovely evening." Her cheek was bruised, and her left hand various shades of purple and green.

"What happened?" My shin hit a clear container that was hanging down the side of the bed, half full of a brownish orange liquid. "What's that?"

Luella stared at her bedcover. "It's just for a little while."

I lifted the blanket to reveal a tube running from the bag under the bed sheet. Some liquid dripped into the sack.

"Luella?"

She wouldn't look at me.

"What do you think you're doing?" I dropped the blanket. Mother folded her arms, waiting for my answer.

"What have you done to her?"

"None of your business." She strode to the window and pulled the curtains shut. "Luella needs to rest. Scoot."

"But—"

"She had an infection, a fever that she was too weak to fight. The bag helps get rid of the poisons."

I didn't believe her. She may be a nurse but she was cold and cruel and mean.

"I said what... have... you... done?" In the pauses between the words I imagined bashing her face in.

"And I told... you... to... scoot. I've done what needed doing. And like I said, it's none of your business."

"Yes it is," my voice raised even though I knew it would rile her. "She's got a tube from the inside of her going to a bag on the outside and—"

"She let you down. She let us both down, going with a boy in this house."

"What do you mean? I don't—"

"She let a boy move on her, in her." Mother jumped forwards and thrust her hand between my legs, squeezing where they met.

"What are you doing?" I pushed her arm away.

"See? You're not a fool like her. You back away whereas she begged for more." Luella had tears streaming down her face as she looked at her hands, moving the fingertips to touch each other over and over, one two three four five four three two, one two three four five four three two, one two three four. "Don't look at her. You look at me. Don't you dare look at her." Mother gripped my chin, turning my head so I faced her.

"Stop it. Get off me."

"I'm your mother," she bellowed. "Where is my respect? You'll do as I say you damn freaks, the pair of you."

"Don't. Don't you dare call us that. We're not freaks. And if we are different it's because of you. You're the freak, not us."

Her shock at me speaking back at her gave me a slight head start but as I ran to the door she caught my neck and spun me round before pulling me from the room, dragging me up by my arm when I started to fall to the floor, shoving me against the wall in the landing.

"Say that again and I won't be responsible for what I do. Dare to say that again and your sister will suffer for the both of you. Do you understand? Is the message clear? All my years of medical training where I learnt how to under-administer this drug or over-administer that one and lo and behold her lips are turning blue and she can't breathe and *oh no what shall we do? I tried everything Mr Ambulance Man* – I'll act so distraught. *Why you poor lady* they'll say *of course you did, you mustn't blame yourself.* And sympathy and flowers will pour through the door, filling the house from the hallway to the attic. Flowers and messages of love from strangers I never want to meet." She loosened her hold. "Or is it only you who'll care? Will you be the only person crying at her grave?" A glob of her spit landed on my chin. "Well? Is that what you want for your sister?" As my strength crumbled, I slid to the floor. She pulled me up. I bowed my head, couldn't bear to look at her. She grabbed my cheeks and squeezed them tightly, making me look into her eyes.

"No."

"What?"

"No."

"Once more for joy."

"No, it's not what I want for her."

Satisfied, she let go and went downstairs.

The Lake

"Luella might be joining us for dinner tonight." I didn't react as I picked up my lunch, in case she changed her mind. "Have a good day darling," she called out, as if she was a normal mother.

The tremor started in my toes and moved up my calves to my knees, through my thighs and hips, right into the middle of my body. I hated her so much. I really, really hated her. Tears flowed but I knew the route so well I didn't stumble or slow down with the blurred vision. And I didn't see the car pull alongside me until the sun bounced off its orange metal casing, tanning the pavement in front of my feet.

"Lara. I've been calling you. Hey. Lara! Are you alright?" I stood still: nose crinkling, shoulders hopping, breath aching. "Here. Get in. I'll give you a lift." And I was so used to orders that I did as he said, utterly exhausted. Home was foul, school was rotten and in between them was a journey that never lasted long enough. Sean drove slowly. I wiped away the mucus trailing from my nose to my chin, suddenly conscious of the stub where a thumb should be. I sat on it. He stopped the car two roads from school and when he turned towards me I kept staring out of the window rather than look at him.

"Has something happened?"

"No."

"I might be able to help." No-one had ever offered before. But Mother mustn't get mad. We hadn't told a soul about anything that went on; we'd been so good at keeping quiet. "What have you got this afternoon? Swimming?"

"Yeah."

"Would you mind missing it?"

"What?"

"Would you mind missing it?"

"I don't know."

"We could go for a drive. Just to talk. And I'll make sure you're back by the time lessons finish. She'd never know." The thought of a whole afternoon away from school and home made my stomach churn. What had Luella said, that I needed to find some guts, to live a little.

"Alright then."

"Excellent. See you here at 12.30."

He briefly touched my hand before opening his door and I bit my tongue so hard some blood oozed through my teeth. I pursed my lips so he wouldn't see it. He was very handsome, like the movie star in the white T-shirt and blue jeans on the poster by the side of his mother's shop.

~

The morning was dragged along by the monotonous droning of the teachers. I willed the bell to ring signaling the end of each lesson and repeatedly moved my fingers to my hand to feel where Sean had touched me.

In English I wrote a note, forging Mother's signature as well as I could from when I'd seen her writing cheques, and after Geography I gave it to Kate Simons asking her to please hand it to the swimming teacher. Before she had time to protest I ran away, knowing she would give it in, knowing she was an obedient girl like me, like I had been. I slid out of the school gates and sprinted down the road, turning the corner to find Sean already sitting in his orange car. My run turned to a walk as he nipped out and opened the passenger door.

I hid my awe at him knowing how to keep shifting the stick and punching the different pedals. His hands were tanned from the sun, the small hairs standing upright on his arms, trying to cool him. We'd learnt about that in Biology.

"Where are we going?"

"Not far, a surprise."

The car protested and slowed to a crawl as it climbed a steep hill. At the top he stopped so we could take in the view of my lake.

"I've been here before. But I came from the other side."

"Yeah. I know."

"How?"

"I followed you the other day, when you ran out of class. I wanted to check you were alright. Marj said—"

"Did you watch me in the water?" He squirmed and let the car roll down the hill. "You shouldn't have done that. It was private. That was me by myself time."

"I left nearly as soon as I got here. Some people in school, they can be such idiots and—"

"They all are."

"Thanks a lot."

"I didn't mean you." I put my hands under my thighs, unsure of what to say. "What now then?"

He tapped the steering wheel with his fingertips. "I was thinking a walk. I like to walk, do you?"

"I guess."

There were trails on either side of where he'd parked. Sean headed for the path to our right so I moved alongside him. It was cool and shaded in the tree tunnels that were protecting us from the fierce heat. Being protected felt good.

"You don't have a father either, do you?"

"No. He died. Did yours? Is he dead?"

"Nah. He just left, didn't want to live with us anymore."

"Why not?" His shrug made me want to make him feel better. "Your mother's nice. Is she nice? She seems it."

"Yeah, she's pretty cool. How about yours?"

I could tell him. I could recant the hundreds of times that she'd been mean and have Sean drive and hide me and Luella somewhere far away. Mother would be happier with us gone, I was sure of it. For years it had been obvious that's what she wanted, and we'd be happier without her too, having a Saturday night treat where we ate toffees and drank lemonade and watched a television.

"She's alright." As we walked in silence I kept nearly telling him then didn't because it was wrong to speak badly of your family, no matter how rotten they were. And Mother wasn't all bad. She made sure we were clothed and fed and watered and educated. What more could a child ask for? "Your mother, I mean Marjorie, does she get cross?"

"God yeah. So fed up if I don't do my chores, if I'm late for dinner after promising to be back on time. Can't say I blame her but—"

"And when she's furious?"

"What?"

"What does she do to you when she's furious?"

"It depends. She might shout, flick me with a dishcloth but then I'll flick her back to make her laugh, try and calm it all down a bit."

"You have a go back at her?"

"Sometimes. Just to ease the tension and stuff."

"Doesn't that make her hit you even harder?"

"Flick, not hit. You mean flick?"

Mother didn't mean to hurt us. She said so. And we were the ones who made her cross. I felt guilty for betraying her and too embarrassed to admit my house might be different to his. I lived in a wrong house. What if I told him and he thought I was strange, like Sylvester had, and didn't offer to drive me a second time in his bright orange car?

"Sure. Of course. I mean flick."

"We'd better get going. You mustn't be late." His lips rolled together and inwards as he breathed through his nose. He walked a bit in front. As we neared the car I tripped over a tree root and went flying. He turned and caught me, scooping me up and along so I could hear his heart pumping, could feel him looking down at me. I raised my head. "You're really pretty, you know that."

~

Sean pulled in three roads from home.

"Is this far enough? I can park somewhere else."

"It should be fine."

"You sure you're okay going home?"

"Yeah, it's—"

"Would you like to go out again?"

My heart somersaulted through the open window.

"Yeah. That'd—"

"Great. When? Week after next maybe?" My heart fell backwards and crashed on the bonnet of his car. "I reckon we should give it a couple of weeks as otherwise the school'll notice, get suspicious. And it gives us time to think of another excuse."

He rubbed his hand on my arm as he reached across to open the door. I walked as elegantly as I could, conscious of him watching me, but as I neared the house my smile thinned and as I walked up the path my stomach twisted violently. I had a bad feeling in my gut. Tiptoeing across the porch, I gently eased open the door, holding my breath as I entered the hall, willing myself to act as normally as possible. Instead of being in the kitchen pointing to a glass of water on the table, Mother was in the hallway holding a piece of paper, pacing, her voice alternating between muttering and shouting. When she looked up, I froze.

"Know what this is?" She held out the sheet, the same pose she'd struck when holding out Luella's underpants. I hooked my foot in the closing front door, ready to flee. "Interfering fools. How dare they write saying they're concerned?" As her voice got louder her face turned redder and the veins on her neck pumped up, turning blue. "Missing school eh?" My bladder nearly let loose as I stayed frozen to the spot, too rubbish to run. "Goddamn it!" she screamed, picking up an umbrella from the coat stand and whacking it against the wall so hard she dented the paneling. I flinched but said nothing, not wanting her to remember I was there, not wanting to be dented like the wall. She pulled her arms back and bounced the umbrella against the sofa. "Think I don't know, think I can't see."

So the school had written quicker than I thought they would and I'd been so wrapped up in my afternoon with Sean that I'd forgotten about the danger that was working its way towards the house and now it was all coming back on me and I'd made a mistake so I had to suffer. Fair enough. But I wouldn't let her harm Luella. I'd rather die than let one more hurt be inflicted on my sister. I took my foot out from behind the door, letting it shut behind me. The latch clicked. She stared at me. She moved closer, the umbrella still in her hand. She held the letter out. I wasn't sure whether to take it or not, terrified of making the wrong move. She tutted, full of contempt. "Read it." She watched my eyes and ears and nose and mouth, looking for someone to blame.

Dear Mrs Jeffries,

It has come to our attention that on Tuesday afternoon your daughter Lara Jeffries was absent from school. This was an unauthorised absence and as such we ask that you visit the school with Lara to discuss this matter.

Please call the office to arrange an appointment.

Yours sincerely,
Mr Parker
Deputy Principal, Head of Student Services

"That's nonsense. Of course I was there." I dared to look up. "Stupid administrators. Look, they didn't even spell our name right, they've done Jeffries with ie rather than the Y. I wouldn't bother going down there after a mistake like that. They're useless." I watched her hand, watched the umbrella, got ready to duck.

"You're such an idiot. They mean your sister not you. And it's only now they've noticed she's been missing. Fools." She snatched the letter back and sat down on the arm of the chair. "Go and drink your water."

Once the kitchen door was closed behind me, I started trembling. I wished Sean was in the room, a witness. She threw open the door.

"Go and do your homework. And don't scrape your chair. How many times must I tell you?"

"Sorry."

"Go on. Go."

"Sorry. I didn't mean to be noisy. Sorry."

~

"Please may I see Luella?"

"Please may I see Luella?" she mimicked. "Her room's not locked now. Keep up girl."

"So I can?"

"Yes. Jesus."

I contained my urge to sprint. Luella's door opened without the key and she turned her head towards me.

"The pain's easing and the infection's nearly gone."

"Great. That's great."

"How was school?"

I wanted to tell her everything, about skipping school, visiting the lake, Sean.

"The usual. It was good." She raised her eyebrows. "What?"

"Something's happened."

"Yeah. Did you hear her? A letter's arrived about you not being there. She's furious. Are you hungry? Thirsty? I'll get you some water."

I walked quietly downstairs hoping Mother wouldn't notice me, and was in luck. She was so focused on writing a letter that she didn't look up. I got a glass from the cupboard and filled it with water, slowly, slowly so the pipes didn't moan like when they were on full blast.

"Here you go. Luella?" She looked dozy.

"She—"

"She's downstairs."

"She wants me to sleep, gave me a—"

"What? Here, have a sip." When she tried to drink, she dribbled. "Are you alright? Shall I—"

"Time's up." Mother walked brusquely to Luella's side and pulled back the sheet to check her piss bag. Luella closed her eyes, mortified. "I said it's her bedtime Lara." I tried to connect with Luella but she wouldn't look at me.

The Meeting

Mother stepped around me as I washed the wooden floor, a mug of hot chocolate in her hand. I stopped scrubbing and listened for signs of distress, trying to translate the murmurs from upstairs. When it stayed quiet and she didn't come back down I went up, pretending to need a pee. As I reached the top of the stairs Luella's door opened. Mother recoiled as if spooked to see me, a towel in her hand.

"I need the bathroom," I said.

Her breath smelt of potatoes. One huff and one puff and she could blow me right down. I gripped the banister. The towel distracted her.

"Hurry up then. I have to go to the post office, and when I get back, we need to talk young lady."

As a sharp pain twisted in the left side of my chest, I wondered if this would be the day my heart gave up on me, unable to cope with the strain. When the front door slammed shut I ran to Luella's room. She was sitting up in bed with the curtains open. The bruising had nearly all faded from her face.

"Oh God, Luella. I think she knows."

"Knows what?"

"I've caused so much trouble."

"What are you talking about?"

I tried to swallow more air.

"I didn't go swimming yesterday. I went to the lake, with a boy, with Sean from the store."

She smiled triumphantly. "I knew something had happened."

"She's gone to the post office where she'll have a go at Marjorie and Sean before coming back and getting me."

"I thought I was meant to be the dramatic one?"

I banged my fist on the wall. "I'm not exaggerating. We have to get out of here. Now. Come on." I pulled the covers off her legs.

"Stop it." She slapped my hand hard. "How do you know where she's gone?"

"She said."

"When?"

"There now. Come on, we've got to go. Please." I picked the blue dress from her wardrobe.

"Did she say why she was going there?"

"I know why. It's obvious. She's playing with me, getting me scared before she comes back. I'll help you dress. Quickly."

"It's for me. She's gone to the store for me. She ran out of dressing for my hand."

I faltered. "Really?"

"Yes. Why do you think this is on it?" A pale blue flannel was wrapped round her thumb, held on with an elastic band. "Go downstairs so everything's normal when she gets back. Hurry." I put the dress away and closed the wardrobe door. "Sean, is he nice?"

I blushed. She shooed me away.

The front door opened as I was polishing the dining room table. I rubbed the duster harder over the wood.

"Did you get everything you needed?" I asked, copying Mother's trick of not looking up.

"What?"

"Did you get all you—"

"The beds need weeding."

"Right." I hesitated before blurting out, "Is Luella eating with us tonight? Is she nearly better?" Mother stopped at the bottom of the stairs but didn't turn round to face me.

"Get on with your chores."

As I shut the back door some flakes of paint fell on the steps. The woodwork was shabby, the pale green paint bubbling and popping off as the sun showed up thick, dusty stains on the glass. A sharp tap on the far right stirred me; Mother was pointing to the bottom of the garden.

I weeded all afternoon, daydreaming in peace, thinking of Sean, Luella and our future which would be ten thousand miles from Mother. When she called me in, I scrubbed my mucky hands then trudged downstairs to find Luella sitting at the table, pale, fragile, motioning at me to go and help in the kitchen.

"Well?"

"Sorry?"

"Aren't you pleased your dear sister's back?"

"Yes."

"Christ. Are there no other words in your head? What do you do at that school all day?" She tapped her finger hard on my right temple. "You" tap "were" tap "meant" tap "to" tap "be" tap "the" tap "clever" tap "one." Tap. Tap.

I picked up the three plates of food and carried them through. When Luella put the first forkful to her mouth it slipped and she missed. She tried again and got some meat and potato in on the second go but the sweetcorn fell back down. By the time we'd finished, only a third of her plate was eaten.

"You clear the dishes while I help her to bed."

Mother led Luella by the elbow and when they reached the bottom of the stairs Luella's chin dropped to her chest. By the time I'd finished the dishes Mother was in her chair sewing a border around her precious cushion. I faked a yawn.

"I think I'll go to bed."

"You think or you will?"

"I will."

"And?"

"Nothing."

"Go on then. Go."

If I repeated her words to a stranger they wouldn't sound mean yet they made my heart flip. I retreated to my room, my sanctuary full of alone hours. It was still light outside and the freshly turned soil was dark and moist compared to the dry earth from this morning. I tried to open the window but the handle wouldn't budge. My palm hurt where I gripped and tried to push up, sideways, down. As I gave up, flakes of brown paint fell onto the floor. I brushed them into the cracks and looked towards town, trying to spot the roof of the store and post office.

~

Mother unfolded a crinkled piece of paper and spread it flat on the table, repeatedly rubbing her hand across it.

"I'll be walking to school with you today."

I choked on my porridge, spitting some out, snatching it with my fingers and mixing it back in the bowl. She only went to the school once a year on parents' night. She couldn't. She mustn't be seen entering the grounds with me; life there was hard enough without being seen with her.

"Why?"

"I need to sort this nonsense out."

"I'm sure it's been forgotten already. They're so busy."

She looked at me like I was stupid. "That's not the point. They've made a clerical error and need to know about it. I can't stand to think that they think I'm in the wrong when I know that it's them who've made the mistake. I need to see this Mr Parker and make him understand that."

As she put the paper back in her apron pocket I frowned at my sister. She half smiled, blinking slowly as if it were a moment to be enjoyed, stroking some hair that had fallen across her forehead. Although she'd been constantly scooping her spoon in and out of her bowl, she'd eaten none of her breakfast.

I washed slowly to delay leaving. Mother called me down, yelling the second time, impatiently shifting her weight from left to right as she waited by the door in a blue and ivory skirt and cream blouse. The colours suited her; she looked brighter, smart, as long as you ignored the hairs on her legs trying to pierce through the tanned tights, thick and long, all huddled together as if there was safety in numbers. The hairs on mine were finer and lighter but there were still lots of them. Girls at school had legs that were smooth and golden.

"What about Luella?" I asked.

"She's in bed."

As I walked down the steps she locked the front door with the three keys she used at night time.

"What if she wakes up or—"

"She won't."

"She might. She—"

"She's had a strong hot chocolate, nothing'll disturb her." And then she was ahead of me, storming down the path so I had to jog to catch up then purposefully stay three steps behind. I would close my eyes when we got there; what I couldn't see wouldn't hurt me.

The orange tail end of Sean's car turned left in front of us as we neared the school. Other feet started to share the pavement and interfere with my thoughts, and Mother had to slow down to dodge the dawdling painted toe nails and white sneakered feet. The boys had such big feet. How did they all miss stepping on one another, the white leather not crushing the girls delicate tippy toes? I wanted to run away, to shrink under their stares.

"Good morning Lara!"

Mother stopped and turned to the voice. I knew who it was without peeking.

"Who are you?" Her sharp tone wiped the smile off his smug face. He shifted uncomfortably in his pale blue loafers. "Well?" Her expression turned bemused.

"Sylvester," he murmured.

"Speak up."

"Sylvester."

"Lara, Sylvester said good morning." He bowed his head, embarrassed. No-one sniggered. I saw Mr Jonas out of the corner of my eye, scuttling into the flower garden, and Miss Simpson by the entrance gate, not taking her eyes off him. "Is there anything else you want to say? Well? Answer me child."

"No Ma'am."

"Thought not. You're a bit of a fool aren't you Sylvester? Think you're worth more than you are, I can tell by looking."

The crowd parted when she stepped past him, creating a path for us to swoop through, all eyes averted rather than risk having her notice them. She turned left down the green corridor that led to the school office and knocked hard on the glass partition that separated the staff from the students, making the receptionist jump, a piece of toast falling from her fingers onto her desk.

"I'm here to see Mr Parker." Mother produced the letter from her pocket.

"Oh. It's a bit early. I don't think he's ready for—"

"Would you mind telling him I'm here please? Thank you. So kind." She read her badge. "Mrs Hawkins." Mother never smiled at us like that.

"What time's your appointment?"

"No time."

"Pardon?"

"What?"

"Sorry. Have you got an appointment? Mr Parker only sees parents who have appointments."

"He'll see me." She grinned broadly.

Mrs Hawkins left the room. I wished I had a different mother. The receptionist was sniffy on her return.

"He's very kindly said he'll pop down in a minute."

She glared at Mother before sitting down.

"I should get to class."

"You'll stay right where you are."

Mr Parker grinned at Mrs Hawkins as he came through the door then casually strolled up to us, hands in his pockets.

"Good morning. Did we have an appointment Mrs…?"

"Jeffreys, spelt with a y, unlike in your letter." She put

it on the counter. He held his hand through the hatch for her to shake. She touched his fingers briefly with hers then pushed the letter closer to him and while he scanned it, she wiped her fingers on her skirt, under the counter where he couldn't see.

"Ah. Shall we talk here or in my office, whichever you prefer?"

"Private would be best."

"My office then; do come through."

When he opened the white door to our right, Mother went first. He put the latch back on, smiled encouragingly at me and led us down a corridor with doors on both sides. After a left turn and eleven doors we reached one with a rectangular sign above the handle, 'Mr Parker – out'.

The room was small but bright thanks to a window nearly the height of the outside wall and half its width. There was a desk sideways on to the window, covered in stacks of papers and text books. There were more books on the shelves above it and a record player, a stack of vinyl, plus three chairs, one at the desk. Mother sat in the spare one nearest the door which meant I was on the inside, left knee touching the wall. To look at Mr Parker we had to face the sunlight, eyes squinting to deal with the glare.

"Now," he leant forward. "How can I be of help?"

The nail of my left hand was digging into the palm of my right. I pulled them apart, not wanting to bleed in front of the adults. I squashed my fingers under my thighs; neither of them had noticed. Mr Parker was smiling at Mother, waiting for her to speak. Mother smiled back at him but he didn't bend, didn't try to fill the silence. Her patience cracked.

"You've made a mistake."

"You think? Let's see now." He re-read the letter. "You're Lara?"

Head down, I looked up through my eyebrows. It hurt the middle of my forehead.

"Yes sir," I mumbled.

"There's the mistake," Mother said cheerily as if that explained everything.

"I'm sorry?"

"Lara didn't miss school last week." Mr Parker leant back in his chair. "It's an error, easily done by some. Sloppy. Rushed. Someone rushed, I guess. The receptionist, I imagine."

"We wouldn't have sent you the letter if we didn't think she'd missed school."

"Except you did. And she didn't."

"Lara?"

"You can speak to me," Mother answered.

"I understand that Mrs Jeffreys but I do like to hear from the students themselves. It often helps solve the mystery quicker."

"No mystery. It's a clerical error. I've already told you."

"Yes, you did say that." He clapped his hands together twice and bounced out of his chair. "Excuse me for a moment." Before Mother had a chance to protest he'd left the room. I sank into my seat, wanting to disappear.

"I've a good mind to leave right now. Wasting my time, leaving without saying why, making me wait, acting all superior, the jumped up little squirt." As the word squirt left her lips Mr Parker came back in carrying a blue cardboard register.

"Right then, let's have a look." He sat down, opened the folder and scanned through the dates. His finger ran down the column of names and across the horizontal line to a tiny box.

"I'm sorry but there's definitely a cross against Lara's name and that means she wasn't at afternoon registration on the—"

"There's a near identical name below it," Mother snapped.

"Pardon?"

"Read her name and the name below."

"Lara Jeffreys, Luella Jeffrey—"

"Lara and Luella, see. It's any easy mistake to make. They're identical twins. Luella's been off sick with a virus; you can see that from the other absent marks."

Mr Parker looked directly at me.

"Lara, did you leave school without permission on—"

"I said you're to speak to me," Mother said. "This is ridiculous. I've another appointment to get to." She stood up.

"Lara?" His eyes were kind, cross, panicky, pleading for the truth.

Yes. But I can explain. Please. Don't make me go with her, let me stay here, keep us away from her. "No. I was in class. Ask Miss Simpson, she got my homework."

"You see. She even gave in her homework. What more proof do you need?" Mother grinned as she put her hand on my shoulder and poked four fingers under the back of my neck. I caught my leg on the chair but managed to stay upright. "So clumsy," she sang.

"I hope Luella feels better soon. She'll need a medical note for having so many days off. Obviously."

Mother stopped in the doorway.

"They're sixteen tomorrow. They don't have to attend school after that, with their parent's permission then it's legal to not be here. Isn't that right?" She'd always told us eighteen, everything was 'wait until you're eighteen'. To not go to school, to not see Sean, to be stuck at home with her, it would be unbearable. "Schooling never suited Luella. She's been bullied terribly by your students."

Relief that she meant Luella; guilt that I'd been relieved. And worry. How would Luella cope with being caged in with Mother but without me? Mr Parker tried to walk beside us but the corridor wasn't wide enough.

"I'm sure we can work something out. It may have been a mistake. We can sort this out and look forward to welcoming Luella back to class. We'll help her catch up, no pressure though, not after she's been so poorly."

He was too late. Mother had made up her mind, was ignoring him and storming ahead. When we got to main door he gave up. When we got to the arches she let go of my elbow.

"Work hard, knowledge is power," she hissed, before stomping out of sight. I leant against the wall, dizzy from the questions and orders.

"Are you alright?" Jonas asked.

"Jesus. You gave me a fright." When he let go of the wheelbarrow, some mud fell over its side onto the concrete. "Where did you come from?"

He pointed to the field at the back of the office, a sheepish expression coating his face. I started walking to class.

"Are you sure you're alright? Your mother looked angry."

"Nothing new there," I muttered.

The Ring

Luella sat on the bottom step as I set the table for dinner: a neglected doll, her hair lank and greasy, shoulders drooping, nightdress creased, eyes dull and vacant. When I moved towards her she scuttled up the stairs, out of reach.

"We'll sort this. She can't keep you here. The school have noticed. They said it's not right, that you should go back." Mother barked my name from the kitchen. "I won't let it go on, I promise. We won't just imagine leaving, we'll actually do it."

"Lara!" Mother shouted.

~

Before bed, I peeked in Luella's room. She was lying with her back to the door and there was an empty hot chocolate cup on the bedside cabinet. I heard Mother on the landing, too late for me to get to my room without her seeing me. She squirmed past me and picked up the cup.

"She's asleep."

"I know."

Her face hardened. "Go to bed. Big day tomorrow."

What did other girls do on the eve of their sixteenth birthday? Did they look forward to fun, presents, people thinking them special, wanting them to be happy? Or did they lie in bed wishing it would pass so fast it could be hidden away like every other day.

~

"Happy birthday."

"Happy birthday," Luella chorused.

I hugged her. Her arms were spindly and weak; mine would be strong enough for the both of us. We held hands as we walked downstairs where Mother was waiting, foot tapping, ready to lead us through the kitchen, unlocking the basement door, turning on the light, motioning for us to go down the dusty steps, past the recently disturbed cobwebs on the crumbling brick walls.

We stood in front of Father's wine collection with the five conspicuously empty spaces. A photo of him dead in the morgue was resting against one of the bottles. His eyes were closed, face swollen, skin blue. Luella turned a paler shade of grey. I held her right hand with my left, our eight fingers all wrapped up in each other.

"Luella's gone bad like I thought she would one day, a drunk like you. Lara's the lesser delinquent." My fingers were getting sweaty holding so tightly onto Luella's but when I tried to loosen the grip she squeezed our palms closer together, refusing to let me go. "Say goodbye then."

"Goodbye Father," we mumbled.

After pulling the photo off the rack, she twisted my shoulder so we all faced the stairs. "Hurry up. You'll need to leave for school soon."

Rather than sitting down in the kitchen, Luella and I carried on to the dining room. Our birthday treat was to have breakfast served and the morning dishes done for us. Mother brought us two glasses of orange juice, followed by honey on toast. She left us alone to eat it.

Luella smiled and took a big bite of toast so a droopy gloop of honey dribbled down her chin. I took a small bite to savour the rare sweetness, chewing the same mouthful again and again until there was only a squashed up ball of dough in my mouth, so small that my teeth grated against one another. My second bite was as minute as the first and the honey stuck to my teeth, oozing through the gaps, coating the enamel. Luella's first piece was nearly gone. She picked up her juice and swallowed it in three big gulps. Some of it dribbled down her chin. I took a sip of mine. The citrus smell made my nose tingle. I pushed the juice around my mouth with my tongue and cheeks, and bits of orange stuck between my teeth, mixing with the honey. The coolness soothed my throat, easing away some of the tension from the trip to the basement. Luella finished first so I passed her half of my last piece of toast, unable to carry on eating with her watching. She gobbled it up and I was glad. It was the least I could do as even though it would be our first birthday apart, I wanted to run away from her to school, like a traitor.

I leaned away from Mother as she reached over to take my glass. Luella started to fold in on herself, wilting in her mother's shadow.

"It's time for you to go."

"What's Luella doing today?"

My sister's body tensed.

"She'll be here. Now don't make me say it again, school." She balanced the dishes on her right arm and took them into the kitchen.

"You shouldn't have asked her that. Hurry up and go."

"I feel bad leaving you here. How do you cope with her on your own?"

"I pretend stuff. Like I'm not here. And when she's near me I force my skin not to prickle. It's fine. You go."

The kitchen door started to open so I grabbed my bag, wanting Mother to be in a good mood when I left her with Luella. I could feel the sugar rushing through my body as I ran down the road. I stopped and turned to see if an orange car was near and after the fourth look my persistence was rewarded. Sean slowed down, pushing open the passenger door. I sidled in. He pulled out a small white paper bag from his pocket and held it out for me. I'd never been given a present before. I didn't know what to do with it.

"Happy birthday."

"How did you know?"

"Mr Parker told Marj who loves birthdays, goes nuts choosing presents. Soooo there you go. Open it."

A ruby red flower sticker sealed the paper shut. I carefully unpeeled it, not wanting to damage a single petal, and opened the bag, taking care not to rip it. Inside there was a navy blue velvet box. I tipped it out of the bag. It was harder to pull open than I thought it would be and snapped shut on me before I could see what was inside. I tried again. There was a silver ring with a purple stone in its centre. I took the ring from the box and put it on the finger next to my littlest one on my right hand.

"We know you can't wear it at home but thought it was small enough that you could hide it somewhere. If that's okay? It suits you."

"Thank you."

"Come and meet me in the flower garden at lunch time, as soon as the bell rings."

In lessons I stroked the silver, twiddled it back and forth, relished the feel of the metal against my skin. It made my hands feel more elegant, my finger nails clipped and neat, narrow on the sides where I'd chewed the skin off. As I day dreamed through Literacy, I understood why girls giggled and wasted their time talking about boys. If I had someone to talk about Sean with, I'd ramble on and on.

"Lara, I said do you know the answer. Lara?" Miss Jones repeated.

"Sorry Miss, what was the question?" The bell rang for the beginning of lunch break.

"Never mind. Go and eat, the lot of you."

Did she notice my ring? She probably had, it was so pretty. I ran to the toilets and checked my reflection in the mirror. It felt unfair; there was nothing I could do to style my hair and I didn't own any make-up. Sean was waiting at the hedge by the entrance to the flower garden. He took my hand and led me to the wooden bench that was now covered in a blue and white checkered cloth with food laid along the middle. He shooed a wasp away from the sandwiches.

"Guess they were bound to go for them, who can resist a bit of sugar?" The last time I'd tasted strawberry jam had been at Sally Spelling's party. "Help yourself." He popped the lid off a juice bottle for me. I took a few big swigs and coughed and spluttered when some went up my nose. "Are you alright?"

"Yeah, sorry. I didn't realise it was fizzy."

I took a smaller sip and the sweet bubbles burst on the back of my throat. A burp rose. I put my hand to my mouth but was too late to stop it and so mortifying to make that noise in front of him but he just laughed, broke off a chunk of bread and offered it to me with a pot of creamy beige goo. "Have some homous."

Already embarrassed by the burp I couldn't admit that I didn't know what homous was. It obviously went with the bread so I tipped the pot over the crust which felt like it took forever as it was so slow at dripping. When it started to fall over the edges of the bread I licked to stop it landing on my dress. I licked my fingers where it coated them, the texture strange, rough and creamy, a deep smoky flavour. I used my tongue to rub it over the inside of my mouth where it stuck to the roof of it. I took a bite of the bread. The crisp crust and soft dough merged with the homous and together they rolled around my mouth, jarring against my teeth. Sean broke off a small piece of bread and dipped it into the pot. I was ashamed. I'd done it wrong. My cheeks burned.

"I've not had homous before. I didn't know what to do, how to eat it." Beads of perspiration dripped down my back.

"Don't worry about it. We only have it because Marjorie says it reminds her of when she was little. Her ya-ya, I mean her granny, they were Greek, Greek Melbourne. She used to make it. Where's your family from?"

"I don't know."

He held out a doughnut. I licked the frosting and sucked on the ruby red jelly. It was stickier than I remembered from Sally's party. When a wasp flew near, Sean flicked it away.

"Shit. I guess there's going to be loads of them in the middle of a flower garden. I should have planned it better."

"It's perfect." A wasp crawled over my drink and slipped under the rim of the bottle landing right inside the bright orange liquid. It struggled and dipped and dived, surfaced, then fell under again.

"Frigging wasps. Here, share mine."

As I took a sip I thought I could taste his lips which made me want to for real so I started to lean towards him then drew back at an angry buzz.

"Damn it," Sean exclaimed, flapping his hands to scare it away. I rubbed the stone on my ring, not caring if a thousand insects attacked us. "Close your eyes a sec," he said. I shut them and waited for a kiss but there was a flicking sound followed by a hiss. "Now make a wish."

Between us was a chocolate cupcake with a lit white candle on top of it. My first birthday cake. I blew out the flame, wishing the moment would last forever. A small trail of smoke rose in the air.

"I wished—"

"Don't tell me. If you tell me it won't come true."

After insisting I ate the whole thing, he packed everything away and the wasps got cross because they couldn't find more food so we had to run from the garden and I smashed right into Mr Jonas.

"Sorry."

"No worries. What's the occasion?" He pointed at the tablecloth and packet of candles sticking out of Sean's bag.

"It's her birthday."

"Right. Happy birthday then. Hope it's a good one." His cheeks were red where he was overheating from wearing too thick a brown jumper on a warm summer's day. It had clusters of holes in it, the largest at each cuff where he'd put his thumbs through. His hat was brown and shabby but worked in keeping the sun off his face. It hid his eyes, hid what colour they were when his head was bowed. "The bell rang already. You better get to class."

The grounds were nearly empty, just a couple more strays near the doors by the canteen. Sean took my hand and we ran together. He never let go, even when two people near the main entrance looked over and saw us. We sprinted up the steps.

"I've got Geography. What about you?"

"Domestic Science. Thanks for today. I—"

"Shall I take you home later?"

"Better not. She might see us. We could have lunch again tomorrow, or the next day or—"

He started running down the hall. I sprinted to room 3Q where Mrs Sanderson was standing next to a table laid with sugar, margarine, butter, flour and eggs.

"Sorry I'm late. I needed the bathroom."

"For goodness sake Lara. Go before the end of lunch break next time. What's wrong with you girls? Now hurry up and take your seat."

I felt the eyes of the class on me, eleven of us now Luella was at home. The teacher's monotone voice was hard to hear over the motor of the mixer. We wrote what she dictated then followed and copied what she'd done. While the cake was baking I prepared the icing and as I beat the soft butter and icing sugar together, the light white dust drifted out of the bowl and settled on my ring turning it a dull grey colour. I raised my hand to my mouth and sucked it clean; more sweetness in a day than I'd tasted in forever. I licked and sucked, imagining I was kissing Sean, my insides going gooey like the mixture in the oven.

"What are you doing?"

I took my finger from my mouth. "Sorry Miss."

"Wash your hands. Immediately. Hygiene, hygiene, hygiene. How many times?"

She went on to tell us about other types of icing we could use: royal, marzipan, fondant, shop bought, ha ha, that was her joke. I rinsed my hands under warm water, taking care to hold onto the ring. Where could I hide it so Mother never saw it? When the class ended I started to panic because I still didn't have an answer. The other girls put their cakes in tins to take home. I'd leave mine with the teacher. Although Mother wanted us to know how to cook, sweet desserts weren't welcome.

"Lara, can I have a quick word." Mrs Sanderson stayed quiet until there was just her and me left in the room. "I'm sorry to hear Luella won't be returning to class. I hope you'll be staying on?"

"She'll be back when she's better."

"I don't think so, not according to Mr Parker. But you're definitely staying on?

"Yeah. I—"

"Good," she smiled kindly. "How would we cope with you both gone? Your cake had a perfect rise today; you're a natural."

There was that gentleness, making me want to cry. I hurried out of the room before she saw my weakness and in the rush, turned on my ankle, falling against the windowsill. I swallowed the pain as I held onto the ledge, carefully moving my foot from left to right and up and down. It hurt. I took my shoe off to rub it and when my ring caught on the sock, I knew what to do. I checked up and down the corridor. No-one was coming. Ignoring the throbbing, I peeled off the sock, took the ring from my finger and tried it on my toes. The smallest was too small, the second the same, third nearly and fourth just right. It felt peculiar as I put my foot down, uncomfortable, but when I wiggled my toes the ring stayed on. I tied my shoelace up just as Mrs Sanderson opened the classroom door.

"Still here? Is everything alright?"

"Yes Miss. I twisted my ankle but it's fine."

"Are you sure? Shall I take you to the office? They can call home and—"

"No." She paused at my snapping; I had to be careful. "It's fine. Look I can walk now." I put my weight evenly on both feet. It hurt like hell and the ring was digging into the bone of my toe but I turned and smiled at her. "All fine now. Thank you." The further I walked the more I got used to the ache and the more comforting my ring wrapped toe felt. By the time I reached home it was a part of me.

In the hallway I slipped off my shoes and tidied them neatly by the skirting board, double checking that you couldn't see the outline of the ring under my sock. We never went barefoot as there were verrucas and other viruses on the ground waiting to latch onto our soles. As I drank my water, Mother entered the kitchen, making the hairs on my arms stand on end.

"Did anything out of the ordinary happen at school today?" I held my breath. It was lucky I'd already swallowed. "No more meddling teachers, no chit-chatting from that awful Mr Parker?"

"No, none of that."

"Good. Homework then dinner then bed." She started peeling three carrots.

As I sat at the dining room table, I rubbed my big toe over the ring, enjoying the hidden rebellion. Luella came downstairs.

"You're home. Did you have a good day?"

"You look better."

"Yeah."

"How come?" She shrugged as an answer. "Mrs Sanderson was asking after you. She said you're not going back to her lesson, like ever. Is that true? It's not true is it?"

Luella raised her eyebrows. I squashed my left foot with my right one so it hurt, punishing my big mouth. My sister blinked too much as she said, "How was your day?"

"You already asked me that." She looked befuddled. "It was good thanks. Quiet."

We ate dinner without talking, chewing the beef and teasing out the bits that got caught in our teeth with our tongues. Afterwards, Mother went in the kitchen to make Luella's hot chocolate.

"Don't drink it tonight." I gripped her arm but she pulled away from me.

"You get to escape; I want to as well."

"But—"

"Stop it."

She downed her drink and was in bed by the time I'd cleared up, leaving Mother tightening the narrow wooden frame on a virgin tapestry.

"The dishes are all done." I took a deep breath in and out to be brave. "Why does Luella still need hot chocolates?"

"For the pain."

"But she looks much better."

I held her stare.

"Well thank goodness my years of medical training weren't in vain, and I can see that she's not. I often find that what's going on outside can be very different to what's going on inside, wouldn't you agree darling?"

"Yes Mother."

As I climbed the stairs the ring pushed into my toe reminding me there was good in the outside world.

"Are you awake?" I whispered, knocking gently on Luella's door.

The curtains were drawn. She lay still, her breathing quiet, regular. I'd wanted to say happy birthday, had decided to risk showing her my present, tell her about the lunch, the homous, the fool I'd made of myself, but she'd gone off into her drugged up dream world. Things were so different. I sat on my bed and cried. I missed Luella. She felt a million miles away.

The Love

I went to school; Luella stayed at home.

I felt guilty; Luella was dozy.

I was happy with Sean; Luella didn't know that we had lunch together every school day apart from Mondays when he had hockey practice, so that was my most fractious day, already wound up and tense after a weekend at home.

I noticed the other students more: how they spoke, how Sean talked about them and liked them and laughed with them so if he liked them maybe they weren't all bad. Maybe if they giggled when I passed, it wasn't always about me.

In Science, missing my only ever partner, Sally Spelling took pity on me, the girl so pretty that all the boys looked over when they thought no-one else was sneaking a peek. Except for Sean. He winked like he only had eyes for me, making me feel less of a plain Jane beside her. And he dropped me off three streets from home each afternoon. And we'd kiss. And I wished I could go back to his house with him one day.

When I walked through the front door, the stale air suffocated me and my breath became shallow, only reaching half way down my ribs. I tried to talk to Luella but all she was interested in was hot chocolates and her room. I wanted to shake her awake but what alternative could I offer with no money to feed us and nowhere we could run to. At night my mind went blank as I tried to decorate an apartment with four rooms. It was easier to picture Sean and I in a house, chatting at a table, him coming home from work eating some cake I'd skillfully baked, iced with his favourite vanilla frosting. Marjorie would knock on the back door and we'd welcome her in. She'd look upon me as a daughter and we'd go shopping together, be the best of friends. If she flicked me with a dishcloth as we dried the dishes I'd laugh and flick her back and she wouldn't hit me. Instead, we'd all laugh, because we were all having such fun, because everything was so easy, compared to before. Everything was perfect with my new family.

~

"Can we visit the lake again?"
"Sure."
"When? Friday?"
"This Friday? Maybe. What about your Mother?"
His liking me had emboldened me. "What about her?"
"Look at you all rebellious. Okay then."
"Definitely? This week?"
"Yeah. No problem."

~

I scrubbed my hands extra clean and brushed my teeth especially hard, so much that the gums above my front top two teeth bled. As I forced myself to eat breakfast I fretted that Mother would sense a different energy about me but I needn't have worried, her mind was more focused on Luella since she'd started staying at home.

Sean's car slowed down as it passed me on the walk to school. We'd agreed I wouldn't get a lift, didn't want to risk anything spoiling our adventure. He stopped and started, stopped and started, his brake lights going on and off to say hello.

After morning lessons I went to the staff room for the very first time, my shoulders bumping others as I walked up the wide wooden stairs against the flow of students rushing down to the canteen. On the square landing, instead of heading straight ahead to the library, I turned right and climbed the twelve empty stairs that led to the staffroom door. The dark wood reminded me of home but I refused to let it plague my confidence and knocked three times. No-one answered. I raised my fist to knock again when Mr Parker appeared from behind me.

"Lara?" I was sure he disliked me for the Mother I had, for the trouble I'd caused. "How are you doing?"

"I need to see Miss McCullen please."

He smirked as he took his hands out of his pockets and opened the door. "No problem. Wait there a second."

Miss McCullen was broad shouldered but only an inch taller than me. Her hair hung past her collar bones, the redness of it matching the hundreds of freckles dotted over her skin. Her brown eyes looked tired.

"Yes?"

"I have to miss swimming today please Miss."

"Why? Do you have a note?"

"No. It just happened, it's my ladies day." Some boys at the bottom of the stairs sniggered. She frowned at them before looking back at me.

"Alright. You can read in the library."

"Yes Miss, thank you." She'd already turned back into the room and I heard the words *why do I bloody bother* as the heavy door swung shut behind her.

So that was me. Free. As I ran down the stairs I saw Sean at the bottom and nodded. "My go," he mouthed. I hung around the foot of the staircase watching him from the corner of my eye, pretending to study the notice board by the main hall door, posters about choir practice, netball, orchestra, a jazz club, nothing that I'd been to, Mother insisting that we go straight home from school each day as school was meant to be a place of learning, not fun. I dared to look up. Mr Johnson's expression was stern, his hands moving erratically up and down, left and right. He shook his head. I bit at the skin on my good thumb; Sean had to get the afternoon off too, he had to. Finally the teacher slammed the staff room door shut.

"Everything alright?"

"Yeah, he'll get over it."

"Are you sure? I—"

"Let's go. You first."

Students were milling around the playground, eating lunch and chatting. I dodged through them to wait near the main entrance. Sean followed me, stopping by the lavender bushes. My heart was pumping hard, adrenaline rushing as I took a chance and ran through the gate, down the road, wanting to check that Sean was there but not daring to look back in case a teacher was sprinting after me. I turned left and ran faster, then right by the post box and there was his car where he'd promised it would be. I held onto its roof with both hands, catching my breath. Hands clasped my waist, moved me to the left, unlocked my door. He ran to his side.

"Bring on the sunshine!" he whooped as we drove up the road. I laughed, my life full of firsts, and as we drove over the hill the sun shone on the water, welcoming us, welcoming Sean and I to its beautiful shore, proving we'd done the right thing. He parked under our tree and we strolled and talked and he stroked my bad hand and when I tried to pull it away, he held it tighter.

"You're beautiful."

"Don't."

"What?"

"I know I'm not."

"What?"

"Oh come on. Short hair, short thumb, horrible clothes."

"I—"

"I used to have long hair, all wavy on the ends."

"Yeah?"

I dipped my toe into telling a truth.

"She cut it off when I was little. We. The both of us."

"Why?"

I shrugged. "We'd been really naughty, pushed her too far."

Luella had snipped a few strands of her own hair off with the nail scissors. Mother hadn't been happy. We'd needed to be taught a lesson.

"Jesus."

"It's fine."

"It isn't. I won't let her hurt you again you know." He was so sweet and naieve. "You've got me now. And Marjorie. She knew something was going on, she kept saying. When I told her about that cut on your head she said she didn't think it was the first one."

I pulled his arms tighter round me needing to believe

he meant it. I put my hand behind his neck and our hip bones rubbed against one another, chests touched, arms wandered up and down each other's backs. I ran my fingers under his T-shirt. His hands moved low. I stepped back against a tree, feeling the roughness of the bark on my spine and the smoothness of his belly on my front. He leant right against me, pushing us together. I pulled him to the ground, on top of me, and all I could think of was the waterfall of tummy tickles as his hands rubbed over my thighs. He moved them under my dress. When he hesitated I pushed my hips into his, wanting him to keep going.

"We shouldn't do this," he said.

"Why not?" His head tipped back as he laughed. "What?"

"Girls don't usually say that."

"Oh."

"I haven't done it before."

"Me neither." But if I did, I'd be like Luella.

"I've not got any protection. I wasn't expecting, you know…"

We'd be fine on the ground. I pulled him closer, the soreness bearable because it was him. I felt warm inside. Stillness with him on top of me and inside me. Cheek to cheek, the sun playing hide and peek on our faces.

"You're getting heavy."

He rolled to the side and pulled his zipper up. I pulled my dress down. All of one side touching, we walked along the path to the car. My lower half stung and my head felt all relaxed like after one of Mother's hot chocolates but with the thoughts staying clear rather than blurring. I didn't want to go home. I watched the lake as he unlocked the door, memorising the afternoon.

"I guess if my family was normal we'd come here after school; there'd be no need to hide."

"Are you alright?"

"Yeah. Fine. Good." I smiled. In the car, I pushed my toes down, enjoying the pain of the ring as it locked on the bone.

~

On the walk to the house I brushed my hands over my dress, making sure there were no stains or bits of dirt caught on it. Mrs Franklin was in her garden. Could she tell what I'd done? Would Mother guess? Would she smell Sean on me? Jesus. But I didn't need to worry. One look at her as she knelt in the front garden, angrily pulling out weeds, dampened my mood so much there was no happiness to hide, no need for an actor.

"Your water's on the table." She didn't look up.

I drank it and rushed to the bathroom. After pissing, I wiped myself clean, between my legs and the top of my thighs. I smelt different. I didn't want to wash him away but couldn't risk being discovered so wet more toilet tissues and wiped as much as I could. My knickers, that's what Sally called them rather than pants, they were still damp where the gunk had dripped but they'd dry when they were on me. A sharp knock rattled the door.

"What are you doing? Homework and dinner. Hurry up child."

The Bubble

Sally was already in class. I wanted to be more like her, pretty and kind with different clothes to wear each day. She moved along to the stool by the window so I could sit next to her.

"Christ, you're so lucky having such nice skin, it's glowing, I swear." I blushed. "Oh. My. God. Who is it?"

"What?" I went even redder. She clapped her hands together, jumped in her seat and squealed.

"I always pick up on these things. It's a sixth sense. My granny reads the tea leaves you know. It's a gift. It runs in the family."

Instead of finding her high pitched tone pathetic like Luella and I used to, I enjoyed being the reason for her excitement.

"Ms Spelling, keep it down please."

"Sorry Mrs Jameson." She winked at me. "Don't worry, your secret's safe. Is it Sean? I've seen you with him. It is isn't it? It's Sean, yeah?"

"I don't know what you're talking about."

I shouldn't have blushed. Her knowing meant she might tell someone else. I watched out for her as Sean and I sat on a bench round the corner from the main playground at break time.

"I got you something." He passed me a chocolate bar.

"Oh wow. That's so delicious." The peanut middle had a texture similar to the homous but was sweeter and covered in a layer of chocolate so thick that chunks fell on my lap when I bit into it. I wet my finger to make them stick when I touched them, quickly so they wouldn't stain my dress; Mother would go mad if she knew I was rotting my teeth with sugary goo a boy had given me.

We sat so our legs touched but not our torsos or hands, the teachers on duty mustn't notice us. I pressed my thigh harder into his.

"How was your weekend?"

"Dull," I replied. "Yours?"

"Yeah, good." He fiddled with his sandwich bag. "I was thinking about the lake and—"

"Me too. We should go back again."

I put my left hand over his right one. A shadow fell over us. Sean and I pulled our hands apart as we both looked up.

"Mr Parker."

"Sean. How are you today?"

"Good thanks Mr Parker. Yourself?"

"I'm very well thanks Sean. Very well." He paused. "Lara."

"Mr Parker."

"How are you today?"

"Fine thank you."

"Recovered from Friday?"

"Excuse me?"

"I believe you weren't well, when I saw you at the staff room. Miss McCullen—"

"Yes Mr Parker."

"And Sean, you missed hockey practice?"

"Ah. Yeah."

"But you're better now?"

"Fully recovered, thank you."

I wished I had his confidence.

"Well, that's good to hear. And you were both in the library for the afternoon, studying?"

"No sir, I had to go home."

"And you Lara?" When I didn't reply he spoke more gently. "Were you in the library on Friday afternoon?"

I was trying to decide which lies would work best but my mind kept going blank and even though Mr Parker didn't look cross I began to fret.

"Lara had to go home too Mr Parker so as I've got the car, I gave her a lift."

Mr Parker half smiled.

"Indeed. Very good then; I'll leave it there. Best not miss games again, the both of you, on the same day."

"We won't. Thank you for your concern Sir."

Mr Parker started to walk away but changed his mind, coming slowly back and sitting on his haunches in front of me so I had no choice but to look down at him.

"If you ever need someone to talk to, you know where my office is."

I nodded. His hip clicked when he stood up.

"Christ. Did you hear that? Bloody hips, they're going to go on me like my Da's did." Putting his hands in his pockets, he hurried into the main building.

"Do you think he'll tell on us?"

"Nah," said Sean. "Don't worry about it."

"But—"

"It's fine. He won't say a thing. He's alright when it comes to stuff like that. Trust me, we can trust him."

~

Luella grinned. She kept grinning.

"Are you alright?"

"Oh yes, you betcha."

"Are you sure? You seem different."

"Do I?" She span on her toes, laughing.

"Hurry up!" Mother called from the kitchen. "The food's going cold."

During dinner Luella played with her roast chicken rather than eating it. Not one mouthful went through her lips.

"Is she alright?" I asked. "What's going on? Something is." I was more forceful, putting down my cutlery, carefully so as not to mark the table. "I—"

"Does she look ill to you?"

"No."

"Unhappy?"

"No—"

"Then why ask?

"She looks different. She's different."

"And that's a bad thing?"

"What do you mean?

"Is her being different to what she was before a bad thing? If she's happy and content, why is it a problem?"

I stared at Luella. She hadn't looked up once through the entire conversation.

"It's like she's not here."

Mother smiled, deeply satisfied. "I know."

"It's not right. What have you given her?" I felt sick.

"Nothing bad. Look how happy she is. Now don't you dare go causing trouble, do you hear me?"

In my head I had shouts and ravings and reasons why what she was doing was wrong but none of them would come out and confront her. I couldn't force the words through my lips.

~

Mother sat Luella down on a kitchen chair in the middle of the grass in the garden then went back into the kitchen. Luella closed her eyes, pointing her face towards the sky. I shifted along three beds to the one nearest where she was sitting.

"What are you doing?"

She stroked her neck. "Enjoying the feel of the sun; I've not been outside in a while. It's gorgeous."

Her hand moved to her other arm and she ran her fingers along it, the blunted scarred end of her thumb standing out brighter and whiter than the rest of her skin.

"You have to stop drinking the hot chocolates. I—"

"Oh shush." She flicked me away with her hand as if I was a tiresome bug that kept flitting in her face, and stretched her bare legs in front of her. "I'm fine, better than fine. I feel great."

"No you don't. You can't. This isn't you, all dopey, think of the energy you used to have, the—"

"God, you talk such rubbish. Always going on. Yakety yakety yak yak."

She shifted her hips forward, resting the back of her neck on the chair.

"Luella." I went to shake her shoulders but she grabbed my wrists and as she squeezed them, a coldness like Mother's glowered at me.

"Don't you dare come all high and mighty with me.

This is the first time I've felt relaxed, knowing what to expect each day. What can you offer that's better?" I tried to break away but her grip was too tight. "There's nothing is there? You've nothing more for me."

"That's not true," I cried. "There's us. Please. We'll run away. We'll do something—"

"What about Sean? Three's a crowd, that's what they say." She let go and softened her voice. "You keep doing what you're doing and I'll keep doing what I'm doing, and then it'll all be fine, peaceful."

She pointed her face back up to the sky, dismissing me. I saw a figure at my bedroom window. No doubt she'd enjoyed the whole exchange, proof of how she'd gotten between us, with Luella hooked on whatever she was feeding her.

~

The leaves were still as the town held its breath waiting for Sunday to end and a new week to begin so it could feel alive again. I wriggled my toes to feel my ring and listened carefully. The house was quiet so I slipped off my sock and moved the ring onto my finger, where Sean had first put it. It was strange to see it as well as feel it. I leant against the window ledge imagining Sean and I living in a house with a garden and three bedrooms, when the door behind me opened with no warning footsteps.

"We're going out. Your sister needs some air."

The whole house was full of air, stale air from closed windows but still it was air. Why did Luella need different air? I waited for the door to shut behind her.

"You've only got one sock on."

"I—"

"What on earth are you doing? Put the other one on. You'll get a chill as well as a verruca. Cold feet are no good to anyone." I didn't move. "What are you waiting for? I said, put your sock on."

I tried to keep my ring hand from her view, covering it with the other hand as I bent down to pick up the sock. Her eyes narrowed at my peculiar movements. I took deep, slow breaths to calm my nerves and improve my balance and I nearly did it, the sock was almost on my toes when I started to tilt. I'd been about to slip the ring in the sock before pulling it up but instead I fell forwards, my hands clawing through the air like a tiny baby searching for comfort in a weird new world. I landed on the floor.

"Stand up. Now!" Her voice sounded lower than a man's. She coughed to clear where she'd hurt her throat from shouting so loudly. I did as she asked and she gestured for me to go to her, her hands out, eyes gleaming, rejoicing at catching me out.

"What's that?"

"A ring."

"Really? It's a ring? I'd never have known." Her tone turned sinister as she pulled at my hand to examine it. "Where did you get it?"

"I found it." I tried to remember the lesson in school where they'd told us that people look left or right to cover their lying. The whole class had practised, the most involved they'd ever been. Unable to remember which way meant what, positive that I'd get it wrong, I did neither and looked down.

"Eyes to me." Hers blazed as she pinched the skin on my hand. "I said where... did... you... get... it?"

I copied her pauses in my reply. "I... found... it."

She pulled it off my finger, wrenching the joint.

"Ow."

"Shut up," she snapped, examining it. "What a piece of tat." I winced. "It looks new. Where did you find it?"

"At school."

"Some common creature's piece of trash."

"I think it's pretty."

"Of course you do, you've got no taste."

"Please may I have it back?"

"No."

"What? Why?"

"Because I said so. Now go and put your shoes on, we're going out.

Anger nudged some courage out of me. "That's not fair."

"I beg your pardon?"

"Please can I have it back? It's—"

"Which part of the word no don't you understand? You're starting to make me think there's more to this than meets the eye."

"I just don't see what's wrong with wearing a little ring. It's—"

"But it's not *your* ring is it Lara? Some poor soul has lost this and we must make sure they get it back. I'll post it to the school. Someone's bound to claim it."

"I can give it in."

"I don't think so."

"I'll be there anyway."

"I said I'll post it. Now, we're leaving in five minutes and you're to come with us so hurry up. We've not got all day."

She took my ring with her. I cried silent, violent tears as I paced the room, banging my fists hard on my thighs, wishing she was dead. Four minutes to get my head together. My toe felt bare, aching for the band of silver.

"Lara! Hurry up! You're driving me crazy!"

They were waiting by the front door, Luella in a floppy blue hat, blue flowery dress, green cardigan, white socks and brown shoes. Her legs looked thin, pale and hairy. She used to be more of an olivey brown and I'd envied the way she tanned rather than burned. I was almost identically dressed, my hat being brown, dress red. Luella followed Mother; I dragged my feet behind them.

"For goodness sake Lara, no sulking."

She pulled me out of the door and locked it behind me. As we walked round and round three blocks I spied on the families inside their happy homes wishing I lived with any of them. Luella delighted in all she saw.

"What a pretty butterfly! Oh look, have you ever seen a flower so pink? See the cat? Here cutey cutey kitten."

Her childishness grated. I wanted my ring. I wanted Sean. I wanted to be away from my family so trailed further behind them to increase the distance between us. They were walking to the same rhythm, leading from the shoulders, big strides, arms swinging in opposition to their legs which were a little too long for their bodies. Luella skipped. Mother tutted and stared at her which slowed her back down to a stroll. I was embarrassed to be with them; they weren't me. When they turned the corner, I heard a familiar voice.

"Mrs Jeffreys. Luella." I hoped she was on her own but when I reached them Sean was standing beside her. Mother started to walk on but Marjorie continued. "How are you feeling honey? How's your hand?"

I didn't dare look at Sean. I pushed my nails into my skin to try and stop the shakes. Did Marjorie know about me? She couldn't do, her attention was all on my sister.

"She's fine," Mother smiled.

Luella giggled. Marjorie glowered.

"I heard she's still not back at school."

"Oh?"

"And we never see her at the store." She beamed coldly at Mother.

"We'd best get on or the meat'll be burnt. So lovely to see you," Mother smiled back. Luella whimpered, her eyes darting between us all, feeling but not understanding the tension. She liked Marjorie, used to tell me she thought her flowing skirts and dyed hair meant she was free and wild and exciting, like Luella wanted to be when she was older. "Girls." Mother put her hand out, meaning go this way, immediately.

Sean's chest swelled. Marjorie put her hand on his arm to keep him still and I couldn't take my eyes off their touching. I wanted to feel that arm on me, have it pull me from the humiliation of being my mother's daughter.

"Lara!" she shouted, even though they were only a few steps ahead. She grabbed my elbow under the pretense of linking arms and I had no choice but to go with her. I could feel them staring at us. My body went as stiff as Mother's bony hand that was holding onto mine. I needed her to let go. I imagined peeling back the fingers and them dropping to her side, click, click, clicking like a skeleton in a lab. I repeated the sentence *get off me, don't touch me* in my head, eighteen times until it worked as Luella stumbled so I was cast aside by Mother who reached out to stop her spaced out daughter hitting the pavement. When we climbed the steps to the porch, Mother's shoulders dropped.

"Go to your rooms. I'll call you when dinner's ready."

~

I couldn't look at him.

I was too ashamed that he'd seen the three of us together, the weirdness of where I came from. I wished I was alone in the world, or that some other mother was mine and the real one would magically disappear. Luella too. And that was a terrible thing to think but life would be so much less complicated if the both of them didn't exist. It would be better. I could be whoever I wanted to be with no history to tie me down, no madness to hold me back, no explaining to do. If anyone asked what had happened to my family I'd block their nosiness with *there was a terrible accident. I'd rather not talk about it, sorry* and they'd be too polite to press for more details though they'd always long to know more, be desperate to hear the plot of the tragedy. They'd skirt around asking outright whilst pouring on the sympathy and treating me like a precious doll, amazed at my strength and resilience. I'd be a winner in every way: not missing my mother and sister so not lonely, not tense at turning the handle of a front door, no past dragging me back to their level. There would be me, looking like a normal person, relaxed and free. My conscience chastised me but I shooed away the niggles as the visions pushed themselves to the front of my head. I had to physically push them back, pressing both palms hard against my forehead, *no* escaping as a low mumble from my mouth. I pushed and twisted the skin, rolling my hands over my forehead, shunting the ideas to the base of my skull, burying them beneath numeracy, literacy, history, geography, biology, chemistry, English.

All through Miss Simpson's lesson, I sat close to Sally, never looking at Sean, not even risking a glance. When we'd been alone my family hadn't mattered, they'd seemed so far away they couldn't affect us, but Sunday was real and the reality was I couldn't escape them, so Sean and I couldn't be together and I had to make sure I needed only myself from now on. No-one else must complicate my life. I would ignore him; if I ignored him he'd go away.

"Are you alright?" asked Sally.

I wanted to run away but couldn't risk another afternoon off school. I raised my hand. "Miss, please may I go to the bathroom?"

The teacher sighed. "Class is nearly finished. You can wait five minutes." I felt Sean's eyes on me.

"I can't. If I don't go now I'll piss myself."

The class fell about laughing; someone called out oh yeah.

"Enough! Lara, what's happening to you? Go on then. Go. And take your homework on the way out."

I grabbed the top sheet from a pile on her desk and ran down the hall towards the science block. It didn't matter that break was in between, I'd wait beside the lab rather than risk being in the same space as Sean, couldn't have him touching me. At the steps I saw a pink sheet on the notice board.

"Ring found.

Visit the school office to describe and collect."

Detouring to the toilets, I dived into a cubicle, battering the wall with the flat of my palm. The birthday picnic sprang up. Someone banged on the door.

"Are you alright?" I tried to shut up. "Lara? It's Sally. Do you want to talk about it?" Her niceness made me kick the wall in frustration. I didn't know how to say what I felt out loud. "It can help to share."

"Thanks Sally but I'm fine," said my cheery voice.

"Are you sure? You didn't look fine." She was whispering so others who'd entered couldn't hear: kind, sweet Sally.

"No, really, I'm fine, just being silly." My voice cracked. I made it perkier. "You go on or you'll be late for class."

"I don't want to leave you like this."

"Honestly." I wiped the tears that kept pouring and smiled through the door, making myself believe the expression. "I'll be out in a minute. You go."

I heard the main door shut. It opened and shut again a few times, getting less busy as the start of classes neared. When it was totally hushed I blew my nose, peeked through the cubicle door and, sure that Sally wasn't there, stepped out. I splashed water over my face. The coldness made me focus. I went to the main door and pushed it open a couple of inches. The playground was nearly empty with only the odd student running as fast as they could to class. I counted to five, sprinted over the tarmac, and was the last student to arrive for Biology, meaning I got the seat nearest the door, nearest the teacher, which suited me fine. Forty five minutes later a dull dingdong told me I'd made it to the end of the day. I darted out before others had even picked up their bags and bumped right into Mr Parker. We fell against opposite walls.

"Sorry."

"You're keen." He looked bemused. "Is everything—"

"Yes Sir."

"You look upset."

"No Sir." The hall was getting noisier with students criss-crossing each other, all less clumsy than me, never bumping their bodies into teachers. "I'd better go."

He looked disappointed. Sean appeared out of his classroom. I walked fast the other way, feeling mean, knowing he'd seen me see him. Sally caught up with me and put her hand on my arm. She smiled gently.

"Are you sure you're okay?" My lower lip wobbled. "Oh no, sweetie. It's alright. It's all going to be fine. Don't worry." Her kindness made me grimace with pain. She held my hand. "Come on, nothing's that bad. Come with me."

Sean was waiting round the corner, he must have double backed.

"Not now," Sally put her hand up. "You can see her later. She's all mine for now." She winked and led me to the toilets I'd hidden in an hour ago. "Only place a girl won't get bothered."

Only place you'll not get bothered, I thought. The room smelt of perfume, flowery and too sweet. I tried to block my nose.

"What's up? Boyfriend trouble, sister trouble, mother trouble?"

"What?" I stuttered.

"It's usually one of the three. Let's take a wild guess, the big clue being Sean out there. Does it happen to be boyfriend trouble?" Tears welled up, sixteen years of crying let loose. "Hey, it's only a boy. Don't worry. It may seem bad now but it'll work itself out." I pushed my nails into my hand again and again, always on different spots so no blood leaked out, embarrassing me. She put her hands on mine. "You'll hurt yourself."

Of course I couldn't tell her anything. It was all too shameful.

"I need the toilet." I pulled my hands out of hers, not wanting her touching me.

"What—"

"I don't do talking."

"I—"

"So there's no point in you being Miss Nightingale. It's best you leave me alone."

"I was only trying to help."

"I know. And there's no need."

I shut the cubicle door, watching under it until I saw her salmon pink pumps walk away. When I washed my hands, a bubble rose from the suds growing bigger and bigger until it surrounded me with its film. I was protected. As I walked out of school, it cushioned me from the questions, comments, and giggles. I smiled as I passed Sylvester, bounced back his catcall so it hit him hard on the head. Sally and Sean were so deep in conversation they didn't notice me. I rolled along in my bubble, enjoying the smooth clear surface, the lack of sharp edges, the sound proofing. Until Sean burst it. He walked right up and popped it with his finger, stepping forcefully into my world.

"What's going on?" he asked. I started walking past him. "Hey." It was easy to barge past his weak attempt at blocking. "The least you can do is tell me."

I shrugged. He went to hold my arm; I lurched back.

"What the hell. Why are you doing this?" The veins at the sides of my head felt like they'd pop, pop, pop, splattering blood all over his face. Bet that would make him go away. "I don't understand. Is it your mother?" Him mentioning her made me wretch. "Are you sick? Do you want a lift home? You shouldn't walk all that way like this." I shook my head and ran, ignoring his call. "Why won't you let anyone help you?"

I left him.

I got home.

And one look from Mother at my grey skin, suffocating under so much sweat, meant I was sent straight to bed. My stomach twisted and cramped. My throat and mouth opened and closed at random as I heaved and breathed, heaved and breathed. She appeared at my bedside with water and a pink pill.

"Swallow this."

"I can't. I'll be sick."

"Take it. It'll make you better." When I raised it to my lips a dry heave threw my hand back. "Get it down you," she snapped. I put it in my mouth. It stuck to my tongue making me retch again. She pushed the glass to my lips so it cracked against my front teeth. "Now." She tipped the glass so water poured into my mouth, down my chin and I had to swallow rather than choke. "Close your lips, tongue to the roof of your mouth, do NOT let it fall out." She pushed her fingers under my chin so my teeth clamped together. I did as she said. And the water went down then rose again but I forced myself to swallow back the acidic mixture. It rose a second and third time, burning more each time but I kept my mouth shut and swallowed, kept swallowing.

"You're such a bloody drama queen, making a fuss over a silly pill like a stupid baby."

The walls span gently round my body as it fell deeper and deeper into the cotton wool mattress. My eyelids drooped as the ceiling twisted.

The Test

I tried to lift my head but it was too heavy, my neck couldn't support it. A slim shaft of light broke through the gap in the curtains. My stomach was hollow but I couldn't bear the thought of food. I willed my hands to move but when only a finger twitched I gave in and let them be. I was happy enough staring at the creases on the sheets, counting shadows I'd never noticed before.

"How are you feeling?"

"Fine." My voice croaked, my mouth was dry and my throat was sore.

"Take this." She held out another pink pill. "You're sick. You've been running a fever so sleep's the best medicine. And you'd better go to the bathroom before more tiredness kicks in."

She stood by the bathroom door, to hear in case I fell. Such a considerate mother. I sat on the toilet not sure if I'd finished pissing or not.

"Hurry up." Her fist rattled the wooden panels.

I couldn't be bothered washing my hands and when I had to lean on her arm on the way back to my room, I didn't recoil from her touch. She sat me down on the edge of the bed and told me to lay back. As I did, she lifted and pushed up my legs to the middle of the bed then pulled the eiderdown all the way up to my neck. As her face passed above mine she looked amused. Her breath smelled of carrots; I turned my head to the side, trying to miss its scent.

Before leaving the room she swished the curtains fully shut, no gap for the light. As I wondered if she and our father had watched the leaves on my tree, a ringing sound brought a regular rhythm to the room. The pattern on the bedsheet twirled to its tune. My eyelids shut, my legs and arms twitched as the muscles shuddered, deep relaxation alien to them. I heard Mother's voice murmuring, travelling further away. My head fell down onto my chest then rebounded back into the pillow. That was better; life was so cosy, so comfortable.

~

"One more."

Mother put the pill on the back of my tongue and the glass of water to my lips. I was falling through the clouds, the sun bouncing off me, my fingertips throwing sparkles across the sky. I reached out to catch them but they flew away same as fairies. I landed on a cloud. It was smooth and warm, folding itself round me like the softest blanket in the world. I nuzzled my cheek against it and closed my eyes, such peace, blissful. But then the cotton wool covered my mouth and I couldn't breathe deeply enough. I tried to move but my arms and legs were trapped. I cried out for help, twisting and shunting my weight, still unable to escape. Fingers prodded and pulled, the pillow was lifted and I was free.

"You were caught up in your blanket." I fell back on the pillow. "Now you're awake, you can go to the bathroom."

I didn't want to. I didn't feel like moving. She pulled the blankets off, leaving me exposed and cold. She held my ankles together and swung them over the side of the bed making my body twist and the ceiling whiz by. I shut my eyes to banish the swirling. "Oh no you don't. You open those eyes young lady. You're getting up." She moved her arms across my body and with a whoosh I was sitting upright. When she hooked an arm across my shoulders and the other underneath my armpit, I opened my eyes.

"On three you stand. One, two, three."

In my head I stood up but when I looked down I was still sitting.

"I said on three you'll stand." It hurt where she was gripping me too tightly. "One, two, three."

I flew.

I soared upwards imagining I was an angel on my way to heaven, but without wings I began to fall. She caught me, dragging me to the door, and I was overcome with remorse at being such a failure, creating so much hard work for her.

"Sorry." She said nothing, confirming my doubts in myself. I was nothing but trouble. I started to cry. "I'm really sorry. I didn't mean to be such a trial in your life." She was concentrating on getting me into the bathroom. My feet were like jelly, wibble wobble jelly, sitting on a plate, shuddering over the floor.

"You can see to yourself," she said.

The room span. I held onto the wall and shut my eyes but that made it worse. I sat on the toilet and gradually the tiles went still. I lifted my nightdress just in time. When had I changed into it? I heard the trickle of liquid more than I could feel it. When the sound stopped I wiped, rose and flushed, leaning on the sink to wash my hands. The warm water felt so delightful I cupped it in my palms and splashed it on my face, scooping some around the back of my neck, not caring if my nightdress got wet. Then I spied my toothbrush. I put some paste on it and started to brush my teeth. The texture of the froth was rough and stuck to my tongue, making me gag. I spat it out and rinsed with water, sticking my mouth as far under the tap as I could, letting it spill over the edges of my lips and dribble down my chin and neck. I was sitting on the bench, ring on my toe, Sean holding my hand, exhausted.

"I'm tired."

"Of course you are. You're sick."

"What day is it?"

"Don't worry about that. Let's get you to bed now. The pill will have started working."

I'd forgotten I'd taken one. It was lucky Mother was a nurse and knew how to make people better. The water sloshed in my tummy.

"I think I'm hungry."

"That'll pass. You need to sleep now."

Her face multiplied by eight and started to fly in circles in front of me. I snapped my eyes shut to calm the rocking of the bed then opened them to check if the room was still but it all twirled round even faster. I tried to go with the flow of the walls but they were too hectic. I shut my eyes again, drifting into a dream where I ran but got nowhere. People passed me by: Luella, Sean, Marjorie, Mr Parker. I tried calling their names but no sounds formed. As I reached out to touch them they went beyond my grasp so I tried to race after them but my legs were stuck and when I looked down, my feet had melted into the ground. I put my hands on my thighs to pull them out but that made my fingers melt into my dress. I pulled and pulled but couldn't move. With a jerk I woke up and my arms and legs were stuck under the blankets, a ten tonne weight pressing on my body, not hurting me, not totally crushing me, allowing me to breathe but not letting me move. I tried to cry out. I willed my lips to part, wishing my jaw would unlock, pushing my teeth forward to separate them but they stuck fast. A hum sounded in my head. I pushed against the force that was imprisoning me, desperately willing Mother to hear me, in need of any form of company. I pulled together enough strength to shout but it came out as a whisper. The terror grew. I summoned all my strength, urging every muscle, bone and nerve ending to do what my brain wanted. With a heave I screamed, lifted myself up, and ran from the room, waving my hands around me to punch away the evil. The light was on in the landing. I smelt dinner cooking and stumbled down the stairs to find Luella sitting on the sofa, stroking a cat cushion. When I landed by her side, she stroked my head with her free hand. As I moved closer to her, Mother laid the cutlery on the table. I didn't tell her about the fear; she may have another pill for it. Her nose twitched.

"I only cooked enough for two, but luckily for you Luella mainly plays with hers and your stomach will have shrunk from being poorly."

We sat at the table and I was still so scared, I wanted to be with them rather than on my own, in my room. The meat was tough, blood dried, veins shrunken. After a few mouthfuls I felt full.

"I don't think I can eat any more. Sorry."

"I didn't expect you to; time for a pill." Luella frowned. "You can have your hot chocolate." Luella smiled.

"I feel a bit better," I said. "Maybe I don't need one."

"Oh?"

"What day is it?" Mother continued eating her dinner. I bit the inside of my lip, rolling my tongue on the skin between my teeth. "I think they gave me a bad dream, the pills."

"That's not the pill's fault. That's the bad thoughts in your head trying to escape. Hardly surprising." She drank some water. "I've got one that can stop your dreams."

"Do you take them?"

"What?"

"Pills."

Her face flushed a sun burnt red. "All I've ever done is look after you. Worked to feed you and clothe you, have nothing for myself."

She started to clear the dishes.

"Sorry. It's just, I feel much better, I really do. You've cured me I reckon. I'm not sick anymore."

"Yes you are. Of course you are. You're very poorly. And you know nothing compared to me, nothing. You've not even finished school let alone been to college, so don't tell me, the nurse, that you're cured, that you know what you need. Do you understand? Do you hear me?" The plates were wobbling in her shaking hands.

"Yes."

"What?"

"Yes Mother. Sorry."

She smoothed her apron in acceptance of my apology, pushing the anger down her thighs and out through her feet before calmly going into the kitchen. Luella's shoulders dropped in relief. I planned to fake taking the medicine but Mother stood by me until I'd swallowed the orange tablet, checking behind my teeth, tongue and lips to make sure it had gone down.

"Bed."

The stairway was gloomy, shadows dancing along the walls. The landing was cold, dismal. I imagined someone was about to jump out at me and hurried, expecting a hand to grasp my shoulder, a presence to push me down the stairs. In my room I was still frightened and didn't want to go to sleep in case I woke up with the weight paralysing me again. I sat up in bed; being uncomfortable would keep me awake so I could fight. My head fell back, banging against the wall. I moved my hand up to rub away the pain but it crept through the air as if submerged in treacle. The pain disappeared. I tried to raise my left arm to help move my right one but it didn't reach, the muscles wouldn't obey me. My chin gurned from side to side like a cow chewing the cud. I wanted to moo but my lips wouldn't peel apart. I slipped lower down the wall and my arms thumped onto the mattress, so pale compared to the brown bedcover. They should be covered and cosy warm; if I kept the blankets up to my chin and my eyes closed, maybe nothing would get me.

~

"Get up. It's time for school."

"What?"

The sun hurt my eyes.

"You're better so you have to go back to school."

I'd have been happy to never go back to those buildings, the classes, the too many bodies rushing round; the only thing I missed was the smell of lavender from the gardens. The brightness in the room made my head ache.

"I don't feel well. I need another day at home."

"You're fine. Get dressed." She pulled back the covers and dumped them on the floor. "You've got seven minutes."

My legs were wobbly on the stairs, knees unsure of how to hold up the rest of me. The few spoonfuls of porridge I managed to swallow sat heavily in my stomach. I gave up. There was no way I could eat it.

"Your insides will have shrunk. You'll eat more eventually. Off you go then. You mustn't be late."

My legs were leaden and clumsy on the walk to school, their pathetic weakness making me want to curl up in a garden to get some rest until I felt stronger. But the trouble that would cause. I had to keep moving. I worried about the work I'd missed; I understood how to cope with one lost day but more than a week, maybe two? How long had I been missing?

~

Mr Parker was stationed by the gates. He stared at me. The students didn't; they hadn't missed me. Their voices were too loud, grating compared to the quiet at home. Girls clicked and clacked whilst the boys guffawed at the slightest thing.

When I handed in my sick note, the teacher said, "Mr Parker would like to see you, midday at the office. Give this slip to your eleven o'clock teacher." He continued to drone through the register; no welcome back, no nice to see you, no we're glad you're better Miss Jeffreys.

At break I sat on a bench and no-one joined me. At 11.55 am Miss Jones stopped writing on the board, "Lara, you can go now. Your midday appointment."

"Yes Miss."

Mr Parker was sitting on the edge of the receptionist's desk, chatting away, not a care in the world, and she was smiling up at him, eyes bright, fiddling with the silver pearls that were hanging loose on her neck. He jumped off when he saw me.

"Lara, welcome back! So good to see you. Come through, come through." He opened the door. Mrs Hawkins smiled warmly at me as I entered their territory. I didn't smile back. "Through that door," he motioned encouragingly. He walked much faster than me and with each of his steps, the gap between us lengthened. He turned left and out of sight then his head popped round the corner followed by his short, jumping body. "So, you've been pretty sick huh?"

He found it hard to walk at my slower pace, taking three steps forwards and two steps back or turning sideways and then back to front, moving his hands from his pockets to his sides, crossed to uncrossed and back to his pockets again. I was serene in comparison. He unlocked the door to his office; memories of our previous meeting flooded back.

"May I move the chair please? It's a bit bright."

"Of course. Whatever makes you comfortable. I should change the furniture around. The feng shui's all wrong but it's so small there's not much choice with the layout."

I moved my chair so the sun was out of my eyes but that meant my neck twisted awkwardly to see him.

"Are you sure that's alright? It doesn't look very comfy. I could try and hang something over the window." He reached for a towel that was lying on the floor by the corner of his desk. As he picked it up some bright red shiny Speedos fell out. "Oops." He laughed kicking them under the desk and when he couldn't reach the top of the window, he moved his chair to stand on it.

"It's fine. I'm fine. Just leave it."

"Are you sure?" Relieved, he threw the towel under his desk and sat back down. "So. You've been a poorly."

"I gave in a note."

"I saw that. And you were off school for a week was it?"

"Yes."

"Are you better now?"

"Yes thank you."

"You look tired."

"Yes."

"Do you mind me asking what was wrong?"

"I was sick."

"With what?"

"I had a fever. Mother said it was a bug."

"Right. And the doctor?"

"We don't need doctors, Mother's a nurse."

"But you must go to a doctor too, sometimes?"

"No." He wrote something down. "Is that a wrong answer? Are you testing me?"

"No."

"Then what are you writing?" He put the pad and pen on the desk, flipping the cover over to hide the words. Perhaps Mother was right not to trust him.

"I won't write anything else." He put his hands in his lap. "Lara, part of my job is to look after the welfare of our students. If I see one in trouble, I want them to know that I'll do my best to help them."

"Am I in trouble?"

"No," he spoke softly. "Not in school." He paused. "But I don't know about outside of here."

"What do you mean?"

He sighed as he rubbed his eyes with one hand. "How's everything at home?"

"Fine."

"You're sure?"

"Yes." This was it then, my chance to save Luella and I from our mean old mother. "You're making my head hurt."

He sat forward, keen to engage.

"I spoke with your form teacher, about that afternoon. Don't worry, you're not in any trouble, but she's sure she didn't muddle you and Luella up, said she's never mistaken one of you for the other the whole time you've been here. Is that right?" I moved back in my seat, not wanting him in my space. "You seem so sad all the time." His sincerity took me by surprise. I held my breath to stop any physical reaction: no tears, no frustration, no confession. I thought about being saved by him but couldn't face the humiliation. I'd deal with it by myself. I'd get Luella away from the house and we'd be fine by ourselves in an apartment with two rooms, that would be enough for us. My knee hit the edge of the chair. My neck was sore from being twisted too long. "I didn't mean to upset you."

"You didn't. I'm fine. Thank you."

I closed the door behind me and heard it open as I hurried down the corridor.

"You just have to knock if you want help Lara. Or to talk. My door's always open for you."

I scooted past Mrs Hawkins and out of the double doors behind her desk which opened onto the top field. There was still half an hour of the lunch break left but I wasn't hungry so dropped my food in a grey metal playground bin and headed to the library. When I got to the stairs Sally called my name. Why would no-one leave me alone? Where was some godamned peace when I needed it? I climbed up four steps hoping that if I ignored her she'd go away.

"Lara! Hey! It's Sally." I had to stop. I couldn't be that rude. I held onto the banister and turned to look down on her.

"How are you feeling?"

"Fine."

"I missed you last week."

"Sorry."

"Are you still poorly? You look –"

"I'm fine, a bit tired that's all."

"Oh. It's just, I saw you with your lunch and—"

"I'm not hungry. I've got a shrunken stomach from being so ill." She studied my tummy as if she wanted to look right inside it, making me so self-conscious I moved my hand to rub it. Her eyebrows raised.

"Were you sick all week?"

"Yes."

"God, you poor thing. You must have lost so much weight."

"What?"

"You must have lost weight, what with not eating and that." She looked at my belly again.

"I don't think so."

"I guess you didn't have much to lose you lucky thing." She smiled. "Do you want to sit outside with me?"

"I've got a lot of work to catch up on." I walked backwards up a couple of steps. She stayed where she was. I shut the library door behind me and sat in the nearest free chair, the shakes spreading down my arms to my fingertips.

"Are you okay?" asked a stranger.

"Yeah. Tired."

"Too much partying this weekend eh?"

She was a younger girl. I must have stared meanly because her smile froze on her face, then cracked and disappeared as she bent over to carry on studying. I got a book from my bag and pretended to read it. Head bowed, hands covering my forehead, I waited for the bell to ring.

~

Mother was waiting in the hallway when I got home. I saw her lips move but didn't hear the words until a few seconds later. Gradually the sounds and movement tuned into each other and I replied.

"It was fine."

"How are you feeling?"

"Fine."

"Anything unusual? I suppose there were lots of questions about you being sick?"

I pictured Mr Parker but couldn't face an interrogation. "No."

"None at all?" She was suspicious, sensing my lie.

"At registration the form tutor asked how I was so I said better and gave in your note."

She sniffed but let it go. After dinner I tried to persuade her to give me an orange pill but she wouldn't and when I woke the next day my head was clearer but my limbs ached like their insides were covered in bruises and I understood why Luella accepted the medicine for making the pain disappear and time pass quickly and life with Mother bearable, though her pills must be less strong than mine had been because she slept less, at least on weekends she did, I didn't know what she was prescribed on weekdays.

Idiot.

I'd been such an idiot.

I needed to help her; she wasn't strong enough to save herself.

~

"Good to have you back," said Mr Jonas.

"Jesus. Where—"

"Sorry. Didn't mean to scare you. Are you feeling better?"

"Yes."

"Good. That's good to hear."

Why was he always round a corner? Sean was standing by the main doors, half hidden by Miss Simpson, but as I neared them he slipped inside. Served me right. I took my time getting to class, not caring if he'd be sitting close to me or not. I could pass him by, no problem.

He was two rows back from the teacher's desk. As I walked towards the seat next to Sally, head up, eyes facing front, he brushed my hand with his finger. I dropped my books. Someone at the back of the room whistled, laughter rippled through the room.

"Oh joy," drawled Mr Magnus. "It's going to be one of those lessons is it?"

"Sorry Sir." I scrambled for my books. Sean held one out to me and smiled at my kneeling figure.

"Hurry up Lara, for God's sake child."

I accepted the book and sat next to Sally.

"The homework's so hard. Do you understand it?" asked Sally. Turning to answer her made me wince, my neck stiff from too much lying down. "You wouldn't be able to help me with it would you, at lunchtime? I don't want to get more behind. My Dad'll go mad if I get another C minus."

I bet he really loved her. And her mother and her brother. I bet they were a perfect family.

"Sure."

As soon as the answer was out I knew I'd made a mistake. Stupid girl. I'd told myself I'd be alone at lunchtime, uninvolved with anyone at school. As we walked out of class, Sean was near the door, talking to another boy, not looking me.

"See you in the flower garden?"

"What?"

"It's such a lovely day out. I thought we could sit in the flower garden."

"Why?"

Sally hesitated. "To do the homework. Like we just said. I thought it'd be nice but we can meet somewhere else if you'd rather?"

Her mind bounced round the place too much; it was beginning to get on my nerves.

"No, that's fine. See you later."

~

Mr Jonas was tending a flower bed that looked perfect to me. I hurried past him into the garden where Sally stood waiting.

"Thanks for this Lara. You're so much better at Geography than me." I fiddled with the buckle on my bag. "Shall we sit on the grass?"

I got my text book out. "Which bit didn't you get?"

"Umm…."

She looked behind me then smiled at me then checked behind me again and this time she smiled over me. I should have listened to my gut; it had been right not to trust her. I sat very still. Sally fidgeted with her text book. Grass was crushed as Sean walked around me and stood next to her kneeling figure, his fingers resting on her right shoulder, like they were together now. In my head I ran.

"Hey Lara. How are you feeling?" he asked.

"Fine." Furious at the thought of them kissing more like. "This obviously isn't a coincidence."

"How are you really Lara?" Sally asked gently.

"I'm fine. Why do you keep asking?"

"You're not still feeling sick?"

"What?"

"She said are you still feeling sick?" Sean added.

"Yeah, I heard her. I just don't see what it's got to do with her. Or you."

Sally spoke more forcefully whilst Sean blushed. "Of course it's his business."

"Why?" I asked.

"Well, I'm just saying maybe it's his business. You—"

"What are you talking about?"

Sally nudged Sean with her elbow.

"Are you still feeling sick?" he repeated slowly.

"No, I'm not." I put my book back in my bag.

"We got you this, just in case." Sally took a brown paper bag from her pink canvas one and held it out.

"What is it?" Neither of them replied. "You two are pathetic."

Sally stepped forwards. "It's a test."

"For what? I don't want it." I felt like crying, not under-standing their game. "What is it with you two? Why are you being so strange?"

"Don't get upset," said Sean.

"Why are you ganging up against me?"

"We're not against you. We're on your side."

"Against what?"

"Jesus!" He kicked the ground. I watched them working out what to do. Sally gave the package to Sean and moved to block the entrance to the garden.

"You two need to talk."

"No!" I cried out.

"See? See what she's like?" he raised his arms out to Sally like I was impossible.

"Just talk to each other." And she left.

"Easier said than done eh Lara? Will you actually talk to me?"

"Of course," I mumbled, fighting the urge to run out like Sally had.

"Really? Because you've been blanking me so much you wouldn't think it. What did I do?"

I couldn't move my arms, only my good thumb twitched. I nearly shouted *Did you see that Sean? Did you see my thumb move towards you?* but he wouldn't get it and I'd seem crazier than he already thought I was.

"Nothing."

"What?"

"You've done nothing. It's me not you." He took a big breath in, his ribs showing up against his white polo shirt. "You should go. Go and find Sally. I'm sorry but I can't do this."

"I can't. We're stuck together now."

"What do you mean? Please Sean, there's so much going on. I'm sorry I can't control the hating, I—"

"You hate me?"

"No. Not you."

"Your mother?"

I hung my head, ashamed at the huge betrayal. "No."

"You know she's not normal?"

One of my knees buckled. "I'm too tired for all this."

He frowned. "You're more tired than usual?"

"I guess."

"And sick?"

"A bit."

The tan drained down his cheeks. "That's why we got you the test. Here. Take it. Please."

I took the bag from him and instead of a jewellery box inside it, there was a cardboard box with the word Answer in blue lettering on its cover.

"What is it?"

"What it says."

"Don't be so cross."

"I'm not but you can see what it is and you can read can't you?"

"Why would you give me this?"

"Because you've been sick and tired and—"

"It was a bug."

"Because of what we did." I looked blankly at him. "At the lake."

"I don't—"

"I know it was only once and it's not fair. I—"

"What's not fair?"

"That you might be pregnant." He looked as wound up as Mother when she was ready to hit something. "Lara—"

"Get off me."

"Why are you laughing? Jesus, what's wrong with you?"

"Everything! Everything's wrong with me." I brushed

bits of grass off my dress. "My mother's wrong, my sister's wrong, this is wrong." I held up the test. "Everything's absolutely, completely and utterly wrong." He looked as if he was about to cry, like a little lost boy. His hand reached for my face. "Don't be nice." He stepped forward and put his fingers behind my ear, moving his other arm around my back, all gentle. "Stop it. Please. Don't be nice." I saw my reflection in his sunglasses, scared and hollow, hair sticking up where it had been unevenly trimmed in the bathroom, my face pasty and blotchy from being ill and upset. I was ugly and pathetic. The reflection blurred as my eyes welled up. I wiped my cheeks with one hand then frowned, realising I was still holding onto the test. He put his hands around mine and the box. The corner of it dug painfully into my palm but I didn't move, didn't want to.

"This is our problem, not yours."

"But—"

"No buts. I'm with you on this."

I'd been going to tell him I didn't understand how I could be having a baby. I tried to remember what Luella had repeated after she'd heard some girls talking in the changing rooms at school. He gestured behind my back. Sally looked nervous as she approached. I wiped my cheeks again, deranged and disheveled next to her perfection.

"Sorry I was mean Sally."

She waved my words aside.

"No problem. I'd be a lot worse in your situation." She put her hand to her mouth wishing she'd said nothing.

"It'll be fine," said Sean.

We stood in a triangle, in our grown up mess. A whistling sound floated closer.

113

"Quick. Put it in your bag," said Sally.

"The test," urged Sean, "before he gets here."

Sally opened my bag and pulled at my wrist so the box fell inside it. Mr Jonas strolled into the garden.

"Lunch has finished guys. Lessons are starting."

"Oh no. We didn't hear the bell. Thanks for letting us know." Sally feigned brightness and led the way. I glanced at Mr Jonas as we walked past him but his eyes were focused on my bag which was open with the top of the test showing. I flipped the flap over and hurried to catch up with the others, trying to persuade myself he hadn't seen it.

That afternoon I kept the bag on the floor between my feet, feeling the edge of the box with the side of my shoe, making sure it was there, confirming it was real. I tried to imagine myself with a baby but the idea was preposterous. I thought of telling Mother then shut that picture away, determined it would never come out.

Sean and Sally walked me home, one on either side, my protectors.

"You can't come down our street. She mustn't see you."

"Are you going to do it?" Sally asked

"What?"

"Are you going to take the test?" I chewed my lips. "I could be with you," she offered. I stuck my finger nails into the palm of my hand, kneading away at the flesh. "It might be best not to do it alone," she continued. "We could do it at school."

"Have you done one before?" I asked her.

"What? No!" She looked appalled.

"Right. Yeah, thanks but I'll be fine."

"But I can help you."

"I said I'm fine."

Sally looked at Sean then back at me.

"You're going to take it then?"

I stopped and their reactions were so slow, they came to a standstill four steps ahead and had to turn back to face me.

"Sally, this isn't your business. You need to back off."

"Christ. I wanted to help, that was all." She stormed up the street, round the corner, out of sight. Sean and I stood awkwardly apart.

"That was mean. She's nice."

"You should go too." He smacked his palm on a fence. "It's nothing personal."

"Yeah right."

"Please Sean, you have to understand, that day at the lake, it was nice but..." He kicked some dirt back and forth with his foot. "I can't explain it. Sorry."

"I think you might need help Lara. Marj said professional—"

"I need no-one."

"Everyone needs someone."

"Why? Why's being on your own so bad? Why do I have to have a family, friends, you? Seems to me it just complicates things."

"That's the way it is though."

"Well it's not my way."

"That's not natural."

"Then I'm unnatural. So be it." And there it was. And he was right. I didn't fit into his world.

"That's such bullshit. You do need people. You daren't let it out that's all. You're scared. She's made you scared. If you get away from her you'll be free you know. The world isn't so bad, think of—"

"I don't mean to be horrible."

"I know." He stepped closer to me. "I'm sorry too. I'm all over the place with this. Please, can you do the test?"

"You really think—"

"I don't know. It all adds up, that's what Sally said, so it's best we find out and—"

"Lara!"

"Oh God."

She would destroy me.

"Keep calm," he muttered. "We weren't doing anything wrong."

Ignoring Sean, Mother grabbed my arm and squeezed. "What are you doing?" she asked through gritted teeth.

"Coming home." She squeezed harder. It really hurt.

"Oh really? Because it looks like you're standing in the street chatting to—"

"Mrs—"

"Shush now Sean," and he did. He'd not seen her fuming before. She pulled me forwards so my back was flung in front of him.

"Hey!" But he stepped back when she glared him down.

"What have you been up to?"

"Nothing."

"Tell me the truth." She squeezed so hard I knew there'd be finger sized bruises in the morning.

"Please, I haven't done anything."

"Then why have I been called to the school?"

"What?"

"Mr Parker and the Principal want to see me." Mr Jonas must have told them about the test; I knew he wasn't to be trusted. "Why have they called me in? What have you done?"

"Nothing."

"Have you been messing about, playing with boys?"

"No, of course not. I haven't." Sean was hypnotized by the scene being played out in front of him. "It must be because I was off sick."

"What?"

"Mr Parker stopped me this morning, asking how come I'd been off sick for so long."

"But you gave in the note?"

"Yes."

"So why are they calling me in?"

"I don't know. You know how they are, what they're like."

She looked like she might believe the blame I was putting on them.

"Go home Sean." She flicked him away like an annoying fly and me, she pushed in the direction of our road. I wanted him to go, to not see me anymore, to not make this trouble worse. Once he was out of sight she poked me in the shoulder. "You. Straight home." She started off in the direction of school.

I tripped as I got near the house, falling heavily onto the pavement, cutting both knees. I pulled my school bag towards me and checked the box which was now bumped and bent. I sat on the curb with blood dripping from the cuts wondering if the test itself was damaged. The blood gathered in pools then rolled down my shins. If it all ran out of me, I'd be at peace.

In the house I called out for Luella and found her in bed. There was an empty hot chocolate mug on her bedside table. She was sucking her good thumb. Her lips were closed around it, one finger on her nose, three others

117

below, just like I used to. She rolled onto her other side, knees curled up to her chest.

I rushed to my room and took out the box. The back of it said ten minutes was all you needed so I had time to try it while Mother was at school; her anger with *that man* and the Principal would take hours to vent. I carefully unsealed the edges and found a foil packet inside. I pulled where it said but it wouldn't come apart and my nails were too short to rip it open. There was a leaflet. I glanced over facts and diagrams I'd never seen before. It said I had to urinate. I had to open the packet and urinate on a stick. Simple apart from I didn't need the toilet. Leaving the test on the bed, I rushed downstairs to the kitchen where my after school water was on the table. I gulped it down, and a second glass, then ran back up the stairs where I checked Luella again. She was still sleeping.

I took my bag, the test and the box into the bathroom, constantly listening for the open and close of the front door. I wedged the bag and a hand towel against the base of the door, making sure it would get stuck if I missed Mother's arrival and she tried to open it, then I re-read every word of the leaflet. It was 99.8 per cent accurate and fast as can be. With the super sharp nail scissors I cut the packet, just managing to catch the white plastic stick thing as it fell out. I checked the little window. It was blank like the instructions had said it would be. I pulled the lid off. It looked too innocuous to be able to change my entire life, the end like the litmus paper in school, like the blotting paper on a calligraphy desk. I sat on the toilet working out where to hold it to make sure it got wet, unsure of where exactly the liquid would come from. I bent over, head down, and started to go to the toilet. Only a dribble came out and the stick was in the wrong place so I missed it. Holding my waters in, I moved it further under me. The urine came out fuller and faster and I managed to place the paper in its stream. It went over my fingers and as I finished, warm liquid dribbled down my right arm.

Carefully I put the test on the floor, replaced the lid and started to count the six hundred seconds, an elephant said in between each one. I wiped then washed my hands and arms, making hundreds of suds, determined that no smell from my insides would remain on me. I rinsed, counting ninety one elephant, ninety two elephant, ninety three elephant. I pictured myself holding a baby and lost count. I couldn't comprehend how it worked, that what we did could make a child. I heard a noise and stiffened, waiting for the sound of her steps on the stairs but none followed and I wondered if she was trying to trick me but surely she'd be too furious to creep about.

I washed my knees, the blood off my legs. The flannel turned varying shades of pink as the red mixed in with the water. I picked up the test with my good hand, unsure of what its answer would mean for me. I looked in the window to see my future and there was one line, which meant one life, mine, me only, no baby. Relief trickled through me. A smile, followed by an urge to run, to see Sean, to tell him it was fine, that there was no need to be anxious.

"Lara, get down here! Now!" She shouted so coarsely she had to cough to clear the anger. I shoved the test and packaging to the bottom of my bag.

"Coming," I flushed the chain and commanded myself to act as though everything was normal.

"Sit down." She registered me holding my bag, but said nothing. I put it on my lap, desperately trying to act naturally.

"The school thinks you're unhappy." I fiddled with the strap. "So I told them that you've got a good home: your mother's a nurse, you get a home cooked meal each night and clean clothes every morning but that didn't satisfy them. Oh no, they didn't want to know about all that. They said they're concerned about your inner feelings and lack of outer emotions." Her tone changed from mimickry to a murmur. "I felt like throwing their patronising words right back in their faces and walking out of there. But I didn't." Her eyes lit up at the memory of it. "I played their game. I'm a poor widow, doing my best, oh the guilt of you having no father but I didn't want to rush into another marriage, I'm not that kind, and now I'm being told I've failed. I even managed a tear. The Principal was easy enough, full of 'there there's' and embarrassed coughs, pulling the collar from his thick neck, with that redness in his face I'm surprised he didn't have a heart attack right in front of me, soon though Lara, it won't be long for him, but that Mr Parker, now he was a different matter. He said nothing, just stared right at me. I'm not sure he ever quite believed my reasoning but never mind, as long as the Principal thinks he's got control we can afford to let it be. I need to watch out for that Parker man though, and you," she pointed at me, "you need to cheer up when you're there and be careful around him."

"Yes Mother."

"They suggested counselling and I had to say yes."

"But—"

"Your form teacher will tell you when your appointment is but of course, you'll forget to go." Having to sit still made the madness of the day overwhelm me, my body empty of energy and my head full of a post-fizz fuzz, like that time we had coca-cola. "So. You can do that?"

"I'm not sure."

"Why not? Christ. You're never sure of anything, it's always this or that with you, dawdling at something in between. At least Luella had some spark in her." And now look at her, I thought. "What were you doing with Marjorie's boy?"

"Pardon?"

She stepped forwards. "You heard me."

I couldn't stop looking in her eyes. I gripped my bag tighter, aware of the explosiveness of its contents, terrified she'd ask to see inside it, that she could smell my piss.

"I was upset."

"What about?"

"Someone at school shouted out stuff. Bad words. About you, the boy that was in the playground when you came to school that time. Sean was checking I was alright, that's all."

"Why?"

"I don't know. He looks out for everyone."

"A nosy creature like his mother."

I didn't defend him; I needed the conversation to end. My knuckles were white where they were squeezing the bag. She padded to the sofa, plumping the cat cushions that were already full of feathers and air. She punched the back of them and stroked the front as if they were real, little kitty cats smiling for their mistress. I waited to be told what to do next.

"Get on with your homework then."

I took out the top book, holding the bag at an awkward

angle so she couldn't see in it, closing the flap before a glimpse could be taken. All the while she stared at my face, trying to read my thoughts. I built a blank wall hiding babies, tests, Sally and Sean. It was a green book, green for biology, the power of plants. Those were some of the lessons she'd made us miss, the workings of the body, people and the new lives they can create, the love, the overpowering liking one human can feel for another. If only she'd let me go to those lessons. If only we'd both known, things could have been different. Luella might not have invited Sylvester and Daviid with two iis. She'd be sitting opposite me now, wanting help with her homework.

As if sensing my need, she drifted down the stairs.

"Is it morning?" she asked.

"No," Mother replied. "Sit on the sofa while I cook dinner."

Luella lay across it and half smiled in her drugged out way. I wouldn't tell her about the test, it was a secret for me and Sean only.

"How are you feeling?" I asked.

"Good. Tired." She yawned again as she stared at me. "You look different. I can see purple all around you."

"Don't be silly." I dismissed her comment but she wouldn't let it go; I hoped Mother wasn't eavesdropping in the kitchen.

"I think you're happy, deep inside. I can see it."

"You're talking nonsense."

"So says you. No need to be rude."

I started my homework but couldn't focus. There was some hope: there was no baby, Luella sounded slightly coherent. It could all get better.

When Mother brought out dinner I still had the leaves of the plant to colour in.

"You're slow tonight."

"Sorry."

"After dinner you can show me what you've done."

"What?" My heart shot too much blood to my head, making the room spin.

"It's pardon."

"It's boring. You won't—"

"Shut your mouth."

She hadn't missed my anxiety then. She'd been biding her time, her thoughts festering as she chopped and boiled and served.

After Luella finished her hot chocolate, Mother led her to bed. It was my only chance to get rid of the test. I stacked the plates and they clumsily clattered together in the sink. In the living room, I grabbed all the evidence and shoved it to the bottom of the kitchen bin, right at the bottom so I was up to my shoulders in peelings, paper, cartons and scraps. It smelt putrid but I needed to make sure it was deep down where she wouldn't find it. "Box, foil, leaflet, test, box, foil, leaflet, test," making sure I'd not forgotten to hide any part of it. Convinced that I'd got it right, I piled the condiments high and took the rickety pyramid into the kitchen. There was a sonorous smash after the pepper pot fell to the floor and broke into hundreds of pieces. Mother ran over the top landing. My arms stank of the rotting rubbish. I immersed them in the washing up bubbles then whipped both out, drying them as much as I could before she reached me.

"What did you do?" she shrieked.

"Sorry."

"What happened? You broke the pepper pot?"

"It slipped."

She spied suds on my arms. "Your hands. Wet hands. You carried them with wet hands?"

"Yes. Yes I did, I—"

"You idiot. You've become such a flaky fool. Why would you do that?" She moved closer to me. "Up here. Use... up... here." She poked her bony finger twice into my temple. "Use what little of that stupid brain you can Lara. Do you understand me? God, you drive me crazy."

She was using every bit of willpower not to turn the pokes into punches. I needed her to stop. I moved my hand up to my temple ready to thwack her finger away. It poked my hand.

"Stop it," I said.

Instead of shouting, she smirked at me.

"Clear it up – every last peppercorn, every shard of glass. I'll check. You know I will." She crunched the glass beneath her slippers into smaller pieces on her way to the door. "And Lara," I looked up from where I'd knelt, "know how precious that was to me; how you've hurt me. Your father bought it as a gift and I've used it every day since. Each turn of the screw reminded me of his love. You think on about how you've taken that away, as you're kneeling, as you're sweeping."

My guilt made me meticulous, finding every bit, reaching under the cooker and moving the table when I spotted a fragment that had got caught half under a leg. A dull ache settled in my throat, the almost tears but too sad to cry feeling. My knee slipped. I saw blood. I watched the red running through the soft hairs to my ankle. The earlier cut had opened up and it stung. I looked more closely and saw a piece of glass sticking out of the open wound. I plucked it out with my finger and thumb. It was quite beautiful, sharp like a dagger, jagged and ruby red. I imagined running it over all my skin, slitting the veins and watching a red river flow over the kitchen, through the doors, over the porch, down the steps, a torrent of blood brightening this dark house, drowning the unhappiness in its sticky flow, too thick to swim against, no chance to float. Then she came back in and spoilt my imaginings. As my empty eyes looked up, nurse mode overtook her. She went upstairs and came back with her medical kit and I sat still as she wiped, picked out more glass, disinfected and dressed the wounds, almost as if she cared.

"Thank you."

"I don't want any more blood on the floor. It stains. Do you want something for the pain?"

I'd promised myself there'd be no more pills but her words had smarted and I felt an overwhelming desire for sleep and the peace that only medicine would bring. I accepted the tablet and glass of water she was holding out. As the drugs took hold I merged with the sheets. I tried to remember her hugging us when we were small, tried to remember laughing and playing as normal families do. But I couldn't.

The Trap

After breakfast I didn't shout out goodbye to Mother and Luella. There was no point. Living under the same roof was our only connection, we might as well all admit that none of us cared for the other. Sean was waiting near the bank. He opened his car door for me, quiet, nervous about the answer that would define his future.

"There's no baby."

He thumped the steering wheel and whooped for joy. "Yes! No offence but we're too young and oh my God, the trouble it would have caused. We have to tell Marj."

He turned the car round and headed in the direction of the store.

"What? What are you doing? Why does she know?"

"It's okay. She understands."

"What must she think of me? Oh my God, I—"

"She likes you. Don't worry about it."

"But why did you tell her? I didn't tell anyone. We said it'd be our secret."

"I had to. She was worried about me and kept going on about it, could tell that something was up. I couldn't keep such a big thing from her, she's my mother."

"But the more who know, the more might find out."

"It's fine. She won't tell a soul. Honestly."

He parked outside the store and offered me his hand but I wasn't ready to see her so he ran in alone, gleeful. A few minutes later he jogged out. And Marjorie followed him. I sank down in my seat wishing it would swallow me up but she knocked on the window so I had to wind it down.

"Hey Lara."

"Hello Mrs… Marjorie."

"I'm glad you're feeling better."

"Thank you." I studied the dashboard.

"We'd better go," Sean piped up.

"Sure. Have a good day honey." She gave him the biggest grin full of love. "You too Lara."

I wished I was her daughter so I could take a little of that smile and feel safe in its warmth. I wanted to jump out of the car and hug her and tell her how strange everything was and then she'd help us. She'd come with me to rescue Luella and help us run away so we never had to see Mother again. If I told her what it was like at home she'd feel sorry for me and see how nasty Mother is and tell everyone in town and then we could leave, conscience clear. Or she'd want to be our friend. We'd stay and she'd paint our nails, be the daughters she never had. As I envied Sean, her face darkened.

"Get down."

"What?"

Sean started pushing me to the floor.

"Hey," I protested.

"It's your mother."

"Go," Marjorie said. "Quickly, go now."

He drove too fast. I stayed on the floor, curled in a

ball. My neck ached but I didn't dare move. I banged my head on the underneath of the dashboard when he took the corners too fast.

"I need to go home."

"What? No way."

"I can't leave Luella."

"She'll be fine. It's you who'll be in trouble."

"If she saw me she'll be angry and—"

"She'll be angry with you."

"You don't understand, that won't matter to her. It's not what it is that's made her angry that's the problem, it's who's near her when she's feeling it." I ripped a piece of loose skin off the edge of a nail and chewed it, desperately trying to decide what to do.

"I don't think she saw you. She was right at the other end of the street and if she thinks she did, well, Marj is a wonderful storyteller. She'll persuade her you were someone else."

As he parked, my breathing slowed. If I went home and she'd not seen me what lie would I tell her? He had a point, it could create a problem that didn't exist yet. As we walked through the gates, Mr Jonas nodded hello then carried on planting white flowers. Sally left her girlie group to walk with us.

"Alright?" she asked, linking her arm through mine.

"Yeah."

I let her be near me. She smiled and talked about chocolate, her treat, for lunch.

Which tasted delicious after my abstinence. I appreciated each mouthful, picking layers off the bar so that it coated my bicarbonate cleaned teeth. I brushed aside the sense of foreboding that crept up time and time again that day. It would be fine. Sean was right. She won't even have seen me.

~

Mr Parker stopped me in the hallway after last lesson, pushing through a group of students, brushing back the unruly brown curls that were falling into his eyes.

"Everything alright Lara?"

"Yes." He didn't go away. "I have to go, mustn't be late." I pointed towards the outside world.

"Of course." He walked with me. "I didn't want to call your Mother in yesterday. It went above me, was out of my hands."

I shrugged.

"You're alright though?"

I speeded up my walk. "I really have to go."

He stopped and I kept on.

My guardians appeared.

"I'm worried your mother's going to be upset and stuff. Maybe you should come back to mine." Sean glanced at Sally.

"No."

"We need a plan," Sally said.

"What?"

"We need a plan in case your mother loses it." She laughed nervously.

"Isn't that a bit dramatic?"

"I don't know. You know her best. Do you think so?"

"It's fine. I can handle it."

"But I thought she was, I mean, that you don't know what she'll do if—"

"You better go. I'll get in such trouble if she sees us

together again." They didn't stop walking with me. "Please. I appreciate your concern, honestly, but it's fine. I'll see you tomorrow." I leant over and boldly kissed Sean on the lips. Sally looked away. I glided forwards as they stood still on the corner.

My confidence lessened as I approached our road which was quiet except for the percussion section warming up in my chest. Our house was so tired looking, sagging at its edges, needing to be released from the burden that was our family. A house needed love and laughter, not fear and shouting. Tiles were missing from the roof and even more paint had peeled off the weatherboarding and window frames in the hot summer. The flower beds were perfectly weeded but not pretty like in the neighbours' gardens.

When the front door shut behind me I instinctively looked back for Sean and Sally but they'd gone, of course they had, I told them I'd be fine. Luella was already sitting in the living room; I could see the back of her head over the top of the chair, Mother's sewing chair that was usually at the other end of the room. I slipped off my shoes and walked down the hall. Luella's hands were on either arm, not resting but clutching the material, fingers clawing over the weave; they'd catch if only her nails had been long enough. Her muscles were tense as if she'd been sitting there for a long time. And as I got closer I saw Mother. She was sitting opposite Luella on a dining chair. Why had she moved it, why not sit on the sofa. Her eyes locked with mine. She raised a hand to stop me, directly behind Luella, creating a totem pole like in the book we'd been studying in History. I couldn't pull my eyes away from her while her focus travelled from me to Luella, to the cushions and their cats, over the back of the sofa until they stared at the dining room table and there, neatly laid out on a bedsheet were the test, the leaflet, the foil and the paper bag. She'd even known which bag it had come in.

"Well?" Her voice was a dull monotone. "Whose is it?" She sounded weary and looked too old, like she'd had us later in life than other mothers. I couldn't see Luella's face but I could imagine her doped up confusion. My breath didn't quicken. I didn't feel sick.

"It's mine."

"What?"

"It's mine."

Her neck cracked back then tipped forward like Luella's when she was at her most high. "Ha! Oh my God Lara, you're taking me for a fool."

"No."

"No mother, yes mother, always what you say mother."

It would be a bad night.

Luella remained stuck to her seat. I felt safer with her and the chair between me and Mother but I was ready to run, ready to dodge, ready to fight back even as Mother's eyes changed from broken to poisonous. I knew that look. I'd seen the results of that hate. My fingers copied Luella's, clawing at the back of the chair.

"Where did I go wrong? How did I end up with you two?" We didn't know the right reply. It was safer to be silent. "They can't even answer me." She stood up, raising her hands to the ceiling. I wasn't sure who she was speaking to. She stumbled and her foot knocked a bottle by the corner of the coffee table which hit another empty bottle that was next to it which rolled across the polished floor. They were dusty bottles, Father's. I'd never seen her drink anything but water and now two whole bottles of wine were gone. I remembered its effect on Luella, but with Mother it was different. Although her limbs were relaxed, they still looked strong and able. Her face was hard not soft, her tone angry not resigned. The morbidity was similar, the pitying martyrdom of the drunk.

"How history repeats itself, well I won't let it happen," she slurred, picking up the test. "I know who used this stick." She waved it in front of Luella's face. "Don't I?" Luella whimpered. I moved to the side of the chair.

"Leave her alone. I told you it was me."

"Shut up. I've had enough of you."

"Likewise Mother." I spat her name out as if it was a piece of rotten food. She hesitated.

"Don't you dare speak to me like that."

"Why not?"

"You will respect me!"

"Why? You've done nothing to earn it." She opened her mouth but I was quicker. "And don't start on one of your 'all I've done for you' speeches. Do you know what? All you've done is make our lives miserable. You made us feel like outcasts in school and town. I look at the other mothers and wish they were mine and dread coming home because I can't handle being near you. I despise you. And I feared you. Don't smirk, don't you dare. That's a bad thing. Don't you get it? To be so cruel that your child's scared of you, to be so foul that she can't bear to be in the same room as you. Oh my God, are you proud of that? Stop smiling. You can't think it means you're a good person, a good mother. Stop it."

Luella, she'd been taking it all in, amazed and terrified, and when Mother stormed into the kitchen, we were left not knowing what to do. Was that it? Was the argument over? Would life change now? It felt good to have stood up to her though my hands started trembling as soon as the kitchen door slammed shut. After a few minutes, when she still hadn't come back, I sat on my haunches in front of my sister.

"I'm sorry. I've got us into a load of trouble."

"No you haven't." She sounded more lucid; there was intelligence back behind her eyes. "Anyway, it'll be alright."

"I'm not so sure about that."

"I am."

"Why? You look better you know."

"I feel it. This afternoon, sitting here, everything became a bit clearer."

"How come?"

"Oh, I'll tell you another time."

"Did she do something?"

"No."

"Really?"

"Yeah. We just sat here."

"What did she say? When you were waiting, did she say anything?" Luella hesitated. "No mad mutterings, no blaming you, no—"

"We just sat waiting for you to get home and you saw the rest of it."

It felt like the wrong time to push for more and my legs had started cramping so I sat on the edge of the chair, holding Luella's hand, watching the kitchen door as it burst open, too slow to stop Mother pulling me up by the shoulders. She squeezed.

"It was you in the car wasn't it? Not my imagination like Marjorie said. I was right. I did see you." I moved my arms up to push hers off but she was gripping me too tightly. "Admit it." Her dark brown eyes were full of anger and hate.

"Get off me."

Luella got up as I struggled against Mother.

"Tell me the truth."

"Get off." It was hard getting the words out with all my strength trying to push her away.

"It was me," Luella cried, tears rolling down her face. "Don't fight. Please. It was me." Mother shoved me as she let go so I fell back against the table, whacking my hip on its edge, banging my knees as I fell to the floor.

"When did you do it? Tell me."

Luella didn't back away. "When you were out one day."

"Who bought it? Who gave it to you? I want details. Who was he? Where was it? Why did you let another one touch you here?" She punched Luella in the stomach. I lunged at her back but she was quicker than me and anticipating my move, turned and whacked all her weight on me before I could stop her. I fell backwards onto the floor crushing my left arm and leg. Mother rocked from side to side, ready to defend her slight frame.

"It's like that is it?" she smiled. "You think I can't see through your little plan? Well, your mistake because I know everything. How many times have I told you, you can't keep secrets from me, I'm your mother."

Luella closed her eyes, dreading what was next. I got up to charge again but Mother flopped onto the sofa with such a weight that her cushions flew in the air, landing all crooked and warped.

"I don't know what I've done." She looked up at the photo of father. "You tell me. What did I do that was so bad?"

She couldn't really believe she was the victim? Tears ran down her face. She bowed her head and stuck her nails into her hands again and again, making indentations on her skin. My hands were doing the same so I pulled them apart and held onto the table. Luella looked at me like I'd know what to do but we'd never seen Mother cry before.

"I did what I could, left alone to look after you both. I wanted to care but you always made it so hard: disobeying me, taking up all my time, my money, wearing me out. I raised you in the way I thought was best, didn't want you to turn out spoilt and precocious like so many brats these days. You were fed and clothed, treated as equals. I didn't favour one over the other did I? Even though I had reason to, I looked after you both the same. People have it a lot worse you know. Was what you had really so bad?"

Luella rubbed her belly. "It was awful."

"Oh really?" Mother sneered. It was not the answer she'd wanted.

"Look at us, always tiptoeing on eggshells, scared of your mood, of being derided and mocked, made to feel worthless. That's not what a mother should do. You kept us in this horrible house, making us fear life outside of your world. What did we do to deserve that? Nothing. We were the children, learning from you, believing your lies and paranoia. And you know what? For years we've plotted about how to leave you and today we're going to. Come on Lara, let's go."

Our time had come. I nodded so my sister knew I was with her and when she held out her hand, I stretched mine out to meet it.

"The money!" cried Luella.

"What?"

"We'll need money."

"What are you talking about?"

She'd already started running up the stairs. Mother chased her. I followed, my injured leg buckling as I put weight on it. Luella was fast, like the weeks doing nothing had given her superhero speed. Mother wasn't as quick and I caught her skirt halfway up the stairs. She slipped and pulled herself up on the banister, trying to kick me away. A shoe hit my face but I kept hold of the other leg, even as some blood trickled by my eye, darkening the vision on that side. She had the advantage wearing her shoes inside. She'd broken house rules; that wasn't fair. Blood ran into my mouth, the familiar metallic taste reminding me I was hurt but this time, fighting back. I gripped tighter. A shadow fell across us. Luella was at the top of the stairs, clutching a roll of notes. I loosened my hold on Mother so me and my sister could head back down together. Mother would leave it there, be glad to be rid of us, it was what she'd always wanted, us gone, but instead she shouted, raising a hand to slap me down. And it all went slow-mo. Luella held onto the banister and kicked her foot at Mother's head, years of rage channelled through her leg, her foot, her toes. There was a crisp crack as it connected with the cheek and chin. Mother fell round, on top of me, and we both tumbled down the stairs, her forwards, me backwards. I could see the surprise in her eyes. I reached for Luella but a thud got in the way.

~

I heard my name.

"Lara. Lara, please wake up. Please."

The hall was dark. Luella came into focus.

"You've got to get up, quickly, before she wakes." I turned my head to the side. It really hurt: my skull, my neck, my arms. Mother's face was two inches from mine. I felt the warmth of her breath. Not dead then.

"Lara, you need to go and get help, please."

She got hold of my shoulders, back and arms, helping me to sit up.

"Can't you go?" I felt my face, blood stuck to my fingertips, there wasn't a part of me that wasn't hurting.

"No," she protested. "I can't leave the house. I'm too scared."

"We'll call an ambulance."

"She tore the phone cable. It's not working, we can't. You go and get Marjorie, she'll know what to do." She hugged me tightly. "You're such a good sister. Thank you."

Everything in me was sore. "I think I need a doctor."

"Yes, definitely. Go and get Marjorie and she'll get the doctor." She squeezed my hand as she led me to the front door. "Go on. You better hurry."

I stumbled down the path, my left leg buckling with each step, the pain overshadowed by an intense anger that Mother hadn't let us go. She didn't want us; she should have let us go. It had all become more complicated than it ever needed to be.

I'd never walked alone in the dark. I had no idea what time it was. The cicadas created a rhythm for my slow steps as the white moon lit the way and the stars took turns to sparkle as if vying for attention. I was tempted to walk forever, to never go back, but that wouldn't be fair on Luella. I thought of disappearing down a dark alley, curling up into a ball and never waking up, but neither would that. A car lit up my solitary figure. I didn't feel vulnerable like Mother had said I would. I didn't even care if they were an enemy come to murder me. I had no fight left, they'd get no satisfaction from beating me, I'd be numb to their game. It ignored me and drove on.

When I reached the store it was all dark. I whispered their names in case I woke up the neighbours. There was no response. I called out a little louder, still no lights popped on. Tears of frustration welled up; I'd hobbled all that way and now no-one was listening. I shouted desperately, using every last ounce of strength I thought my body had but they were stubborn, they wouldn't wake up. I grew hysterical, screaming, "Sean, Marjorie, Sean," again and again so hard my body rolled after the sounds roaring out of me. I missed the curtains twitching but saw the light. I lunged to its source but then other lights came on, confusing me as to which way I should go.

"Lara?" He looked appalled. I was ashamed.

"Mother's hurt."

"You're hurt."

"Mother's worse."

"Come inside."

"We need help. Please."

"Come in while I get dressed."

I shook my sore head. "I can't. You need to hurry. Please."

He checked along the street then ran inside. They came out together. I'd forgotten to ask him to bring Marjorie but that was fine, he'd known what to do and she was with him. Good boy, Sean.

The change of the gearstick and squeak of the brakes were the only sounds in the car as they woke from the sleep I wished I was in. We all knew something terrible might be waiting for us. Sean parked outside the house and they walked slowly up the path with me at my fastest possible pace. As they exchanged a look, I wondered how I'd ever live down the mortification.

I slipped off my shoes, you're not allowed to wear them in the house. Mother's body was still at the bottom of the stairs, a relief that she hadn't woken up and hurt Luella while I was gone. We didn't speed towards her, afraid in case she was dead, but as we got closer you could see dribble from her mouth moving back and forth as her breath controlled its journey. I'd never seen her asleep; she looked troubled even in her dream world, a frown etched between her closed eyes. Marjorie motioned to Sean and he picked up the receiver.

"It's not working. She pulled it out."

"There's a dial tone," he replied.

"Where's Luella?"

I limped to the kitchen to find her. Marjorie called her name with a false jollity as if trying to entice a child out of hiding. It didn't work. I couldn't manage the stairs so sat on the second lowest one whilst Marjorie ran up them. I studied Mother's body. It wasn't twisted or battered. There was one small cut on her head with a tiny trickle of dried blood out of it, the only sign that something was wrong. I moved as far to the corner of the steps as I could, arms around my knees, scared she might wake up and pounce. I held on to the banister ready to pull myself up should she rise and leap on me. Footsteps stopped behind me.

"Sean, we need two ambulances. Say to them to bring two."

I breathed in and in and in, then pushed myself through the pain to standing.

"What's happened? Where is she?"

Marjorie stared pityingly at me. I started the climb, clumsy and slow.

"There's no need," she said. "No. Sorry, I mean she's breathing, she's just..."

Marjorie had left Luella's bedroom door open. The curtains were drawn and the main light was on. It was too harsh, Luella didn't like bright lights. I turned it off. She was lying on the bed, her back towards me.

"Luella." She didn't answer. "Luella, I'm back." I reached across the bed to stroke her head, which felt clammy. "Luella," I poked her shoulder, the lack of reaction making me cross. "Luella, wake up. Now." I pushed her harder even though it jarred my shoulder. She rolled slightly forwards and back again. I turned to find Marjorie standing too close behind me.

"I think she's taken some pills," she said.

I stared where she was pointing to four empty medicine jars on the table by the bed. There were no labels on them but I could see the remnants of herbs in one. The others were empty, who knew what they'd been full of: pink pills, purple pills, yellow pills, orange pills, all the colours of the rainbow pills. My head dropped in resignation. I hadn't listened to her plan. And she'd wanted to sleep, and though I didn't blame her, as I watched her shallow breath I was furious with her weakness, her easy, drugged escape. I'd come back. I hadn't curled up in the dark, beckoning alley.

"Wake up. You wake up right now!" I knelt on the bed, my left hip kept burning as I shook her. "Wake up! Wake up! Wake up!" But she slept on, her skinny ribs rising and falling erratically. "You selfish thing. I got help like you asked me to. I found us help so the least you can do is wake up now." I pushed her meanly, purposefully causing what would have been pain if only she were conscious to feel it. When she didn't react, I punched the back of her shoulder then lay beside her, spooning my body around her perfect one, trying to keep the life pulsing through her veins, wondering if she died would I too, for I had an awful feeling she was nearly gone and we'd come into the world together so we should go out of it together.

Heavy footsteps pounded across the landing.

They should have taken their shoes off, the naughty people, Mother would go mad. A man's face appeared in front of Luella's, asking the room what her name was. Another set of hands gently eased me up and Marjorie awkwardly took hold of my hand. I pulled away from her and stood back to give the ambulance men room. Luella was leant over, touched and talked about, then put on a stretcher and carried out with a mask over her face that looked like it was stopping air from getting in rather than helping more oxygen flow into to her lungs.

Two different ambulance men were kneeling beside the chair, nearly hiding Mother's body, one putting a wide plastic tube around her neck. I stepped around him, hating her.

"Please can I have a lift to the hospital?"

"Sean'll take you. I'll go with your mother. Someone should I guess." Marjorie was watching the body being shunted onto a stretcher.

"What's her name?" the ambulance man asked.

They all looked to me, but I didn't know. She'd never said. The only clue the post gave us was a J, Mrs J. Jeffreys. "Mrs Jeffreys."

The roads were clear with an occasional pinging of light through the night time. I wondered who would be up so late and why. Were they fighting and hurting and fuming like we were? The hospital had all its lights on, a beacon on the sooty landscape.

"You go in. I'll park and catch you up."

I shielded my eyes from the tubular fluorescence trying to probe every part of me. They should have gentle lights in a hospital, easing people inside to confront what's troubling their body and mind. The lady at the desk looked up when I leaned on it.

"My sister's been brought in."

"Right. And you need to see a doctor?"

"Her name's Luella, Luella Jeffreys, with a y not i-e." She took a sheet of paper from a drawer, rolled it through a typewriter and started tapping with her fingers. "She's only just been brought in, by ambulance, if that helps you find her." She smiled patiently and tapped some more.

"And what's your name?"

"Lara. But that doesn't matter. She took all the pills and herbs you see. I think she wanted to die."

The tapping stopped.

"I'm sure she'll be fine. One second."

The lady left the desk and disappeared through a white door behind it. I leant more heavily on the counter with my good arm, trying to ignore the pain that was punching me randomly in my arm, leg, hip, head, neck.

"That's you done. You might as well sit down. She won't be coming back!" a young red haired man chuckled. He was holding his arm which had a gash the length of an apple under the elbow, seeping only a little blood. He must be one of those timewasters Mother talked about. I was about to tell him to go home when Sean came through the doors, reaching me as the white door behind the desk opened and the receptionist came back with a doctor. The man with the sore arm sat back down, dumbfounded at being proved wrong.

"You need to go that way dear, with Doctor Franklin."

The doctor nodded and smiled when she pointed at him, so we followed him through door after door, left turns and right. Maybe I was in a bad, drugged up dream, lost and dazed, unable to find what I was looking for, unable to keep up with his pace, one of those dreams where you think your feet are stuck in treacle.

"Can you slow down please? She's hurt as well."

The doctor turned and let us catch up with him. He looked at me more closely, at my head and my leg.

"I'm sorry."

"It's alright. I'm fine."

He frowned. "We're nearly there."

His uniform was navy blue, the trousers and smock like the ones we used to wear in nursery school for painting. We always had to be very careful of the paint, having been warned by Mother never to get any on our clothes. The other children would laugh as they splattered the vibrant colours on the pinned up paper whereas we'd cautiously choose the smallest brushes and paint without making any drips. And at the end of the day, when the others lined up clutching their works of art with pride, we'd leave ours in the classroom, knowing from the only time we had brought our pictures home how worthless they were, from the way she'd derided our poor effort, was unable to tell what the shapes were, the speed with which she'd ripped them to shreds in front of us. There was no point in bringing anything nice back to our mother.

"I'll send someone to see you." He stopped so we stopped.

"There's no need. I'm fine."

"You're not fine. She's not fine." Sean looked like he needed to either cry or hit something.

"Where's my sister?"

"She's through there," he pointed to more doors, "but you need to wait here." There was a row of six orange, plastic seats, their backs attached to the wall. "They'll be out as soon as they can to let you know what's happening."

There was just enough space in front of the seats for two people to pass side by side but the corridor was empty apart from us. The pain got worse as we waited.

"Would you mind getting me some water?"

Off Sean went, his stride the same length as the distance between the square lights on the ceiling. I wished they were dimmer. I wished they didn't glare so much as then my head might hurt less. I closed my eyes which momentarily lessened the throbbing but a second later it pounded again, ruining the peace. I couldn't hear anything through the doors. I wasn't brave enough to push them open. I heard the footsteps but because they didn't sound like Sean I assumed they weren't to do with me. They stopped too close to my feet.

"Now young lady, I hear you need a check up."

He was wearing a pale blue smock. I wasn't sure if that meant he was a higher or lower grade than the man in navy, a different kind of doctor.

"I'm fine."

He sat beside me, speaking brusquely. "You don't look fine. Your head's bleeding." I pursed my lips, willing him away. "Who's in there?"

"My sister, my twin, Luella."

"Right," he kept looking at the doors. "How about I check you over properly once you know how she is and for now we get you some painkillers. Is your head hurting?"

"Yes."

"I'll be back in a minute then. You stay there."

I ran my finger over my stump, hoping Luella would be okay. She had to be. She couldn't die, that would be too awful. Sean arrived, followed by my painkiller man, giving me the choice of two cups of water to help me swallow one small white pill.

"I don't want to go fuzzy. I—"

"It'll just help with the pain. No fuzziness, I promise."

I swallowed it and shut my eyes, my signal to be left in peace. The man wiped the blood off my face so gently I wanted to sleep, then he murmured to Sean who sat down beside me. Through my closed eyes I watched the darkness, a never ending darkness, no daydreams, no night dreams, nothing.

The Discharge

She wore a pale green smock as bland as the expression on her face.

"Luella Jeffreys family?"

"Yes."

"Would you please come with me?"

We followed her through the doors I'd not dared enter. Now there were another three routes to choose from. We were taken down the right hand corridor, into a room with the word 'family' on a plastic sheet by its side. She motioned for us to sit down and before she sat, opened a cupboard and took out a box of tissues, placing them on a low table between the sofa and three chairs that were crammed into the small, beige space. Sean moved closer to me. I sat in the middle chair as they both angled their bodies towards me.

"Luella had taken a lot of drugs and I'm afraid we weren't sure what they all were. They brought in the containers but without labels it was impossible to know." I watched her; there had to be more. Sean's hand brushed onto mine. "I'm very sorry. We tried everything we could." I kept staring at her. She squirmed. "Do you understand what I've said?"

"Lara?" added Sean.

"Lara, do you understand what I'm saying?" She looked at Sean who put his hand completely on mine and then she spoke more gently. "We did all we could but I'm very, very sorry, your sister died."

"She's my twin."

"Your twin. Sorry. Yes. Apologies." She offered me the box of tissues but I didn't take one. "She wouldn't have been in any pain."

I wasn't crying, not like Sean. I was strong. I didn't need tissues.

"I'm so sorry Lara. It's all so shit, so sad." He was right. It was. It was terribly sad. "What about her mother?" he asked.

"Excuse me?"

"Their mother was brought in as well."

"Oh. Right. I'm sorry, I didn't realise. I'll go and check for you now."

She almost smiled as she got up, relieved to have an excuse to escape, glad to have a job to do that might bring her back bearing better news. I needed to get out of the family room. I had no family. Sean followed me into the corridor where I saw an open window with a gap wide enough for me to put my head through. He grabbed my waist but he'd got it wrong. I wasn't going to jump. Stupid boy. I wriggled out of his grip.

"There you are. I've been looking everywhere for you. The receptionist didn't know where you were. She was useless, completely useless." Marjorie rotated the brass zippo in her hand, out of her depth, in need of a cigarette. "Your mother's in theatre and—"

"Is she?" Sean said.

"Has no-one told you? Unbelievable. Honestly."

Sean didn't want to say the Luella words out loud. I got that. If you said it, it made it real, that's the way bad news worked. And then it would hurt too terribly.

"Marj—"

"How's Luella?"

I started to shake.

"No?" Her hand rose to her face, trying to block the truth. "That can't be right." She gripped the windowsill. "Oh Lara." She didn't wipe away her tears. She let them roll down her face like she wasn't ashamed of them. I clenched my fists. I wouldn't cry in front of them, I wouldn't. I brutally shoved Luella out of my mind and concentrated on trying to control the trembling in my legs.

"Oh look at you, you poor thing. We'd better get you checked out." Marjorie's voice broke, her nose ran, her hand grabbed one of mine and I went with them because it was easier than refusing. They found a different man in pale blue who pointed us down another corridor where we met a lady in violet who took us into a room and sat me on a cushioned bed with wheels underneath it.

"Would you like something for the pain?"

"Yes please."

She came back with a cup of water and a bottle of pills. She shook out an orange one. I knew how good those were.

"Everything really hurts, so badly."

She looked pityingly at me and shook out another then passed me the two perfect, orange tablets. After I'd swallowed them, I lay my head back on the pale green pillow so the drugs could take over and make the real world disappear.

~

"The poor love. Do you think she'll be okay?"

"Physically yes, I mean her injuries are superficial but—"

"Lara, we've moved you to a more comfortable room. That's why it looks different."

I frowned.

"How are you feeling?"

I wanted to stay numb.

"Everything hurts." It was hard to form the words.

"I'm afraid it will. Would you like some pain relief honey?"

"Yes please."

I swallowed the two orange pills and closed my eyes before they began to work. I did not dream, so that was good.

~

"They say it'll rain tomorrow."

"Really?"

"Umm."

"I thought it was meant to—"

"Hey Lara."

I snapped my eyes shut.

"Lara, how are you feeling honey?"

"Everything hurts."

"Awww, you poor thing. You've been through so much."

I waited to be offered more painkillers but the nurses didn't speak again. I forced my eyes open and watched them fuss round the bed.

"It all really hurts."

"I know sweetie. The doctor'll be here soon. She wants to see you before we give you any more medication. You've already had your quota for the—"

"But it hurts so much."

"She'll make sure you get what you need. She's very good, used to be a nurse so really knows what she's doing. Ha. She'll help you get better as quick as can be, I promise."

She winked at me. I stared at the door.

"When's she coming?"

"Shouldn't be long. Would you like some water?"

"No."

My right arm was bandaged and out of the corner of my left eye I could see the edges of some sterile strips on my face. I raised my fingers to feel them. There was a second set of strips on my forehead. I'd been cleaned up. My brain felt blurred but not dim enough. I remembered Luella was dead. My body started to twitch. The spasms got stronger and my back arched high, chest rising as though someone was tearing my heart out. I clamoured for breath. Bodies whizzed around as I thrashed about. Arms held me down, a pin pricked my skin and I was done with.

~

A lady in white was standing by the left hand side of the bed.

"Is this it? Have you seen my sister?"

The smile left her lips as she shook her head, and I wept. I wanted it all to be over so I could be with Luella. The lady rushed nowhere when her beeper sounded.

"Your injuries are healing well. How are you feeling?"

She crinkled her nose up as if it was itchy. "Lara, I'm sorry about the loss of your sister."

"She's not lost, she's dead."

I pushed the nail from my little finger into my left palm. I couldn't feel any pain; some drugs must still be in my system. Good.

"Would you like to know about your mother?"

I stopped pushing and looked up hopefully. Encouraged, she stepped closer to the edge of the bed. "She's stable, unconscious but stable."

Two tracks formed on my face where the tears rolled down, tears that she misread, taking them to be a good sign when they were actually very bad. She touched my shoulder. "I'll give you a moment. Be back in a minute."

The pillows were so full of feathers that I was almost sitting upright. I tried to define what unconscious meant. Could she wake up and storm in the room, furious with me? I needed to be further away from her, in a different room, in a different building, a different state. The doctor came back in; I grabbed my chance.

"I'm well enough to go home now thank you."

"I don't think so."

"You've no reason to keep me here. I'm sure you've more poorly people to heal." I didn't mean to sound so arrogant, so like Mother. I had to be the opposite. "Please, if you don't mind, thank you so much." I was not her. I didn't have to behave like her. "I'm sorry if I sounded rude. I don't like hospitals so please may I go home now?"

"We need to make sure you're all better first."

"I am though. I feel fine. And if you let me go home I'll heal quicker and there'll be less chance of infection, won't there?"

"You can't go home now Lara." Her tone was turning impatient.

"Why not?"

"For a start, it's the middle of the night."

Damned pills muddling up time. "What about in the morning then?"

"Would you like something to help you get back to sleep?"

"No thank you. I can sleep without help. I'm all better you see."

I wasn't sure she believed me. Maybe she'd rather I was under her control and out for the count, that'd make her job easier because I bet she was one of those inexperienced young ones Mother moaned about.

She turned the light off on her way out of the room leaving it dark apart from a continuous bright light from the corridor straining to get under the door and through its hinges, finding any gap it could to go through. I watched until it disappeared, swallowed up by the sunrise shining through the cream blind. I dared not sleep in case I woke up with Mother beside me.

~

After forcing myself to eat a few bites of the toast they'd put in front of me, needing them to think I was on the mend, a hand with bubblegum pink painted nails held the door open for the nurse carrying the tray out before letting her son enter the room ahead of her.

"Well good morning," she said. "So nice to see you awake. How are you feeling?"

"I want to go home."

"They've done a neat job over your eye. I bet there won't even be a scar." Her fingers moved to scratch her right eyebrow. "So you're feeling better? Better than before?"

"I want to go home."

Sean coughed as he checked his watch. He and Marjorie would have talked about me in the car on the way here and they'd carry on with their conversation on the way home. Right now, I needed them to talk for me, to the doctors.

"I really want to go home."

"They've said you can?"

"Not yet, but I feel ready."

"Are you sure? All alone in that big, empty house?" Sean winced at the insensitivity.

"I'd rather be at home."

"But—"

"I'll be fine."

"You might get lonely, honey. I don't think—"

"You could check in on me." I'd thought of that in the night. Sean looked as if he was trying to see inside me to work out what was really going on. The tears came easily. "I don't like hospitals. We never visited them. And Luella died here; it's not the place for me."

Marjorie took me in her arms, hushing and shushing the victim.

"Oh I know. Of course it isn't. Of course it isn't honey."

The tears became real as I surrendered to her comforting hug, the warmth of her cheek, the softness of her yellow, blue and red top.

"I really do think I'll be better at home."

"I know. I don't like hospitals either. No-one does."

"Maybe you could speak with them?" When she glanced quickly at Sean, I pretended not to notice. "Actually, don't worry, I—"

"No. Do you know what? I will. I'll speak with them, but how are you feeling, really?"

"Even the doctor said I'm much better and it's all superficial now so I'd rather go home, then I can start to grieve. And I need to be further away from Mother."

"Well that's understandable."

"Marj," chastised her son.

She made a face at him. I told her she needed to speak to someone dressed in white and she went to look for them.

"I'm really sorry Lara."

"Why?"

"I saw the test on the floor, when we were waiting for the ambulances."

"It's not your fault." I looked for the spider that lived in the top right corner of the room.

"But I made you take it."

"I didn't have to."

"I can't believe it led to all this," and he started crying, which was embarrassing.

"I said it's not your fault; I misjudged her." He wiped his eyes with the back of his hands. "I didn't think she'd search the bins, not that deep anyway."

"What happened?"

I wanted a pill, not an inquisition. "I'm tired."

"Right. Sure. I hear you."

He stood quietly whilst I closed my eyes and pretended to sleep, hands tucked under my arms so he couldn't try and hold them. Every time Luella flew into my head I pushed her out. I couldn't break down in front of him. I'd only do that when I was alone. I could feel him watching me, caring about me, and willed him to stop. I couldn't accept it. I would let no-one in. The door clicked open as Marjorie slipped back into the room.

"Shhh, she's asleep," Sean whispered.

"Did you find them? What did they say?" I asked.

"They'd like to keep you in for one more day, just to make sure you're stable." I sucked in air to stop me shouting out. I could make myself manage one more day; two of the purple pills, maybe some orange ones, they'd help me get through one more day. "But I'm worried about you going home, being alone in that house."

"I'll be fine."

"You keep saying that and I don't mean to patronise, but you're so young and—"

"I'm old enough. I can cook and clean, what more do I need?"

"Why don't you stay with us?"

Sean glowered at his mother.

"No thank you."

"But—"

"It's very kind, but no."

She chewed on one of her painted nails. "How about I visit you each day then? I bet that would reassure the doctors. I'll go and speak with them, see what they say." She ran from the room, glad to have a plan.

"Jesus."

"Don't be mean. She cares about people."

I looked at the black dot, top right, that could be a spider except it wasn't moving, except it still could be a spider getting ready to bite me. I wished Sean would go away.

"Would you mind getting me some water?"

"There's some by your bed."

"Oh." I didn't reach out for it. "You should go."

I felt sorry for my coldness towards him. He hadn't asked to be dragged into this mess, it was me who'd knocked on his door, but I couldn't make myself be nice to him. Alone, my good thumb rose to my mouth and I bit the skin around the top part of the nail, chewing it between my front teeth, concentrating on the tough texture that needed softening before it was swallowed. I hoped Marjorie's conversation went my way. I'd go mad if they made me stay here.

She returned, dismayed.

"They still want you to stay another day. They have to be sure you're alright, which I get. I— Where's Sean?"

"He needed the toilet." When she hesitated, I took my thumb away from my mouth to show I was listening.

"They said they need to know you'll be safe when you leave." She brushed some invisible dirt off her arm. "I think they mean, you know, safe by yourself after all that's happened."

I focused on the bedsheets.

"I won't do anything out of the ordinary. I won't do anything stupid." That's what people said when someone hurt themselves, that they were stupid. Stupid, stupid, stupid. Marjorie played with the turquoise ring on her middle right finger. "You don't need to worry. I'm not ready to die."

And the decent, naive, hopeful, part of her believed me. "Of course not. I'll be back in a second."

There was talking in the corridor, words I couldn't hear clearly, and those I was intermittently able to catch I didn't understand, medical nonsense they could have made more basic. A doctor I hadn't seen before came in, dark hair greying above his ears. He questioned and queried me, writing the answers on a sheet that was attached to a grey metal clipboard, eventually leaving me alone, desperate for sleep, so tired that I'd forgotten to ask for my favourite orange pill. Which turned out to be a good thing. Which helped convince them that the thoughts they'd made me speak out loud were true and therefore all the boxes they'd ticked were correct which meant the forms that proved I was well enough to leave their ward were willingly signed with the required three different signatures.

The Return

They suggested I visit Mother before leaving the hospital.
I refused.

"Can I see Luella?"

They refused, saying they'd look after her until Mother
woke up and then we could have our last goodbye, the
three of us. I locked the toilet cubicle door so they couldn't
see me trying not to cry, mouth twisting, terrified, not for
my sister but for the fear of Mother waking. Her deep
sleep was what made being alive bearable. I couldn't have
her cornering me.

~

Sean's car felt too bright on the drive home, too garish,
and the world through the passenger window looked no
different which was wrong and outrageous, people going
about their business with no idea of what had happened
in my world. I wanted to shout out to them how lucky
they were but they'd think I was crazy and call an ambulance and put me in a ward room back in the same
hospital, and that wouldn't be fair because I wasn't crazy.
I knew exactly what I was doing. Kind of.

The house looked the same. I walked up the path. The

doctors were right about the wounds being superficial, my hip was hardly aching and the bruising on my arm already yellow. Sean irritated me by walking too close. I'd wanted be alone at home, why didn't he get it.

"There's no need for you to come in."

"Marj said to."

Talk of the devil.

She tooted her horn as she parked in the driveway, and hurried over carrying a brown paper bag full of groceries. Balancing them on her hip, she took a set of keys from her pocket and unlocked the door. They were Mother's keys. As Marjorie passed the hall table she dropped them next to the telephone. I picked them up, slipping a finger through the brass ring. Now they were mine.

They'd cleaned the house.

The test was gone, the empty wine bottles cleared away, the cat cushions had been plumped and furniture straightened. Marjorie busied herself unpacking the shopping. Sean stayed near me.

"Are you sure you're alright?"

"Yeah."

"I can stay."

"No thank you."

He kicked the wall, making me jump. I wished he'd leave like he obviously wanted to. I couldn't cope with more anger, even if I understood it.

"Apple juice all round. And there's some ginger biscuits, new in, let me know if you like them."

She put the tray on the coffee table. The juice really did taste like apples but sweeter, stronger. My first apple juice. Marjorie fidgeted as she made small talk about the weather, where was the year going, how her garden was blooming, whether to start opening on Sundays or not, like the big supermarket that was opening on the edge of town, apparently it was going to so what should she do then.

"I'm tired."

"Of course you are. We'll go." She made no move to get up. "Unless you want us to stay?" She looked at Sean. "Or you want me to?"

"There's no need. Thank you though."

"I'll stop by at six then?"

"See you then."

"Right. Right you are then. Six it is. I'll see you later."

Sean was already in his car by the time she'd reluctantly let go of the front door. I watched through the frosted glass as she chatted to him through his open passenger window before he disappeared in an orange blur and after what seemed like an age, she drove after him.

I unhooked the keys from my finger and locked the front door like Mother used to each evening. Then I checked the back door in the kitchen to make sure it was locked and the downstairs windows though they'd never been opened. When I was sure she couldn't get in, I settled on the chair where Luella had last sat, hoping to feel her. The cats glared menacingly from their resting places so I turned them all back on themselves, hoping they'd suffocate where I'd pushed their faces against the sofa.

I searched the room for some trace of Luella but there was none. I climbed the stairs and knocked on her bedroom door before opening it. Her room looked the same, which was impossible because with Luella gone absolutely everything had changed. I lay on her bed, under her sheets, my head on her pillow, catching the faintest scent of her in the flannelette. As I hugged the pillow and buried my face amongst its thin, prickly feathers, I felt her love and her pain and her dreadful unhappiness and thought I'd break in two as I realised I'd never see her again. They must have made a mistake, about her breathing, because she'd been so full of life and we were going to leave this place and rent an apartment with lots of rooms, four or maybe even five, six, seven, who knows, and it would be so wonderful. The pain was excruciating, crippling. Should I leave to be with her? I thumped the mattress, enraged. I knew people had it harder, much harder, Mother had told us so, but my heart had been slashed and no-one understood how much I missed my sister. We'd come into the world together, we should have left the world together.

"We could have been here together you idiot," I yelled. "She's unconscious, nearly dead, but now you're gone too, you stupid, stupid idiot. We could have been together." I sobbed and slept, woke, shouted at her, was filled with guilt as wasn't it mean to shout at dead people, more guilt as I cried, staring at the ceiling, biting bits of skin off the edges of my fingertips.

~

My legs twitched in response to the doorbell. When it rang a second time, I heard my name being called. Banging sounds boomed round the back of the house. They were panicking. I went downstairs.

"You're there." She turned her head to the right. "Sean, it's okay, she's here!"

So Marjorie didn't have the courage to check up on me on her own. Fair enough, the Jeffrey's didn't exactly have a good track record.

"Did you manage to sleep?" I nodded. She didn't ask about my blotched face. "Great. That's great. So good for you. Sleep's the best medicine. I'll cook some dinner and I thought we'd eat with you, if that's okay."

While Sean plonked himself in the living area, I sat on a stool in the kitchen and watched Marjorie prepare the food. It was mainly cold bits: vegetables finely chopped, a white sauce shaken from a bottle, chicken cooked on a frying pan then sliced and mixed with the vegetables and sauce. There was no boiling, no potatoes, no red meat. Rabbit food Mother would have said, not fit for humans. But she was wrong; even though my appetite was minute, the spoonful of dinner I tasted was good with all the ingredients mixed together.

Marjorie wrote their telephone number on a piece of yellow paper and left it half under the telephone so a draft wouldn't blow it away.

"All you have to do is dial the numbers in order and it'll ring straight through. I'm a light sleeper so even if it's in the middle of the night, I'll answer quickly." She looked at me expectantly. "Okay. So. We'll head off and I'll see you in the morning."

Rather than watch them walk down the path, I locked the front door and re-checked the back door. Then I worried Mother would somehow open both so I placed a row of cat cushions along the bottom of each, hoping that would stop them from opening further and make it too small a gap for an adult to be able to squeeze through.

I sat on the sofa.

Which felt wrong.

I ran up to Luella's room, shooting through her ghost that was standing on the stairs, holding onto the money, determined and ready to escape. We'd never had any money but she'd been holding a massive roll of notes. How come? Where did she get them from? I searched her wardrobe but nothing was different. I checked through all her drawers but they were empty apart from socks and slips and pants. I looked under the bed and behind the curtains, not understanding, because where else could something be? Drained, I lay on her bed but without her it was too desolate. I went to the toilet before taking the two pillows from her bed, spreading the bottom one in front of my closed bedroom door to give me an extra minute's warning against an intruder, and the other on top of my pillows.

The house creaked as normal. I allowed Luella to creep in. I remembered her when she was five with long hair and a dimpled smile on her face. I remembered her holding me gently after I lost my thumb and me returning the favour when she lost hers. I'd loved her, honest truth, honest to God and all that. And now we were the furthest apart two people could be.

~

Dawn shone through the gap I'd purposefully left in the curtains. I was tired but couldn't get back to sleep so instead stared at the rays as they searched for something to reflect their light on. Finding nothing, they retreated, heading for another more rewarding home, this house being too dark even when its miserable owner wasn't in it.

When the doorbell rang I was still in my clothes from the night before. Marjorie glanced curiously at the cushions on the floor. I followed her into the kitchen where she started unpacking her shopping onto the table. She put a pan of water on the stove.

"I couldn't see a kettle yesterday? I—"

"We don't have one. There's a pan with a tip on the end for liquids, a different one to that."

I found it at the back of the cupboard next to the sink and handed it to her. She poured the water from the potato pan into the milk pan.

"Would you like a coffee?"

"No thank you."

I'd never tasted coffee but knew I didn't want to become addicted to its caffeine content. Mother had told us how it made people fractious and unable to sleep, and in some it was the cause of heart attacks.

"I put some cranberry juice in the fridge. Did you see it? And I've brought some other bits and bobs to keep you going. I'll bring more tonight. Is there anything in particular you fancy? Would you like some juice? Try this one." She opened a white and red carton and poured maroon liquid into a glass. "Help yourself to a croissant. They're still warm."

"I'm not hungry."

"Just a little? Maybe try?" She sat down in Luella's chair, which was wrong but it would be rude of me to say so. "I know you're going through a horrendous time. I mean, I can't imagine what you're feeling but you should eat, just a little even, to keep your strength up." I turned my cup of juice round and round on the same spot. Some condensation from the glass caught on its base making it stick to the plastic coating of the table. I waited to be told off for fidgeting by Mother's voice that was yapping inside my head. "I'll put one out for you and if you don't want it, that's no problem." Marjorie opened and closed different cupboards and drawers. "Where do you keep your jam?"

"We don't have jam. There should be some honey."

"Honey's good. Which cupboard?"

I pointed to the one where the salt pot stood alone in the corner, a jar of honey a third full sitting on the shelf above it.

"I haven't seen this make in a while," she exclaimed, unscrewing the lid and reading the faded label. "Is this the one you meant?" I nodded. "Okay. Wow. Well it's years out of date. Let's just have butter shall we?"

And she dropped the honey into the bin.

Just like that.

Mother would go mad at the wastage.

When Marjorie served the croissant it felt rude not to take a bite. I nibbled an edge and sipped some juice. They went well together. I ate half of the buttery, flaky layers, wanting to please my guest.

"Where's Sean?"

"School. Now don't you worry. They aren't expecting you for a while. Mr Parker knows what's happened, what you're going through."

But I did worry because education was a big part of my plan. Knowledge meant freedom, meant choice, meant power.

"When can I go back?"

"Why don't you wait for a few days, see how you feel?"

"It hardly hurts."

"Maybe there's more than cuts to heal?" I didn't know what to say to her pitying look. The doorbell rang. Marjorie went to answer it and I heard mumbling but they stopped talking when I stood on the border of the kitchen and the hallway.

"Hello Lara, my name's Johanna. I've just come for a little chat and a check-up."

"I'd best get going, sorry, the shop won't run itself, more's the pity." Marjorie threw her maroon leather bag over her shoulder and left me with the smiling lady who'd been holding out her hand. She lowered it, unshaken, to her side.

"Shall we sit down?"

I chose the armchair. She sat on a sofa. I stuck my thumbnail into my index finger, ignoring her fake smile. There was a burning in my chest and throat but I managed to make it stay there.

"I understand you were discharged yesterday. How are you feeling?"

"Fine."

"Are you sleeping?"

"A bit."

"Okay. Do you need some help with that?"

She flicked open her black case and my spirits rose at the sight of all the pills. I nodded and whispered, "Yes please". She fiddled behind the lid then put a small transparent plastic case on the arm of the sofa.

"If you take it just before you plan on going to sleep it should help to—"

"They gave me more at the hospital."

"Sorry?"

"Two pills, not one."

Her eyes narrowed which made me dislike her because I wasn't lying.

"Let's start with the one shall we and see how you get on."

Awkward silences were punctuated by mundane questions: had I eaten, had I been drinking enough water, had I washed, had I been to the toilet, would I like to go and see my Mother?

"No. But I'd like to see my sister."

"Oh, I don't think that's possible," I stared at my thighs that were sitting on top of my hands, "but I can ask for you."

~

The ringing of the telephone startled me awake. I stared at it, but no matter how much I willed it to, it wouldn't stop. On and on it rang, disturbing my peace. I grabbed the receiver.

"Is that you?" she asked. I held my breath. "Don't you dare hang up, you talk to me." I held the receiver further away from my face but she screeched knowingly. "I know what you're doing! Answer me."

I smashed the receiver down and rebounded from wall to wall to banister, stumbling upstairs to the bathroom where I could lock the door in case she was on her way to the house right now. I knelt facing the handle so I would see it turn. No-one had told me she'd woken up. An adult should have warned me. I pulled all the towels off the rail and blocked the door with them. Surely she wouldn't have the strength to push through, not after such a big bash to her head. I stayed perfectly still, waiting, ready to pounce, never taking my eyes off the handle.

~

A bell sounded three times. I would not let her trick me.

"Lara, are you there?"

I couldn't distinguish the voice through the thick walls, the only thing I could tell was that it was a woman's one. There was no way enough time had passed to mean that Marjorie was back. The lady called my name again but the sound was more muffled and then there was a shout from the back of the house. I peeked through the bathroom window but couldn't see anyone.

"Lara, please answer me honey. Are you there?"

Mother would never use that word; I wasn't her honey. Honey was what we had on our toast once a year for breakfast. I dared to stand up and show my face, jumping as Marjorie smiled and waved up at me, miming that I should come and open the back door. I kicked the towels out of the way and after checking to the left and right, ran straight down the stairs to unlock it.

"You took a while."

"I was in the bathroom."

"Are you alright?"

"Yeah."

"Sure?"

"Yes." My frustration came out as impatience. "What time is it?"

"A quarter to six. Are you hungry? I've brought chicken and rice."

I sat at the kitchen table, twisting my fingers around each other, building up the courage to ask her when Mother had woken up. The oil sizzled angrily, not used to a high heat; our meat was always cooked in the oven, never fried in a pan.

"I hope you like it; it's one of Sean's favourites, since he was little."

I didn't. The rice reminded me of porridge. But I had to force it down, be polite, not create a problem. I tried to speak but the words I needed wouldn't pass from my mind to my lips. Instead I put more food between them.

"You've eaten lots. Well done darling."

I had to steer us away from the unbearable small talk.

"Is my mother awake?"

"What? No."

"Are you sure?"

"Yes. I mean, I think so. Why? Has something happened?"

"I had a dream that she was awake."

"Right."

"It was so real, you know?"

"Do you want me to check for you?"

I nodded and tried to glean the answer she was getting from the little she was saying on the telephone but couldn't work it out.

"They said she's still unconscious."

"How do they know?"

"What do you mean?"

"How do they know she's not pretending?"

"Why would she pretend?" Her face was full of concern. "Lara, she's very poorly, you do understand that?"

"I need to see her."

"Alright then. When?"

"Now. Can we go now please?"

I heard her dialing and murmuring again. She sat back down to finish her dinner.

"Sean's on his way. He'll give us a lift. My car doesn't have enough petrol in it."

She was much noisier than I was when washing up, banging and clattering the pans around, not caring who she disturbed. Soap suds flew onto the wall and over the surfaces but she didn't immediately wipe them up. Instead she let the bubbles disappear until a soapy puddle remained and only at the end did she sweep a cloth over it. I was appalled, worried there might be stains, and her wiping was so slipshod it still left a pool of liquid on the surface so there were bound to be marks in the morning. I took a drying cloth from the drawer and carefully ran it over every missed drop.

Marjorie opened the front door to let in fresh air. Mother had never done that.

"Would you like to sit on the porch? It's a lovely evening."

"No thank you."

Sean knocked on the door even though it was open and she hugged him hard, relieved he was there. They both turned to me.

"You're sure you want to do this?" he asked.

I made them leave the house first. I had the keys; I would lock the front door. When I reached the car Marjorie was sitting on the backseat. It seemed all wrong but she avoided eye contact with me so it was clear I couldn't ask her to swap places.

~

When we reached the hospital foyer, lemon walls led us to the patient.

"Well good evening. You must be the Jeffreys family. How are you all tonight?"

She was a kind looking nurse with a booming voice, her smock too tight across her belly which was ripe for hugging. Mother would have disproved of her undisciplined eating habits but I thought she looked comforting, nice and soft, and she smelt of coconut, like Marjorie did when she put the lotion on her curls. They spoke a few feet from me, heads tilting thoughtfully as they glanced in my direction.

"Right then Lara. Let's go and see her shall we? It's probably best I stay in the room with you. Always good to have a nurse nearby." She raised her hand to near my shoulder, not quite touching it, encouraging me towards a white door which she confidently opened, marching straight through. "I know there are lots of tubes but don't you worry about them. Your mother's more comfortable than she looks. She can probably hear you if you'd like to talk to her?" There were more bits of plastic in Mother than Luella had needed after her thumb thing. They ran from the machines and bags of liquid, disappearing through her nose, hands, arms and mouth. Her eyes were closed. I was so glad of that. "You can hold her hand."

I kept my fists clenched by my side.

"Was she awake earlier?"

"No."

"Are you sure? Could she have woken up and gone back to sleep again?"

"No. She—"

"How do you know? Could she have spoken on the telephone?"

She laughed. "No. There's no way she could have done that sweetie."

I studied Mother's pale, grey face, unable to tell if she looked well for her age or not as she'd never told us how old she was. The nurse was right to laugh; seeing her all tied up in bed made my suggestion sound ridiculous; the tubes would have left a bloodied mess if they'd been ripped from her skin so she could get to a telephone.

"You can stay longer if—"

"No thank you." She followed me to Marjorie and Sean. "Please can I go home now?"

~

Marjorie started to get out of the car.

"You don't have to come in."

She carried on getting out of her seat. Sean stayed in his. Marjorie walked beside me, ignoring my protestations and when we entered the house, asked if I wanted a drink, her solution to everything.

"No thank you."

"Are you sure? I saw some drinking chocolate in the cupboard. I—"

"No."

"Alright. Sorry. Only asking. You don't have to have one." I felt guilty for shouting at her kindness. "I don't mean to nag honey but are you sure you're okay here because you're welcome to stay at ours, you do know that?"

"You've said already."

"It's just—"

"I'm fine. And your number's by the telephone. I'll call if there's a problem. Promise."

As the door closed behind her I locked it, double checked it was locked, took four cat cushions and laid them against it. Then I checked the back door and all the windows. My knees gave way as I loosened the hold on myself. I sat on the bottom stair and remembered Mother's body, lying so still, unconscious, asleep, still sleeping.

Unless she was pretending.

And the nurse was her friend, colluding with her to fool me.

And she was in the house already.

She could have run out of her room and snuck into the house while Sean was driving me back. I listened in case a single sound was out of place but heard nothing apart from my shallow breathing. Which wasn't proof enough. I tip-toed to the kitchen and plucked the fish knife from the drawer, holding it tightly as I climbed the stairs and tapped open my bedroom door. It looked like it should do. I opened the wardrobe doors and checked under the bed. There was nothing else to hide in or behind. She wasn't in there then.

I moved across the landing to the bathroom, turning the handle slowly and stepping in quickly. It was empty. I opened the cabinet. The hair snipping scissors were still there, not taken as a weapon. I hid them inside a toilet roll.

Next I went to Luella's room. My heart pinged erratically as I decided that's the spot Mother would have chosen to confront me. The curtains were closed. I didn't want to blind myself by turning on the light so ran and pulled them apart, screaming as I turned with the knife raised to a fold of the heavy material that had got caught on my arm. No-one was behind me. My cry turned into one of relief but I quickly smothered the noise with my hand. There was still one more room, her room.

I tiptoed to her door, trying to pluck up the courage to go in, suddenly ashamed of the knife that was clutched between my fingers because who the hell carried a serrated blade to meet their mother? I laid it on the floor by the skirting board and gripped the door handle. She'd never let us in her room, never cuddled us in her bed, never chatted to us as she put on make up, never asked us to help choose a pretty dress for her to wear to a party that night. We'd imagined she had though, pretended that one of us was the kind Mother and one was the sweet princess of a child. I wished Luella was with me now to pretend everything was alright plus she'd have the courage to go straight in. The thought of her was a boost. When I turned the handle and pushed, the door opened easily. Mother had never locked it as she knew we'd never dare disobey her.

It was disappointing, the bare room much the same as mine and Luella's, giving no hint of the person lying in hospital. The bed was perfectly made with ward corners like the ones she'd impatiently taught us to copy, aged seven. The eiderdown was dark grey with a hint of emerald from its youth. The pillows were cream. The bed was larger than ours, much larger, built to fit three of four people, and there was one pillow on the right hand side, the space beside it conspicuously empty. There was a threadbare, pale brown and green rug under the bed, slightly wider than its' metal base so that when she put her feet on it in the mornings her toes would only just miss the wooden floor. The top of the mahogany bedside cabinet was bare apart from a brown and cream lamp. There was no cabinet on the pillow free side. The curtains were wide open letting natural light shine through the two windows on either side of the corner of the room.

One wardrobe rested against the wall, the wood so dark it was almost black and when I opened it, my reflection greeted me from a mirror inside the door, a full length mirror like she'd told us we didn't need as that would make us vain and narcissistic. My dress was creased, my complexion ashen. The sterile strips stood out, their white surface contrasting with the yellow, green and grey bruises.

My posture was stooped, shoulders rounded and forwards, head hung slightly too low. I straightened up like how other girls stood. It made me look taller. My stomach was fuller than Luella's, my legs a little shorter and my eyes a darker brown. I tried to put her face onto mine but it didn't work so I told the reflection how much I missed her and went to touch her but the fingers that rose to meet mine were cold and the hand couldn't grip in its greeting.

The wardrobe was only a fifth full, Mother's dresses as bland as ours, apart from her cream and blue suit and blouse which were covered in a plastic sheet and hung on the other side to everything else. A pair of brown shoes rested on the wardrobe floor, one heel touching her brown going away bag. Her other pair must be at the hospital. I started to close the door when a prism of light bounced off the bottom of the mirror. I spun round but no-one was behind me. I stood with my back to the window, hand on the wardrobe door, moving it again, and this time when the light re-bounded off the glass it shot to the ceiling. It was coming from under the bed.

On my hands and knees, I spied a cardboard box. I crawled over and pulled at its edge. It wasn't out of reach or heavy but was tall enough to be awkward to get out, the top catching on the base of the bed. With a heave I pulled it free, ripping off part of the cardboard.

Mother would go mad at me.

I pulled out the object that must have caught the light, a silver photo frame offering up a picture of Mother and Father. They were both laughing. She had a sparkle in her eyes I'd never seen and he wore a wide grin, so unlike the sombre picture on the mantelpiece or the photo from the morgue.

There was a second, identical frame. They were standing together in front of a marble fireplace, him in a suit and her in a white dress, red lipstick showing off a perfect pout. It had to be their wedding day. Again, they were both smiling but while his beaming was wide and free, hers looked forced. He was leaning on her arm and I sensed she wished him gone. I knew Mother, I knew that expression.

I prised out a third identical frame but it was empty. The picture of father's body at the morgue fell on the floor. I put it straight back wincing as my fingers caught on a sheet of thick cream paper which sliced through my skin making paper cuts on the tips of two of my fingers. As I lifted the sheet, a spot of blood smeared over the top right corner. I swapped hands and sucked my cuts. The paper was plain with the letter J written over and over in different sizes, at odd angles, tiny drawings of squares interspersed between them.

My mind ached, tired and fed up from using up all my bravery, her few possessions telling me nothing. I put her paltry memories back in the box and slid it as far under the bed as I could. Back in my room, pillows firmly in front of the door, I sat on the bed, purposefully leaving the curtains open, hoping Luella could see me from wherever she was. I imagined her and Father talking, working out how to send some instructions my way. I needed their help in finding a future. Was I meant to leave or stay? Should I wait for Mother to waken?

Because I didn't want to.

Didn't want her to.

I wanted her to die.

A thought so shocking I knew I could never say it out loud because people would think me evil. Too many contradictions tumbled round my head. I swallowed my pink pill, which turned out to be strong enough to make the whole night disappear. Johanna knew her medicines.

~

A bright dawn blasted through the window.

I felt safer in the daylight.

As I remembered.

And hugged Luella's pillow so tightly that some of the feathers escaped. The pillow became feminine in form with a clinched waist where my arms were gripping so hard. I didn't make a noise as I cried, just rattled my shoulders and soaked the thin flannel where she'd rested her head, sorrow turning to fury as I remembered her running up the stairs to get the money. If she hadn't done that, she'd be alive today. We'd have made it out of the front door and there's no way Mother would have got us. I cursed Luella, punching the pillow repeatedly, taunting it to fight back, throwing it on the floor, despairing for a sister so worn down by life that she'd chosen to leave, to leave me to it. Guilt swelled. I'd thought life would be easier without them, I'd wished them both gone. What right had I to be angry with Luella's choices?

In her room I meticulously searched her wardrobe but found nothing. I checked the bedside cabinet but there were no secrets there. As I curled up on the bed I saw her sitting on a school chair, mesmerised as the teacher told the story of a princess who found a happy ending because she'd felt a lump through all the mattresses, "Lara," Luella would say raising the pitch of her voice, "I am that princess, for my bed is too lumpy and my chores beneath me. Fetch me some water you foul smelling servant." We'd giggle conspiratorially at playing something Mother didn't like.

I shoved my hands deep under the mattress, scratching my fingers on the metal springs, twisting my arms awkwardly to reach the corners. And in the very middle, where her back would have lain, furthest from every edge, I found the cylindrical role. I pulled it out and unwrapped the single blue band. When I unrolled the notes they sprang back like a woodlice poked with a stick. I separated them and placed them in a line. There were thirty two curled up ten dollar notes, all brand new looking. Where had she got them? She couldn't have stolen them; she wasn't dishonest. She must have found them somewhere when we weren't together. I placed them precisely on top of each other but when I rolled them up their edges splayed apart. Frustrated, I tried again but the edges remained uneven.

"Morning! Breakfast time!"

What the hell? I hadn't heard the doorbell. After shoving the notes back where I'd found them, I rushed to the kitchen.

"Dressed already?"

"No, I…" but I was dressed. I'd forgotten to change into a nightdress the night before. "How did you get in?"

"I got some keys cut in case you were sleeping so I didn't have to disturb you. And today we have jam. Ta-dah!" She held up a glass pot full of strawberry conserve as well as a brown bag, the two grease spots giving away the number of croissants. "How did you sleep?"

"Fine."

"It must have been hard seeing your mother like that."

"She didn't wake up did she? There's no way she could have?"

"No. Definitely not. Don't you worry."

I let her squeeze my right hand. Her skin was rougher than Luella's, and warmer, the heat soothing. I ate the whole croissant to repay her generosity in bringing them and when she refused my help with the dishes, I sat and pulled at the skin on the edge of my thumbnail, tempted to tell her about the phone call. I was sure I hadn't dreamt it. I'd felt the phone in my hand, I had, I was sure I had. Marjorie chatted as she washed and dried, pulling me into her world.

"Do you want to visit the hospital this afternoon?"

"No thank you."

"You might get bored here."

"I'll be fine."

"You can come to the store with me?"

"No thank you."

She made do with my shortness, didn't pry further, unlike Johanna, who arrived at ten past eleven with a tall man called Frank who was a grey suit wearing policeman, his hair greasy, demanding answers to a myriad of questions about that night, the night of the accident. When they left I was so tired I put the pill she'd given me in my bedside drawer and lay down without taking it. An hour into dozing the ringing began. I pushed my back against the door to try and stop the noise getting through but it was too tenacious to be blocked by wood. I put my hands over my ears; it seeped through the gaps between my fingers. With a scream I flew down the stairs, crying by the time I picked it up.

"What do you want? Why are you—"

"Lara? It's me. It's Marjorie. What's happened ? What's wrong?"

"What?"

"It's Marjorie. Has something happened? Are you there? Lara?"

"Yes. Sorry, I had some juice bits caught in my throat."

"What? I—"

"I'm fine."

"Are you sure? You sound—"

"How can I help you?"

"Oh Lara, I'm so sorry to do this but something's come up and I don't think I can visit this evening." At least she wasn't Mother. "Lara? Can you hear me honey?"

"Yes. I can hear you."

"There's food in the fridge. And I can get someone else to pop by. Shall I ask Sean or-?"

"No." I forced a smile on my face. "There's no need. I'm fine. It's fine. You have a nice evening and I'll see you in the morning." I added a sing song tone to my voice.

"I feel terrible after promising but it's only for tonight."

"Please. Don't worry. Honestly, it's fine."

"Are you sure? Because you could stay at ours? Sean can—"

"No."

"Well you've got our number, if you change your mind?"

The piece of paper was still half under the phone.

"Yep."

"Promise you'll call if you need anything."

"I promise."

"Okay then, well if you're sure. I'll see you in the morning and—"

She started to say goodbye but we'd already done that so I put the receiver down. It started ringing again before I'd walked away, on and on and on. I picked it up, braced for more apologies.

"Yes?" I asked.

"Is that you?" Legs quivering, I held onto the telephone table with my good hand. "Is it? It is isn't it? It's you."

"Yes."

"Why are you whispering? Can't you speak up?" Her disdain at my weakness was obvious; even from a distance I was failing her. "Well? Are you going to answer me or not?"

"Leave me alone. Please, just leave me alone why can't you?"

After I'd thumped the receiver down, I kept crying the same words out loud.

Leave.

Me.

Alone.

She was meant to be asleep, they said she couldn't wake up, not with all the drugs in her, but I'd definitely heard her question me, command me. I thrashed around the room, anger and fear merging into an hysterical mess. I picked up her precious cat cushions and threw them on the floor. But that wasn't enough. I ran to the bathroom, reached into the toilet roll for the sharp scissors and stabbed, ripped and shredded them, trying to get even with some of the hurt she'd caused, hurting what she loved most. Feathers caught on my lips. I spat and clawed them off my face.

"See what I've done? Come and get me. Come on then!"

But there was no rebuke. The phone didn't ring even though I wanted it to. I sat on the sofa surrounded by mess and looked at Father, serious and serene. I took his photograph from the mantelpiece and sat with it on my lap, wishing I could remember him.

"How could you be with her? Was she nice once? What made her so horrid?"

He didn't answer so I threw him aside. He'd abandoned us so why the hell should I care for him? Darkness infiltrated the room. I sat alert, scissors on one side, father on the other, ready to face her when she came. I watched the hallway and listened for the door, eyes flickering to the windows in between. When morning took over I was still ready for her, my body tense, eyes dry from not blinking enough. When the doorbell rang I didn't move to answer it.

"Lara honey, it's me." Marjorie knocked harder. "Lara!" She let herself in and faltered in the hallway.

I dropped my head, ready to be disciplined, thinking of how best to explain away the mess, but instead of shouting at me she said, "oh you poor thing," and her unquestioning kindness took me so completely by surprise that instead of closing up I allowed her to hug me. She stroked my hair, not minding the feathers sticking to her clothes and hands.

"It will get better," was all she said, but with such conviction I nearly believed her.

"Do you believe in ghosts?"

"Of course."

"Live ghosts?" Marjorie laughed like I was making a joke. "She called, on the telephone, on that." It sounded ridiculous. Her eyebrows remained symmetrical as their centres angled down towards her scrunched up nose. "She did," I insisted.

"When? Tell me what happened." I replayed every word Mother had said, on the telephone, to me, when she was meant to be unconscious. "I do believe," Marjorie said, "that you think that's what's happened, without a doubt, but it's also pretty confusing, I mean... I wonder if there's another explanation." Her arm moved away from my shoulder. "I think better when I'm busy." She used her hands to gather up the plucked feathers and tatters of cushion covers. "Do you want me to call the hospital?"

"Yes please," I said, even though I knew what their answer would be and I was right, they told Marjorie she hadn't regained consciousness. "You think I imagined it."

"Did I say that?"

"No."

"Well then—"

She was interrupted by the doorbell which had been pushed more in the last few days than it had been my whole life. I did not want to see Johanna and sensing this wasn't a good day, Marjorie stayed with me until half an hour later when she closed the door behind our visitor as I rolled the pill case back and forth in my hand.

"Do you want to try and get some sleep now?"

"But what if—"

"I can stay here today, get the store minded. It's not a problem."

"Really?"

"Absolutely. Honestly." She nodded to the stairs. "Go on. You go and get some rest."

I swallowed the tablet with water scooped from the bathroom's cold tap.

The Voice

I ran on woolly legs but Marjorie already had the receiver by her ear. She held a finger to her lips, calming down my fear, lowering her hand from her lips to her thighs, lowering me down as though I was a puppet on a string. I perched on the edge of the armchair.

I'd never woken up from a pill induced sleep so quickly. It was wrong to have rushed, my mind couldn't keep up with where I was or what was going on. I concentrated on the words Marjorie was speaking but the sounds were out of sync with her lip movements. I stared at her lips, trying to make sense of how they were moving but it was no use. I closed my eyes so I could simply listen.

"Yes. No. Really? Unbelievable." I garnered little else. And then I heard the drawer open. "Lara. Lara, do you have a pencil?" She mimed writing. "I can't find one in the drawer." I pointed to my school bag which was in the same spot I'd dropped it that fateful afternoon. "No, not now. I don't think so. I'm just not sure it's the right time. Look, I really think it's best if I call you back later."

I felt Luella sitting behind me so let myself fall back and curl into an imaginary her. I rubbed my head where her hair had touched, trying to remember its exact shade of brown. I stifled a sob. I shoved three fingers into my mouth and bit hard with my front teeth but the tears wouldn't stop. Mucus mixed in with them slowing their journey over my hand. I didn't hear the receiver click down but there was Marjorie crouched in front of me, gently pulling my fingers from my mouth and holding both my hands in hers.

"You poor love."

She moved one hand to my head and stroked my short hair and wet cheek. I couldn't look at her; I didn't want to share my grief. As her crouching turned to kneeling she didn't leave my side. When the tears ran out, my heart hurt. I stared at her perfect, manicured fingers encasing my rough, chewed ones.

"It may not feel like it but it's good to let it out. You've got to roll with how you're feeling each day." My lower lip twisted. "I think we could both do with a drink."

She squeezed my fingers before coming back with two glasses of apple juice and a soft white tissue which must have been from her bag because we didn't own any. She tucked her legs under herself at the side of the sofa nearest to me and cupped her hands around her glass in the same way she drank a hot cup of coffee.

"It wasn't your mother, on the phone."

"Who was it then?"

"It was your aunt." I gripped the glass so tightly my wrists ached. "She was terribly upset, sorry that she frightened you. She didn't mean to. She thought you were your mother."

I felt sick that I sounded like her. I would not be her.

"The actual aunt? Our aunt? Mother's sister?"

Marjorie looked at me like I was strange, an odd one out; our stupid, bloody family.

"I'm not sure whose. I guess she could be your father's?"

"He was an only child."

"Right, your mother's sister then. When did you last see her?"

"I can't remember."

I tried to picture her but just saw Mother's angry face with longer hair, red lipstick, pale porcelain skin, and cackling instead of giggling when she laughed.

"She wants to meet you, to come here and see you. She was so upset. She didn't know about the accident, about your Mother and Luella." The room tipped back and forth in front of me. "You look a bit peaky. I really think you should stay at mine tonight."

"No."

"Have a think about it while I make us some dinner. It might be for the best you know."

I heard a pan bang as it was plonked on the stove and flinched at her clumsiness. I was used to quiet and preferred it that way. And I had an aunt, an angry aunt to go with the angry mother. There were two of them, two sisters. I see-sawed on the edge of sanity, then tipped to Marjorie's end as I decided to accept her invitation. It would only have to be for one night, maybe two, three at most say.

The pasta coated in herbs was too slimy on my tongue, too peppery.

"I'll go back with you."

"Really? That's great." She hadn't swallowed before speaking; a twist of pasta fell out of her mouth. She picked it up with her fingers and popped it back in again.

"How long shall I come for? One night? Two—"

"Why don't we see how it goes? No pressure. You go and pack a bag while I do the dishes."

I took my school bag from the hallway and emptied it onto my bed, filling it with two dresses, a change of undergarments and the spare pink pill. I took Luella's pillowcase off her pillow; I would sleep breathing in what was left of her scent. I pulled the money from under the mattress so I'd be able to pay my way and when I went downstairs, nabbed the photograph of Father that Marjorie had put back on the mantelpiece.

"I can get a bag from home so you can bring more things?"

"I've nothing else."

"Oh. That's fine then. Sean'll be here in a minute. My car's been playing up, such a pain, the stupid thing."

I hadn't heard her phone him. I was usually good at hearing things. He'd hate me coming to visit, be embarrassed by our lake visits which were so insignificant now. Who cared about boys and girls and kissing; compared to Luella dying, it was all meaningless.

He poked his head round the open front door.

She hugged her boy.

Their ease with each other, their sharing of secrets, it angered me. I avoided eye contact, trying not to take it out on them, fiddling with the strap on my bag, knowing now that it would be a mistake to try and fit in with their happy space.

"I'm not coming. Sorry. Sorry, I shouldn't have said I would. I need to stay here."

"But—"

"I've never been anywhere but here and now's the wrong time to leave. I don't think I should."

"Lara—"

"Sorry. I'm sorry to be such a nuisance. I had meant to

187

go with you, honestly, and you've been so good to me but…" All I wanted was to take a pill and go to bed, my bed.

"I'm not happy leaving you here honey. You shouldn't be alone."

"I'm not afraid."

Sean's eyes rolled up in annoyance. I definitely shouldn't go with them. The awkwardness was unbearable, another stress I didn't need. I'd ignore Sean from now on, ignoring would make the problem go away.

"How about I stay with you then?" Marjorie asked.

"What?" Sean and I both said.

"Only for a few nights, until I know you're alright. I'll go to work as usual in the day and—"

"Marj, I—"

"Oh Sean, come on. You'll enjoy less nagging and helping yourself to whatever you want from the fridge." She winked at him. "I'll come home with you now to fetch a few things."

They could talk about it, the situation, about me, in his car. The matriarch had made her mind up so we all had to go along with it and look at Marjorie, clever Marjorie, just as good at getting her own way as my mother.

~

Marjorie kept hold of her multi-coloured stripey canvas bag, five times the size of my school one.

"Where will you sleep?"

"I was thinking in your mother's room. Would that be alright? She won't mind?"

"She will. She'll hate it."

"Right. Oh well, it's you I'm staying with so… you know. I'll explain to her why when she wakes up."

"If she wakes up."

"If," she conceded.

We carried our bags upstairs. She had a softer step than Mother; I might not hear her moving around in the night. I pointed to the door of what would now be Marjorie's room. When she reached it there was a clanging noise by her feet. The handle of the knife had been kicked by her foot, the blade striking the skirting board. She bent down to pick it up, a fear creeping through her.

"That's to keep us safe. It's Mother's, it was. It's the fish knife."

"Well I don't think we need it now. I'll put it back downstairs in a minute. In here then?" She entered the room with absolute confidence. I hovered in the doorway. "What a beautiful room, such gorgeous windows." After throwing her bag on the bed she tried to open one but the sash wouldn't budge. "Come on you." She talked to the wood, pushing and pulling it with her hands and elbows but it wouldn't give in.

"It won't open," I told her.

"It will in a bit, just needs some elbow—"

"No. We never open the windows, never have done."

She laughed as if what I'd said was ridiculous. "How do you cope in the hot weather? How do you air the place?" I let her keep trying, she'd give up soon enough. "Can you pass me the knife?"

"Why?"

"To loosen the paint."

"But—"

"It's so stuffy in here, and I can't sleep without fresh air. She'll understand."

189

I picked the knife off the bed and held it out to her, blade first. She looped her hand round mine to reach the handle and after scraping, digging, pushing and cursing the frame, it gave way and was raised high with a groan. Marjorie lurched to the side, smiling triumphantly. A warm breeze swept over us.

"Oh my God, that's better. Shall we open yours?"

"We'd better not, I—"

"Don't worry. I'll tell her it was all me, that I did it when you were out one morning." She strode past me, the knife in her hand. "Which is your room?" I pointed. She pushed open my door and was at the window by the time I'd sat on the bed. "I like the tree."

"Yeah. Me too."

My window was much harder to open than Mother's. About to give up, Marjorie turned and saw me watching which seemed to renew her determination. She kept on working at it until with a crack so loud I thought the frame had broken, the sash gave way. Branches from the tree poked into the room, relieved to find some space after years of having nowhere to grow into.

"Excellent stuff," Marjorie said, taking the knife out with her.

I raised a leaf to my cheek, running its smooth side over my skin. A cluster of branches were caught under the sill so I pulled them up, welcoming them into the room. My door was open so the breeze blew past me, rocking the bathroom door back and forth, making it catch and click on its frame.

Unpacking my bag, I put the money under my bed rather than Luella's, right under the mattress like she'd done, and I put her pillowcase back on the uncovered pillow that was lying on top of mine. Then I sat on the edge of the bed, glad that I'd not left the house, sure that the right thing was to stay, to face my spirits.

~

Cosy under the covers, I thought of Luella's body being cold in the hospital. If Mother was awake would she take a photo of her dead daughter to go with the one of her dead husband? I couldn't picture Luella without air in her lungs; I could only picture her asleep in her bed, her back to the door, like I was.

I watched the branches on the sill. They were completely still now, not even a hint of movement. A drop of water ran down my forehead and my scalp began to itch where it was overheating. I scratched it and a piece of skin caught under my nail which I swiped onto the sheet, trying to control the fear that was returning, the pressing down dream. I couldn't face it so threw back the covers and flung the door open so violently it bounced off the wall, chipping some paint from the skirting board. In the kitchen, Marjorie jumped at my dramatic entrance. I covered my chest, embarrassed at being downstairs in my nightgown; Mother would have told me off for not being dressed yet.

"You're up early. Are you hungry? I'm making toast." She pointed to the grill. "I couldn't find your toaster so—"

"We don't have one."

"Ah. That explains that then." Her smile was warm. I let her hold and pat my hand. "It's early days, you know?" She squeezed my fingers and I was glad she was there. "Shit," she cried, pulling out the grill pan to reveal two blackened slices of bread. She picked them up and tossed them from one hand to the other, smoke gathering in the room.

"The door's stuck," she banged her shoulder and hip against it. I turned the pot by the sink upside down to get the key, unlocked it and she ran outside, throwing the bread on the grass. "Damn it," she laughed. "I'd better make some more." Plumes of black smoke swirled into the air; I wished I could disappear that easily. "It's such a beautiful morning. Let's eat outside." She dragged out two of the kitchen chairs. "The store's shut today so Sean's popping over in a while."

Again.

Always her and him.

Always him coming here.

When she sighed with worry for her boy, I didn't reassure her. We sat quietly as the sun gathered strength on my pale face and her bronzed one, darkened from making the most of the good weather whenever she could. Mother said it was bad for the skin, making a person look cheap when tan marks showed. Neither of us moved when the doorbell rang.

"Would you mind getting that?" she asked.

"It'll be Sean."

"I know.

"He's your son."

"It's your house." As I squinted at her, she walked down the steps to the grass, picking up the burnt bread. "I'd better break this up before a bird chokes on it."

The bell rang a second time. I pursed my lips and willed her to go inside but she kept her back towards me. She could sense my discomfort, I knew she could, the stupid, mean woman making me see her boy. I stomped through the kitchen and pulled open the front door. He turned from admiring his car which stood out as such a bright orange compared to the pale yellow and brown saloons in the nearby driveways.

"Hey. How are you doing?"

Stupid question from a stupid son. I stepped aside to let him in, standing so close to the wall that my back was right against it, all so I didn't have to touch him. He got the message and walked straight past me looking for his mother.

"She's in the garden."

I shut the door and stayed in the hallway, not wanting to be there when he told her I was acting weird again. Such a bloody misfit. I went to Luella's room and lay on her bed. The curtains were drawn and that was good because my head ached with a vicious, piercing pain above the left eyebrow. It eased a little when I closed my eyes. I stayed still in the dark and heard the door open and close but didn't move. My limbs were too heavy and my head too sore to turn. The room was peaceful, the cool, quiet darkness making the outside world just that, outside, not my world, away.

When I woke up the pain had dulled to a manageable ache. My tongue kept sticking to the roof of my mouth. I opened the bedroom door to be greeted by more darkness, my eyes used to it so there was no need to turn the light on to show the way to the kitchen where I turned on the cold tap. No matter how long it ran for the water always landed lukewarm but I drank a glass full in one breath, then filled it up again and sat at the table. Birds chirped sporadic tunes when the sun rose. Marjorie's soft steps landed on the stairs.

"I didn't hear you get up. How are you feeling?"

"My head hurt but it's a bit better now. I got some sleep."

"Good. Sleep's the best medicine. I'm so glad you slept." She didn't look it; she looked worried. She went for a wash and came back smelling of lemons. The underneath of her eyes were less dark and the skin on her nose wasn't as shiny. After she'd eaten she put on some lipstick. Using a mirror from her bag, she followed the crinkly lines that were the outline of her lips. After applying the first layer she pressed a tissue on the peach colour and added another coat.

"You'll call me if you need anything?"

"Yeah."

"The number's right by the phone. You're sure you're happy using it?"

"Yes."

"Right then, I'd better dash." She kissed the top of my head before rushing down the path then ran back waving. I opened the door for her. "What would you like for dinner? I'll bring something back."

What was I supposed to say? No-one had ever asked me before. "You choose."

"What's your—"

"You choose please."

When I shut the door the walls of the hall closed in on me. I needed to be outside, in the garden which now looked nearly as neglected as the rest of the house. I could fix it.

~

I'd just finished the third bed when she called my name.

"I'm in the back," I shouted, walking towards the side gate. Johanna got there first and tried to push it open as I pulled back the rusty bolt.

"I've been ringing the bell."

"Sorry."

"I guess I'm a bit early." She checked her watch. "You like gardening?"

"I want it to look nice."

"Lovely. That's so great."

I let it go, thinking she didn't mean to sound so patronising. And I needed to act well, then she'd sign whatever forms were needed to disengage herself from my life.

"Would you like a drink? There's some apple juice."

She smiled. "Perfect. Thank you."

She sat on Luella's old seat, which was disturbing. I needed her away.

"How are you today Lara?"

"A little tired but alright." I was so good at sounding like a typical sixteen year old. "Marjorie stayed last night."

She nodded; of course she already knew that.

"And how are you finding that?"

"Great." I forced myself to keep talking. She had to think I was normal so I could be left on my own. "I think it's for the best, with all that's happened."

She took a sip of her juice. I knew what was coming. She was so rubbish at pretending.

"And how do you feel about all that's happened Lara?"

Medical people always said my name as if that meant they knew me. Under the table I stuck three of my right hand fingernails into my left palm to stop any tears mixing with the words. "I miss Luella, a lot, and Mother's still unconscious so—" My voice cracked. I reigned it back in with a cough. "It's hard I suppose but I'm strong enough to cope."

"Did you ask Marjorie to come and stay?"

"She offered."

"Have you been to the hospital?"

"Yes."

"How was that?"

"Fine."

She looked sorry for me being in pain. Wrong. She was so wrong about what was causing it. None of them knew me.

"Shouldn't you be asking about Luella?"

"I can. I wasn't sure if you were ready."

"Ready for what?"

"To talk about it."

"Don't I have to?"

"Have to? Lara, why do you think I'm here?"

"To assure the hospital that they were right in saying it was fine for me to be discharged and go home."

"Wow, that's pretty—"

"It's your job to decide if I can stay here or not and—"

"No. I'm here to check that you're going to be okay, that's all." She moved forward in her seat. "The world's not against you Lara. People care. They're concerned. They want to know that you can cope with day to day life, to make sure you know you're not alone." She handed me a case containing one pink pill.

"How long will you keep coming for?"

"I'm not sure. Talking of which, I'd best get going to my next appointment. No rest for the wicked eh?"

Furious that she'd be coming back, I returned to the garden to pluck, prune and weed, ignoring the bed numbers, working from one end to the other. The middle of my back began to ache and the trowel slipped in my sweaty palms. I rubbed my hands in the soil to improve the grip.

"Oh my God, you've been busy. It looks great. You've done loads." She made me jump, her with her keys. She was right though. "Are you hungry? I'm starving. What did you have for lunch?"

"Yeah. I could eat." Because I'd forgotten to stop for food.

She went into the kitchen, making her presence known by her brusque turning of the taps. My joints protested after a day of squatting and kneeling. The back of my neck was hot where the sun had beaten down on it, Mother's insistence on us always wearing hats was fair enough then.

"Five minutes," Marjorie smiled at me as I walked inside. I washed my hands with the white soap and nail brush. The dirt wouldn't come out from under my nails and the grooves where I'd pulled the skin off. I scrubbed vigorously, wanting to be totally clean. Her lemon bubbles caught my eye and I was tempted to try some, imagine owning such a treat. I sniffed them; the citrus scent would give away my stealing.

She'd put two bowls of pasta covered in a red sauce on the table, and a bowl of green leaves covered in white sauce between them. "You don't have to eat it all. I always cook too much. Just eat what you can honey."

I wondered what little amount I could get away with but the first mouthful tasted better than I'd expected and that with my lack of lunch meant I carried on until there were only a few strings of pasta left on the bottom of the bowl. We only ever used bowls for soup. What would Mother say if she saw them stained with the thick tomato sauce? Marjorie chewed noisily, using her nails to pull shreds of salad from her teeth. I fiddled with my fork, focusing on acting polite, sane, lucid.

"How was your day?"

"It was alright. Busy but that's good. I prefer it to quiet, makes the time pass quicker. How was yours? Did Johanna come?"

"She knew you were staying here."

Marjorie used her fingers to help herself to a handful of salad, not commenting that I hadn't eaten any. "Yeah, she would do."

"How come?"

"I told her."

I didn't like the thought of my life being the topic of their conversation.

"Are you the one that's paying for her? Is she not from the hospital?" Marjorie held her hand up all sorry I can't talk my mouth's full. "I don't need her to visit me anymore. You can save your money, tell her to stop coming."

"That's good you feel stronger."

"So you'll tell her to finish?"

"Oh no, I don't think so. It should be her decision, as the professional."

"Why can't you decide? You see me more. What do you think?"

"I think you're doing really well."

"Really well at what?"

"At coping, at your life being..." she gestured to the walls as if the house explained it then leant closer to me. "Do you want to tell me what happened? You can trust me. I won't tell another soul."

"I'm tired."

She sat back. "Why don't you have a bath to stop you getting stiff from all that gardening? I brought you some lavender bubbles. They're a wonder for relaxing. Here."

I followed her to the hall where she picked up a bag patterned in bright red and blue flowers. She took out a bottle that was as tall as her hand and the width of three fingers, with a picture of a purple plant on the front of it and white liquid inside it.

"Smell. Isn't it gorgeous?"

I sniffed, ashamed at my surliness. "It's lovely. Thank you."

"And I forgot to give you this."

She handed me a white paper bag, all crinkled and tired looking. I took it upstairs and stood the bubbles on my bedside table before shaking a box out of the bag. The case opened first try and there sat the ring, the lost ring, the ring that Mother had taken. I held it in my palm, full of remorse. Marjorie leant against the doorframe. Mother never leaned.

"Sean said to tell you that he understands."

I kept my head bowed, ashamed at being the villain. She moved to sit next to me.

"No. Please. Not now. Sorry but don't be nice to me now."

She picked up the lavender bottle from the table. "I'll start running the water."

The noise of the hot water tap on full covered up the sound of my crying. When it stopped she called, "Bath's ready," before going downstairs.

I took the ring with me. The lavender scent reminded me of walking into school, Mr Jonas bent over a flower bed. The water was milky white. Mother would have mocked that it would make me dirtier than I already was and Luella would have jumped straight in. I stepped in slowly, the water swallowing my toes then heels then ankles then calves. It was a hotter and deeper bath than I'd ever had and even though we weren't allowed to wet our hair at night I couldn't resist submerging my head beneath the bubbles. One hand stayed above the water holding on tightly to the ring. Sounds echoed as I held my breath, without effort, a mermaid with no need for oxygen. Mother would love that, me disappearing through the water, forever. She'd hold me under; she'd get rid of me like she had Luella. I pushed myself up. The air was cold and unwelcoming compared to the world beneath the water. I lowered myself back down until the bubbles were level with my chin and put the ring on, unable to find a spare feeling for Sean or what we'd shared, the pain of losing Luella demanding all my broken brain's attention.

The Stopover

I woke up with a stiff neck, Mother proved right again about not going to bed with your hair wet. I heard Marjorie turning the taps on and off in the bathroom so put some water on the stove for her coffee. Pain shot through my neck when I turned my head to say good morning. Had she noticed I was wearing the ring?

"What are your plans for today?"

"The garden."

She hesitated, pulling a chunk off her toast. She really could do with learning some table manners. "Your aunt called again, last night." I must have been in a deep sleep not to have heard the phone ringing. "She'd like to meet you. What do you reckon? Perhaps we could call her back, maybe this evening?" I turned my juice cup round and round. "Why don't you have a think about it today?" I kept on staring at my juice. She made a show of looking at her watch. "I'd better brush my teeth and get going."

She left the dishes for me to clear but I just turned my cup clockwise and anti-clockwise, then round and round full circle. When she came back down she stood in the doorway.

"Are you alright?"

"Yep."

"I can try and arrange some cover for the store, stay with you."

"No thank you."

"If it's your aunt, I mean, there's no rush you know."

I tried to keep up with the pictures of Luella and Mother whizzing through my head, the unknown relative jumping between them.

~

That evening, Marjorie sat next to me on the back steps, admiring the pristine beds.

"I don't want to speak with her on the telephone. I don't like speaking on the telephone. But I'll meet with her. If she comes here, I'll see her."

"That sounds like a plan. Shall I call her now?"

"If you like."

When I went to wash my hands she was still on the telephone. I scooted past, not wanting to hear their conversation, nervous about what I'd started. At dinner I kept checking her face, all weathered from the sun, not old but less smooth than Mother's pale, thin skin. Marjorie was wearing a fuchsia lipstick to match the silk scarf tied loosely round her neck and the gold and feathered earrings hanging from her tiny lobes. I liked the way they jangled when she moved, joining in with the tinkling sounds of her charm bracelets. She sighed as if her life was full of woe. She was too bright for this house. It was too depressing a place for her, no matter how hard she tried to pretend it wasn't.

"Right then. So. She's coming the day after tomorrow,

at around eleven. I can get cover for the store if you'd like me to be here. I can make myself scarce but be in the house in case you need me. What do you reckon?"

~

I cleaned and polished the bannisters, the table, the paneling, until they were all shining. Johanna was pleased to see me busy. She gave me two pills for my collection.

~

Marjorie patted the sofa for me to sit down next to her. "Is there anything you'd like to talk about before tomorrow?" I shook my head. "I know you don't like to talk but it can help." My silence made her uncomfortable. I didn't want that.

"What do you want me to say?"

"You don't have to say anything but I want you to know that if you do want to, I'm here."

Her wants and don't wants wearied me. I sat on my bed and watched the stars, hoping beyond anything that Luella was now at peace, more peace than there was back on earth. I played with the pills and resisted taking one, not wanting to be fuzzy when I met my mother's sister.

~

I walked through the house checking that all the rooms she'd see were spotless. I went into Luella's room. The edges of her face were starting to blur, mainly I pictured an expression, a smile or an eyebrow raised at one of Mother's moods. And sometimes I heard her laugh but that was already fading. She'd been much better at letting the moods blow over her than me, at least I thought she had.

"How about a citrus bath? It's wonderfully uplifting."

I poured a tiny dribble of Marjorie's bubble bath into the water, not wanting to waste such an expensive soap. It didn't make as many bubbles as the lavender one and the water stayed clear, but the scent was stronger. I eased myself into the nearly scalding tub, my face perspiring within seconds, every pore being thoroughly cleansed. The skin turned red where it was covered in hot water. There was a tap on the door. I sat up quickly to cover my body, splashing water over the sides of the tub.

"It's nearly time sweetheart."

She didn't barge in like Mother would have done.

I pulled out the plug, wrapping the chain in a figure of eight around the taps, the pipes groaning as they swallowed the dirty water. As I got dressed I wished I owned brighter clothes, not wanting the aunt to think the dark dress was my choice, then I waited on the bed, hands squashed under my legs, trying to resist but a finger rose between my teeth so I ripped off a piece of skin and chewed it. I watched the clock, wanting the hands to stop moving but they stubbornly tick tocked forwards and at exactly eleven, as I walked downstairs, the doorbell rang and Marjorie exited the kitchen. She gestured for me to go in front of her but I wanted her to answer it. She put on a beam and opened the door. I stayed at the bottom of the stairs; Marjorie moved to the side revealing a lady in purple.

Who was not as I'd imagined,

Who looked the same as Mother but nothing like her.

She wore flared, grey trousers that had thin purple stripes running through them, and her plum coloured top was short sleeved, letting her show off a big plastic purple bracelet, five rings on her fingers, two chains round her neck and jewelled earrings, their stones the same shade as her top, set in silver. Her shoes were a shiny patent purple reflecting the necklaces on both toes. There was more colour in her one outfit than I'd seen Mother wear in a lifetime.

She laughed then coughed. We had similar features, I reckoned that's what strangers would say, though I was dressed as if I was the older, strict aunt, with cropped hair and dark circles beneath my eyes. Marjorie tried to melt into the wall. A ray of sun shone around the aunt, forcing its way into the hallway, lighting a path for her. She stepped over the threshold, into its centre.

"Lara?"

"Hello..." I didn't know her name. Mother had never said what her sister was called, not that I could remember.

"Alice. I'm Alice." She opened her eyes as wide as she could to try and stop the tears, then squished the corners of them with her fingers, embarrassed. Even her eye make-up was purple. "Sorry, I'm, oh God, I—"

"Alice, it's so lovely to meet you. I'm Marjorie, we spoke on the phone. It's so good that you came. Why don't you have a seat and I'll get us some drinks. You must be thirsty after the drive. Was there much traffic?"

"Not too bad." She looked like the time Luella had toothache and pretended she didn't so the dentist couldn't hurt her.

"You can sit there." I pointed to the sofa.

She sat down and rested her bag between her feet. I was so afraid of what we were stuck in that I kept quiet in case I yelped like the dog who was kicked by its angry owner after it had done its business on the pavement outside Marjorie's store. My stomach cramped and twisted under my folded hands; I had to squeeze my buttocks together to stop any wind from escaping. She noticed my bad thumb and looked away, too polite to ask about it. Her searching of the bare room gave her no clues about our life, there was nothing to see but dark furniture.

"I'm sorry I upset you when I called. I didn't mean to. If I'd known it was you, what had happened, I'd never have spoken like that."

"It wasn't your fault. Bad timing."

"Yeah." The word came out too loud, mixed with a snort. "Sorry. I'm a bundle of nerves. May I use the bathroom?"

Marjorie brought in a tray with three juices and a pot of coffee with two cups.

"Upstairs, first door on your left."

When we heard the bathroom door shut Marjorie whispered, "She seems nice. I'll leave you to talk shall I?" She saw the panic in my face. "Don't worry. I'll be in the kitchen, only a second away if you need me."

The bathroom pipes sounded as Marjorie's cue to leave the room. I sat on my hands, trying to hide my discomfort, while Alice had obviously gathered her thoughts as she came downstairs looking much calmer than when she'd arrived.

"I like your house."

"Do you? I think it's too dark."

She was dismayed; I felt ashamed, acting so awkwardly when she was trying so hard. I tried to focus on our connection.

"Mother didn't like bright colours. There used to be cushions on that sofa but they were mainly shades of brown and grey and we don't have them any more."

"I'm sure they were lovely."

"Not really. Do you like bright things?"

"I like colour, not necessarily bright. I like white. My—"

"You like purple."

"I love purple. It's my favourite. What about you?"

"I'm not sure, not brown." She clocked my brown dress then her eyes searched the room again. "There aren't any photos, if that's what you're looking for."

"No?"

"There was one of Father. It used to be on the mantel-piece but now it's upstairs."

"What about you and—?"

"No. There's none of us." She closed her lips tightly. "You're surprised?"

"Not really."

"Have you got any children? Are you married?"

"No," her face filled with the toothache pain. "So what about you. How are you feeling?"

At least she didn't add my name to the end of her question. I shrugged and swallowed the lump in my throat. It burned.

"I'm sorry. I didn't mean to—"

"It's fine."

"Not really."

I'd made her angry. I curled into the chair, my arms around my knees. "Luella would like to have met you. She'd have liked your outfit."

"I'd love to have met her too."

"Then why didn't you visit?"

"I wanted to."

"But you didn't."

"No."

"Why not?"

"It's complicated. Did you get my cards, the money?" The room span so I held on tighter to my calves. "Every Christmas I sent a card and ten dollars each. I wasn't sure when your birthday was so—"

"Would you excuse me a minute." On the third go of lifting the mattress I was able to grab the roll and when I went back downstairs, I held it out to her. "Luella found this. Is it yours?"

"I don't know. It could be but… You mean is it yours? Did she show you the cards, any of them? I know she posted a bundle back when you'd have been about six or seven but once you were older, I thought maybe she'd soften and—"

"No. We never saw them. She never gave us anything."

Alice let out a pitying wail. I couldn't tell if it was for her pain, or mine and Luella's. She cried too loudly. Unsure of how to comfort her I stared at my feet, waiting for her to quieten down and gather herself.

"Oh God, I'm sorry. I'm so rubbish at this. Maybe I should go?"

I knew that was where I should ask her to stay, but I couldn't. I was numb to her tears, unable to feel sympathy for her feelings when I had my own to hide. She took a deep breath and sniffed up her snot then wiped her eyes. I side-stepped behind the chair so she couldn't hug me.

"Shall I visit again?" She seemed weird, too on edge.

"If you want to."

"Great. Oh that's great. Thank you. When? Tomorrow? What time? The same time?"

She could take Johanna's place; I couldn't face the both of them. I nodded. She moved forwards as if to grasp my shoulders but I stepped back so instead she walked to the front door, turning to smile at me before closing it quietly behind her. A car started and drove away. I grabbed the money as I sat down, my money. I was rich. As for the meeting, it wasn't like in fairytales where lost children are re-united joyously with their families. It was tense, stilted, disappointing, exhausting.

Marjorie sat down where Alice had been. "That was quick."

"She's coming back tomorrow. At the same time."

"When Johanna's due?"

"Yeah."

I didn't look up in the silence.

"Alright. I'll call her. We've got a free afternoon then. Do you want to do something?" I wanted to take a pill and curl up in bed but that wasn't the right answer for someone who needed to appear well. "We could visit the hospital?"

"No."

"But—"

"I don't want to see her."

"But—"

"Why should I visit her just because she's poorly? I don't even want her to wake up, not ever." My babysitter sighed. "You don't get it. You don't get what she was like."

I put a pillow in front of my closed bedroom door and hugged Luella's pillow right into me, understanding why she'd chosen the pills, to fall asleep and never wake up, to let it all drift away and not have to face it any more. I got that now. But I didn't have enough medicine to do the same. And I was awake and I heard the knock on my door and when Marjorie tried to open it the pillow caught at its base.

"Lara." I kept my back facing her head that was poking through the gap. "I'm sorry. You're right, I don't get it." She tried pushing the door but it wouldn't budge. "Can I come in, please?"

She waited; I waited. It was hard breathing in and out without it showing. She gave up and closed the door. I pushed the pillow back against it, and when I woke up, stood before her in the kitchen.

"Sorry."

"That's alright. I'm not doing very well am I? Do you want to go for a walk? We've been inside too long. It's never good for a person, a person's mind."

Away from the house the skin on my head loosened and words trickled. We walked along streets Mother had told us not to go down as there was no need, and stopped at an ice-cream shop I'd never seen before. I hadn't realised there were so many flavours, and Marjorie bought me a lemon cone cold enough to numb my aching throat. I didn't tell her it was my first ice-cream. I'd take the new things and act like they were no big deal. Marjorie's kindness together with the sun's warmth smoothed my barbed edges and I stretched my arms to the sky and back round in the biggest circle I could.

"I'm glad we came out."

"Me too."

"The house is so dark."

"It certainly is, brings a person down after a while."

We strolled through a gate into a botanical garden where children squealed with excitement when a jet of water shot over the grass catching the petals of the red and yellow blossoms that were bursting out of the flower beds.

"I love it here, don't you?" She licked her strawberry gelato.

"I've never been before."

"No? Never? Jesus."

I was lost, a stranger in the town I'd never left. Mothers and toddlers skipped past us, anyone my age was at school. I felt as feeble and lonely as the old people who hobbled past, but to the outside world I must look normal, sitting on a bench letting the day drift by me.

"Can I ask, and you don't have to answer but... Why didn't you say anything? Why didn't you get help, either of you? Tell a teacher, or me, another parent, a—"

"It was too shameful."

"But it wasn't your shame. You weren't acting badly."

She didn't get it. No-one did unless they'd felt it. You didn't say the bad things you were feeling about your family.

Marjorie needed to visit the store on the way home. Inside, a lady with long, straight blond hair, properly blond like a white towel, she gave Marjorie a huge hug and a smile which she then passed on to me.

"All good, no catastrophes," she laughed.

"Excellent. Frida, this is Lara; Lara, my friend Frida."

"Nice to meet you Lara." She didn't need to ask how I was, she'd heard all about me.

"Lara honey, we just need to sort out a couple of things, won't be a minute. Help yourself to anything."

The banned candy canes were stuck together in a clear jar, their glazed coating begging to be licked. I saw the baking soda and toothpaste. Next to them were the toothbrushes. My eyes settled on the lilac ones, pretty, unnecessary, expensive, a frivolity. I couldn't hear Marjorie and

Frida. No-one had entered the shop. I slipped behind the counter and took one, shoving it in the waistband of my skirt, hidden by my loose top. I stood behind the counter, waiting. Still they didn't come, and the temptation was too great. I opened the glass bell jar and snatched a red and green candy cane, tucking it in next to the toothbrush then stepped one foot on the ladder and pushed off with the other, too fast, too much strength making me bang to a stop on the opposite wall, jolting my neck and shoulders but I didn't care. I'd felt the breeze. I flew back again.

~

Alice arrived at exactly eleven, wearing blue denim jeans, open purple sandals showing off her purple painted toes, a cream and pink top and the same jewellery as the day before. I liked what she wore, her outfits as colourful as the ones the girls at school wore but somehow not as brash; a universe away from Mother.

"Would you like to go for a walk?" I nearly said her name but stopped myself, thinking it would make me sound too familiar. "It's always good to get some air."

As we walked, she talked of her regret for not visiting years before, said her own issues with her sister had stopped her from pushing to see Luella and I, and as we sat on my bench in the park, she said she was sad that she'd missed us for so many years, that she'd wanted to visit then would bottle out of coming at the thought of having to sit in a room with Mother. She used the word issues a lot, sounding as angry as I felt. I threw in the odd "um" and let her ramble on.

A boy and a girl chased each other on the grass as their mothers chatted about this, that and the other. An older girl ran up and tickled a younger girl but too hard, for too long, you could see the pain in her tiny face. When she started to cry the mother told the younger one off for making a fuss. The elder walked away, satisfied.

"We've been gone a while. Marjorie'll be getting worried."

I remembered the route home even though I'd only walked it once before and when we reached the house Alice stopped next to her blue car.

"Mother didn't drive."

"No."

"Why not?"

"She never wanted to learn, said others could chauffer her."

"But you did?"

"God yes. Don't you? The feeling of freedom, that you can go anywhere."

"I guess."

"I could teach you."

"Really?"

"Yeah. Why not?"

"But you live miles away."

She fiddled with her keys. "I talked too much today, about myself, sorry. I get—"

"It's fine."

"Your turn tomorrow?"

She didn't try to hug me.

The Union

I entered Mother's room more boldly than before. It smelt less musty, more of Marjorie whose nightdress lay on top of the pillow, matching the royal blue slippers on the floor, which made Mother's brown ones look ready for the bin. I pulled the box from under the bed and took out the photos to show Alice, apart from the one of Father's dead body, there was no need for her to see that. A navy tube rolled out of the blanket that had been on top of them, a lipstick. I popped off the lid and turned the base. It was red, Radiant Red according to its faded lettering, bought and barely used by the look of it. I didn't try it, not wanting a thing Mother's lips had touched to press against mine. When I put the blanket back, a clear plastic cylinder fell onto the floor. The pencilled writing on the hospital label said Luella Jeffreys. And in it was the top of her thumb, nail hanging off the skin. I searched for a second container but there wasn't one. Where was my thumb? Why wasn't part of me worth keeping?

~

I opened the front door as Alice's car pulled up in the driveway.

"I've something to show you." I took the frames from the side of the sofa and stood them on the coffee table. Alice's breath shortened like mine did when I was panicking. "She looks happy in that one." I pointed to the photo that I reckoned was taken before the wedding. "Did you know him?" Alice shook her head. I'd expected her to pick the pictures up but she left them alone. "Have you seen them before?" She shook her head again. "But you were at their wedding?"

On the third shake she exploded. "No, of course not! Sorry. Sorry, I shouldn't snap, not at you, it's just she was so, Christ almighty." She carried on, veering from swearing to apologising to swearing, her thoughts making no sense out loud, all muddled together. I'd got it so wrong. I'd envisioned her smiling whilst looking at them, happy memories in her head.

"Why weren't you at their wedding? Had you fallen out?"

"We never fell in." Alice took a deep breath. "To talk about her when she's not here, it doesn't seem fair."

"She was mean." Whereas I was brave. I was fearless. "I'm going to the hospital today. Do you want to come?"

"I don't think so."

"I haven't got a car so was hoping you'd drive me." She'd found her way to the house. She could follow the red signs to the hospital. "It might be easier if there are two of us." I pictured Luella's body lying on a metal slab like Father's, distorted, bloated, a blue grey face, an agony. "I want to see Luella."

"What?"

"I want to go and see Luella. No-one's let me see her since she died. Please will you come with me? They'll listen to an adult that's family, I'm sure they will."

She accepted the challenge. And I tucked the stolen lilac toothbrush and candy just above the base of my brassiere whilst Alice wrote a note for Marjorie, leaving it by the telephone.

The inside of her car had the same knobs and counters as Sean's but the colours were varying shades of pale blue rather than all black plastic, and it smelt different, like coconut and vanilla were mixed in the air. The gear stick was straight with a navy ball on top and there was a string of purple and pink beads hanging from the middle mirror that jangled together whenever she braked or turned a corner.

My stomach muscles started to spasm as we neared the hospital. I wound down the window and leant my head out, not wanting to be sick in her car. Alice concentrated on finding a parking spot, driving too slowly, without the strong breeze my nausea grew. On the third loop of looking a white car reversed out of a space, making room for us. As soon as the handbrake was up, I jumped out.

"Are you alright?" she asked over the sky blue roof.

"A bit car sick. Sorry."

"You don't have to say that you know. You don't have to pretend that's what it is."

I started walking to the entrance. Alice closed the gap by the time we took to the corridors. She was unused to being led and kept stepping in front of me then stopping, waiting for me to overtake her. When we arrived in the open area that led to Mother's room a nurse looked up from her desk.

"Can I help you?" she asked, cross that we were disturbing her peace. I pointed to the door I'd gone through last time.

"We're here to see Luella," Alice said.

The nurse frowned.

"She means Mrs Jeffreys."

"And you are?"

"Her sister and daughter." I smiled apologetically at the nurse, wishing I wasn't associated with Mother, certain she was rude to them even in her sleep.

Alice gripped my elbow. "What are you doing?"

"While we're here you may as well see her, to see that she's asleep and she can't get you. It'll be a good thing."

"She's had so few visitors, it's shocking really," the nurse tutted.

I cringed; Alice leant over the desk. "Perhaps that says more about her than us."

"She's been moved," the nurse barked.

"What?"

"Mrs Jeffreys was moved to another ward this morning. Of course, you'd have known that if you'd been visiting."

I stuck my thumbnails into my clenched fists. "Where is she now?"

"Ward 7D."

"Which is where?"

Her eyes narrowed as she gnarled, "Back the way you came, take the lift to the seventh floor and follow the green stripe on the wall all the way there."

"I'll be having a word with the sister Nurse Temperley. You're a very rude woman; I'm not sure you've found your proper calling," were Alice's parting words.

"Really? Are you really going to complain about her?" I asked.

"No. I don't know. I doubt it, but it gives her something to worry about and why should we be the only ones? I mean what a bitch. She didn't need to be so snooty."

On the seventh floor a dark green stripe led us to Ward 7D which was much busier than the one we'd come from. Violet, blue, and white uniformed staff rushed around on their rubber soled shoes from bed to door to cupboards to beds again. We waited by the main desk but no-one acknowledged us. After a few minutes Alice stopped a doctor.

"Excuse me, we're here to see Mrs Jeffreys."

"She can help."

He pointed to a lady in the same yellow uniform that Nurse Temperley had been wearing.

"And you are?"

"Her daughter and her sister."

"How lovely. Oh she'll be so pleased to see you. Come with me."

Alice started to follow her but I held onto the desk. The nurse stopped to wait for me which made Alice turn too.

"Lara? Are you alright?"

I was gripping the ledge so tightly my knuckles had turned as wan as my face which was trying not to let sick spew everywhere.

"She's awake?"

"Sorry?" said the nurse.

Alice moved closer to me.

"Is she awake Alice?"

"Jesus. No. I don't know. I don't think so." The blood drained from her face leaving only two streaks of magenta blusher and some green eyeshadow. "Has she woken up?" Alice asked the nurse, who looked crestfallen.

"No. I'm so sorry. She hasn't, not yet. But she's doing ever so well. She will soon, I'm sure."

I breathed in four times before remembering to exhale.

"Do you want to wait here?" Alice offered.

I did, but I couldn't. I needed proof she was still in a coma.

The nurse took pigeon steps and we had to do the same so as not to bump into her. The ward beds were in rows of four facing four, with four sets of eight beds running off the central desk in a cross shape, giving little privacy to those who were awake. Mother was next to a window. It seemed a waste to give a view to someone who couldn't appreciate it. The air smelt of nothing, all aromas regularly, constantly, carefully wiped away.

Alice and I stood as far as we could from the bed while remaining in Mother's allocated space. My calves were touching the skirting board of the wall I'd backed myself into. Alice stepped closer to her sister then retreated as if she was afraid the patient would unexpectedly waken, but she was lying perfectly still with fewer tubes in than last time. There was definitely no movement. Her eyes were closed, her mouth pinched, a look of concentration and confusion on her face. She'd be fighting in the dreaming world. Alice cried quietly. I was tempted to reach out but not in front of Mother.

"I wasn't sure what I'd feel, guilt and anger of course but sadness, I didn't expect that." She hit her two palms together, fingers stretched up and out forming a C shape. "Such a waste." One hand moved over her eyes and squeezed the bridge of her nose. "There we go then. All done. Do you want to say anything?" I shook my head, wanting it to be the last time I ever had to see Mrs Jeffreys. "Be at peace Susan," Alice said, reaching out her hand but not touching her sister, not evening touching the sheet by the foot of the bed. My mother was a Susan. Susan Jeffreys. It sounded too nice for her, too few syllables, too friendly.

"Do you think she'll wake up?" Alice asked a doctor.

He was surprised at her bluntness, with me glad that she'd asked exactly what I wanted to know.

"Shall we go somewhere more private?"

"Here's fine. We just need to know." Alice stepped sideways, closer to me. "So we can get on with things, or not. It's very difficult for her daughter as I'm sure you can imagine."

"I'm afraid the honest answer is we don't know."

"At all?"

"It's hard to say."

"Do *you* think she'll ever wake?"

"I'm sorry, I just can't say. None of us can."

I'd hoped he would say no. Alice found and squeezed my hand.

"Thank you for your honesty."

We left the ward. And walked down two hundred and twenty four stairs to the basement. There were less people in the corridors beneath the ground and the air was colder.

"Can I help you?"

This time it was a man wearing pale green who was asking us. I hadn't seen that colour uniform before.

"We're looking for the morgue."

"Why?"

"My niece is there. This is her sister."

"Family aren't usually—"

"They've made an exception in our case." She was a good aunt, a useful aunt, a confident twister of the truth. "So, if you could just—"

His beeper sounded and for the first time it was a help rather than a hindrance.

"It's down there, turn left at the end and it's the fourth door on the right." He was out of sight by the end of his sentence.

"You're sure you want to do this?"

"I have to."

We found the fourth door and tried the handle, which was locked. Alice knocked firmly.

"We will see her," she reassured me. "Today."

When I heard footsteps coming to answer, I nearly ran away. I could run to the lake and hide beneath the water, no-one would find me at the bottom of there. A man opened the door, squinting from one eye. I tried not to stare directly at it.

"Can I help you?"

"We're here to see Luella Jeffreys."

"Oh really?"

"Yes really."

"Well, I'm afraid there must have been a misunderstanding, we don't—"

Alice walked past him so I followed her. We both shivered. He was wearing a fleecy maroon jumper under his dark green smock.

"Now Mr...?"

"Jones."

"Mr Jones. This is Lara Jeffreys, the sister of Luella Jeffreys and she really needs to see her twin, her identical twin. No-one has let her. No-one seems to understand how important it is for her grieving and healing and—"

He held up his hand, the palm towards Alice's face, stemming the flow.

"You're Lara? My son goes to your school, Daviid, with two I's, Daviid Jones." His poorly eye wasn't from an accident then. "He was very upset about Luella. Everyone was, all the students. They were devastated."

I let my anger seethe inside at the rubbish he was spouting because I needed his help, and nodded slightly as if accepting his condolences, before pulling a piece of skin off the back of my good thumb whilst counting the dirt marks on his shoes.

"Alright then," he said. "She's this way."

I checked with Alice. "I'll wait here. Unless you want me to come?"

But I knew she didn't want to. And that was right, she'd never even met Luella.

"No thank you."

I followed Mr Jones through an unmarked door. There were four rows of three silver doors and two empty tables in the middle of the room. He put his hands on number five.

"You're sure you want to see her?"

"Yes."

He hesitated. "I have to ask you not to tell anyone. It's not allowed, not down here."

"I won't. Cross my heart and hope to die."

He pushed on the thick latch, turned the handle, and pulled open the drawer, his face reddening with the effort. The ledge he drew out was longer than I'd expected. There was a green sheet covering her. I'd pictured white.

"Shall I?" He gestured to the sheet.

"No. I'll do it."

"Right. I'll be just outside."

I touched the crease free cotton with two of my fingertips

then held the sheet with both hands, pulling it back to reveal the head and shoulders of my silent sister. Her face wasn't fighting the death that owned her; her lips were turned up at the corners as if she was content not to speak any more. The lids were closed. I couldn't see the chocolate brown twinkle that used to glint at me. Her complexion was waxy but perfect, no teenage pimples had ever spoilt its hue. Her hair was combed away from her face in a style she'd never worn. Why on earth had they done it that way? She'd have hated it. I brushed it with my fingertips, the fringe falling back where it usually sat.

I stroked her face, my fingers running smoothly over its marble surface. I put my hand under the sheet to hold her hand. She didn't hold mine back. My four fingers gripped hers, eight fingers touching but with no reciprocated love. Tears spilt down my flushed cheeks. It was wrong that she was lying still while I was breathing fast enough for two. "Luella." I leant forwards to try and hug her. She wouldn't hug me back. "Luella. Come on." My pleading fell on deaf ears. She was gone and I was alone and it hurt so badly that I wanted to die as well. I wished it more than anything as I squeezed her fingers scanning her for some sign of life. I stroked her with my right hand. "I got you the toothbrush you wanted, and a candy cane. Can't have one without the other." I wedged them between her right arm and hip. "There you go. Especially for you, no sharing." I kissed her on the forehead as a last goodbye then couldn't let go, couldn't cope with it being the final time I saw her. I pushed my head down next to hers so we were cheek to cheek, my tears rolling down her face, both of us crying.

I didn't hear them come in.

I felt Alice's arms around my shoulders, trying to gently lead me away but I would not let go of Luella. I'd planned to be dignified and mature but now I'd seen her and was back with her I couldn't contemplate a future without her, couldn't believe the boisterous girl that I'd always lived with was lying so bloody still. The thought of her being buried made me sob. It had to be a no to that. She wouldn't like it, she'd hate being under the ground. Alice and Mr Jones tried to soothe me off her but their platitudes weren't working. Then I saw Luella watching, crying in the sky, needing to be left in peace, and her pain at my pain made me pull myself together in the way Mother had taught us. I switched to being fine. I kissed her cheek. I raised two fingers to salute my thanks to Mr Jones but he was wrapped up in his own distress at my upset. The blurred lines guided me up the stairs, out of a side door and onto streets that led away from that place. Alice was behind me the whole time. She didn't speak, she was just there.

I pictured Luella giggling but more recent memories swept that away and all I could see was her drugged, Mother smiling, and me not there, me being out, me being too selfish to care about what was going on at home. I would walk forever; that would be my punishment, my purgatory.

"You must be getting tired."

I quickened my pace to prove otherwise.

"I'm a bit tired," she said.

"You can go."

"You can't keep going like this."

"I don't want to go home."

She pressed two fingers on her temples, pushing and circling the skin. "We could go to the park?"

We could.

We walked more slowly, in unison, and a quarter of an hour later sat on a bench in front of the freshly watered grass.

"What were your parents like?" I asked.

Her expression turned stony. "They tried their best."

"But what were they like?"

"I've got some photos, back at mine."

"Really?"

"You've not seen them before?"

"No. Were they kind?"

"No. That's not a word I'd use about them. Our mother was from England you know; she spoke like the Queen, kind of. From the sounds of it, she acted a bit like yours." I'd dreaded her saying that; I didn't want it to be passed down as that meant I'd turn into one of them. "I mean, I never saw Susan with you but… People say it's hard raising children, especially alone, exhausting, with no thanks or let up and—"

"That's no excuse."

"Hmm."

I couldn't tell if that meant she agreed with me or not.

"I'm not going to have children."

"You're too young to say that."

"I'm not. All it causes is unhappiness."

"I've seen tonnes of families who're happy, lots of my friends are. You can be different to her you know."

"You didn't have any. When they died, your parents, was it a relief?"

She chewed her lip. "I guess." Shame made her slump down.

"Would you be relieved if Mother died?"

"That's not fair."

I was no longer alone in being nefarious.

~

In my room I took a pink pill from its case and swallowed it. I got into bed and pulled the cover to the top of my neck. The breeze blew the edges of the curtains back and forth through the open window.

I dreamt of Luella. We had the best night of our lives, flying over treetops and skimming the lake with our feet. We hollered for joy as we held hands and spun in the air. I chased her and caught her. We embraced time and time again. Then the stars began to fade, replaced by a misty sky and gentle sunrise. She flew in front of me, leading me back to the house, to my bedroom window, pushing me so I went from bouncing to lying on the bed with her stroking my hair, telling me it would be oh so pretty once it was longer, two years was what she reckoned. I reached out for her but she hushed my moaning and wiped my eyes with the edge of the sheet. She glanced at the window before dropping her head to kiss me. I felt her cold lips on my forehead and her fingers closed my eyelids as she whispered goodbye. When I woke up, she was absolute in her absence. Which meant I had to change. I had to leave like she had.

I ran a boiling hot citrus bath and scrubbed every bit of my skin and washed and rinsed my hair three times until I smelt of Marjorie. I made toast, boiled water for coffee and poured two glasses of juice. When Marjorie appeared, the bags under her eyes were dark and puffy like she'd not had enough sleep. As I turned the bread under the grill, she emptied her glass.

"Coffee?" I'd watched her make it so knew to pour hot water in to warm the pot, then two scoops of grains followed by more boiling water and a stir, finally adding the plunger as a lid. I tried some; it was too hot, too bitter.

"You don't like it?" I shook my head, disappointed. "Try adding milk and sugar."

I liked it with milk and three sugars.

"You've got a sweet tooth."

"That's so bad. Mother would be furious."

"Well, she's not here now so don't worry about it."

I emptied the remnants of coffee into the sink and washed up the cup.

"Alice has to go home today. She's coming back, she—"

"That's fine." My voice raised.

"She's dropping by this morning. She's got to sort out some work things then—"

"Of course. No problem."

I cleared, washed and dried, refusing Marjorie's offer of help, ignoring her presence so she gave up and went to get dressed. Feeling jittery, I polished the dark wood paneling in the hallway, hoping a strong shine would make the world brighter. Marjorie came down wearing a white and red sundress with one strap around the neck, her tanned shoulders bare.

"I'll be back around three." She pursed her lips, swallowing her crossness with my rudeness. Well I was angry too. The row was saved by the ringing of the doorbell. On her way out, Marjorie's eyes told Alice that I knew she was leaving.

"I have to go home today."

"Yeah, that's fine."

"You think so?" I turned to face her biting sarcasm but was met with concern. "I wanted to stay. I hoped you'd wanted me to stay."

"I do."

"So it's not fine then."

I twisted the polishing cloth, trying to wring out an honest answer.

"I've got a job, a house. I need to go back and sort some things out." I stuck my nails into my palms beneath the cloth. "So that I can come back for longer."

"You can't want to come back here, no-one would."

"I want to help you."

"I don't need help."

"Right." She cleared her throat. I plucked threads off the sofa, concentrated so hard on picking at the brown fluff; Mother would go mad at me damaging her property. "I wondered if you'd like to come and stay with me for a few days." I plucked and plucked, it would take hours to make it bare. "She said it would be alright, Marjorie, if you wanted to. I think she thought it was a good idea. And Johanna. What do you think?" I plucked and plucked. "Shall we get some air?"

My throat burned as I nodded. Her niceness had mixed my head up. We left the house, still not speaking, and her purple shoes made no noise on the pavement but their silver buckle kept catching the sun so a shot of light danced to the nearest surface be it a fence, a wall or the post box.

"I really do need to speak with my manager and sort out some things at work."

"I told you, it's fine."

"Can you please stop saying that? It's not fine. It's not fine at all. I wish I could turn back time, that I'd come sooner, I do. But I can't change that now." Her eyes blazed but I wasn't frightened; it didn't feel like she was going to turn on me. "Come back with me. Let me look after you."

"So it'll ease your guilt?"

"That's not what I meant."

"That's how it sounded."

"I thought it'd be good for you to get away, to get away from her, and the house. You said yourself it's not a happy place."

I'd never been inside anyone else's home.

"What's your house like?"

She smiled. "I love it. White on the outside, with a small front garden, bigger at the back. There's a driveway and a porch, two bedrooms, one for you if you'd like it. The kitchen opens onto a space for the table and the living room and there's another spare room that I keep meaning to sort out but it gets fuller and fuller of things I don't know where else to put."

"Are the walls wooden, like ours?"

"No, they're plaster painted white. The floors are wood but a light shade, more like that fence than the ones in your house."

"Which walls are white?"

"All of them. And each room has a window that I open wide to let in the scent of flowers from the garden. There are lots of flowers, in the front and the back."

I could see her fitting into that house, but not me.

"It wouldn't work."

"Why not?"

"I'd look out of place there."

"What do you mean?"

"Look at me, all dull, I'd depress you."

"Don't be so silly. And I can get you new clothes, I owe you sixteen birthday presents. You don't have to come though. It was just a thought."

"I want to. I think. It's confusing."

"How about you come for one night, and if you don't like it I'll bring you back the next day."

"But it's such a long drive."

"Not really."

"Then why didn't you come and visit us."

"I wanted to. I told you. That's why I phoned, why Susan came to see me."

"When?"

"Earlier this year. It was the last time I saw her. First time I'd seen her in years. I wanted to meet you and Luella. I'd phoned her saying I was going to visit no matter what she said that she needed to come and tell me something in person first, then she'd let me meet you."

I knew who the liar was. Lying to her children as she headed off for the night.

"Was it nice seeing her?"

"No. We both said pretty mean things. I tried calling a few days later but she was already in a rage when she answered and wouldn't listen to a word. She told me to leave you all alone, forever, that she'd told you about me, and you both said you wanted nothing to do with me, that I'd die with no-one to care." Her hand gripped my arm tighter. "I know I left it too long but I do want to try and be a good aunt now, to show you that I'm not whatever she said I am. She could be a bit harsh sometimes, your mother."

Uncomfortable with her closeness, I moved out of her hold. A crack of anguish shot over her face, pity the poor aunty.

"I lost my thumb." I'd never told a soul. Me and Luella hadn't. I threw the words out before Mother's face shut me up. "I was six and she said I had to stop sucking it but I couldn't and that made her mad so one morning I woke up and half of it was gone. When I say gone, I mean she'd cut it off. I guess it wasn't lost so much as taken though I don't know where she put it, she didn't keep it like Luella's so it is lost, sort of."

Alice cried so loudly a lady on the other side of the road stopped walking her black and white spotted dog to watch us. Embarrassed, I tried to quieten her saying 'shush' and 'it's alright' over and over. What had I done? Luella and I had agreed to never tell anyone and now, as soon as she wasn't here, I'd gone and broken that promise.

"It's okay. It doesn't hurt."

"Did no-one do anything?"

"Like what?"

"Tell on her. Call the police."

"She said it was an accident."

"That's so wrong. She was so bad. What else? What else did she do? What else has she done?" I didn't know what counted, big things or little things, only physical things or were words allowed. "What about Luella?"

"That wasn't Mother, she cut her own one off." Alice's knees went from under her but she grabbed onto me in time to stop hitting the ground. The sounds she made weren't words, more strangulated snorts. "Please, don't be angry. Luella wanted us to be the same again. And she was alright once she got to hospital. The hot chocolates helped. She really liked them."

I pulled a large bit of skin off the side of my little finger, too big, a blood bubble swelled up. The pain was sharp near the wick. I sucked the seepage, feeling a fool. I was too peculiar for Alice's world; she would leave and never come back. And I needed to leave, to start again with no complications, no explanations.

~

Alice picked up the bag that she'd left on the floor by the chair. The orange leather sack hung from her heart to her hip and the wooden beads dangling off the straps bumped together as she swung it over her shoulder.

"I bet you don't want to stay with your mad aunt now?"

"I'm the weird one."

"I think you're remarkably sane, considering."

The heaviness of the house pressed on my tiredness, pushing out a yawn. I turned the main light on. It was such a dark house, always so miserable.

"I'll come."

"Really?"

"It might not be for long."

"Of course, your choice. Come for as long or as little as you like, that's absolutely understood. Whatever you want to do, you do. And I can come back the day after tomorrow. Does that suit? Can you be ready by then?" She hugged me tightly. I didn't hug her back, my lack of response tempering her excitement. "I'll see you soon then?"

"Sure."

I wasn't sure.

I wasn't sure at all of what I was doing.

The Exit

Marjorie gave me a present for my journey, a cream bag, the material imprinted with large violet flowers. Inside it were a packet of multi-coloured candies and a purple toothbrush. I added two dresses, two sets of underwear, the roll of money, the photo of father, the pink pills and the paper bag that contained a box that contained the ring that kind people had bought me.

As we were clearing the table, Sally came in uncertainly and Sean followed, bearing a protective stance by her side.

"We came to say goodbye." She smiled pityingly at me.

"No need. It's only for a few days."

They all blushed at the secret conversation they'd had earlier that day, about how I should leave for good, it would be the best thing for me, for them, for everyone really. There was a knock at the door. Sean opened it and Mr Parker walked in. Marjorie stood by his side, awkwardly. Sean looked cross about something. And I felt like the one who didn't belong, in my own home. Mr Parker reached inside his green blazer and pulled out a brown envelope.

"I found this for you."

I was embarrassed by them all watching me, eight eyes peering as I opened it and pulled out a rectangular piece of navy card. I turned it over. There was a photo of Luella glued to it.

"It's from Year Eight. It was the only one we had. Sorry."

I ran upstairs to be alone with her, holding my arms out straight so my tears didn't fall on her glossy face. She was smiling and looked pretty even with short hair. She would have blossomed so beautifully. I pulled her to my chest and hugged her flat against me. "I miss you," I whispered, cradling her image, pushing it onto my heart so she could hear the painful beating. It hurt so much I was sure it was full of holes from where an invisible blade was puncturing the muscle each time I thought of her. I cried for us both having lost each other. I curled in a ball, protecting my twin, trying to replace the image of her dead body with this live one. Marjorie opened the door a little way.

"Can I get you anything?"

"I think I'll go to sleep now."

I put Luella's picture on the bedside table so I didn't crush it and lay with my head at the very edge of the mattress, facing her.

~

I took the keys from the hall table and held them out to Marjorie.

"Would you mind looking after these for me?"

"Of course not. No problem."

"Here's my number and address. We can get back in no time, sort of, if you need us," said Alice.

Marjorie picked up a piece of paper from the hall table and handed it to her. "Keep in touch."

Alice put the slip of paper in her bag.

"Thank you for everything, and Mr Parker. And Sean, tell him I'm sorry, I—"

"He's fine, it's fine." She hugged me hard. "You take care you hear me? Look after her."

"I will," replied Alice.

I put my new bag between my feet on the floor of the car and as we drove away, saw a familiar figure in the side mirror, running determinedly along the pavement. I twisted my neck round and saw Marjorie wave at him. We turned the corner. I opened the packet of candy and picked out a red one for Alice, a green one for me. The sweetness settled my nerves.

"What have you told people?" I asked.

"What do you mean?"

"About me coming."

"Nothing yet." As the distance between the crossroads increased so did the speed of her driving. "What would you like me to say?"

I tested sentences through silent lips.

"We could just tell them I'm your niece and I've come to stay."

"Sounds good."

"Do you think they'll want to know more?"

"Maybe. We can say you've been abroad or your mother's having an operation or—"

"She said all lies get found out."

"We're not exactly lying. She is in hospital."

She smiled briefly before concentrating on her driving, speeding up so the trees blurred on the main road out of town, my lying mate.

The Gardener

We walked up the path to the white house with purple bougainvillea wilting over its door. In the weeks since I'd lived there, the grass on either side of the path had faded to the palest green, in some places brown. Alice shook her head as she ran her left foot over it; she'd have to water it later, second time that day.

~

"I'll get it," I called after the knocking, seeing as I was nearest the door.

Sunshine bounced off a cluster of crystals hanging in the hallway so that green, red and blue lights danced over the white walls, ceiling and pale, worn, oak floor. I breathed in the heady scent of the cream and yellow freesias on the hall table. They'd become a habit. A new bunch every seven days and a deep breath whenever I was near them.

The bulkiness of the dark shadow in front of the mottled glass made me stop. I listened to where in the house Alice was then opened the door a fraction before pulling it right back. I stared past Jonas's shoulder at the road. He held out two bunches of flowers.

"Hello Lara. These are for you. And your aunt?"

On cue, Alice came down the stairs, all in pink, like a bright flamingo.

"Who is it sweetie?"

I moved out of the way so she could study our visitor. Mr Jonas's shoulder length hair was brushed with a rough centre parting, light brown preparing to go grey and his eyes were the blue of the sapphire ring Alice showed me every time we passed Hatton's Jewellery store. He'd shaved but missed some spots so little tufts of stubble were dotted about his face. His clothes were old but clean, no attempt at ironed. The bulk of his torso was hidden by the two bunches of flowers.

"Can we help you?"

"I've come to see Lara, if that's okay?"

"Lara?"

"This is Mr Jonas. He's the gardener at school, was, at my old school."

"Right. Nice to meet you Mr Jonas."

I gave Alice the hand signal we'd agreed when I didn't want to do something; two taps with my right hand on my right thigh. Jonas looked at the ground while still holding out the flowers.

"They're beautiful," Alice said.

"I shouldn't have come. I'll go. You keep these."

He pushed the flowers further inside the house so Alice automatically moved forward to take them. I backed closer to the wall, my hands behind me.

"Maybe call first next time?" my aunt suggested.

"Yeah. Good idea. I'll do that." He stepped backwards as he spoke then turned and rushed down the path before she could give him the phone number.

"That was odd. You okay? What do you think he wanted?"

"God knows."

I went to my room while Alice put the flowers in two vases, setting one in her bedroom and the other in the living room. At dinner, I fiddled with the woven purple placemat.

"I didn't mean to be rude earlier."

"I know."

"Do you think he thought I was rude? I hope not." I tried to pierce a crouton with my fork.

"No. He looked kind, understanding. You don't know why he came?"

"No."

"Wait and see then. Or you could ask Marjorie and—"

"No way."

"It was just a suggestion."

"I have a feeling, I don't know. I feel like it might be important but I don't know why. That sounds stupid doesn't it?"

"Not at all."

"You don't have to humour me."

"I'm not."

"You are."

"It's your gut instinct."

"Really? I had it that day, before I opened the door. Like I knew something bad was going to happen."

"I'm sorry," Alice said, quietly, as if it was all her fault.

"Should I have not gone in? Would that have stopped it?"

"I don't think so."

"It was my fault for going in."

"No."

"But is it always right?"

"What?"

"Gut instinct. Is it always right?"

"I think so. I don't know. It seems to be." Alice scrunched her eyebrows together, concentrating hard. "I believe in it. There's no scientific explanation but—"

"If it's always right then it was my fault."

"Lara—"

"I want to know why he came."

"Right. Well, maybe next time we should let him in and find out. I can stay with you."

"You think he'll come back?"

"I do."

I allowed a slight pause. "Is that your gut instinct?"

She smiled.

~

I sat up as Alice shut my white bedroom door behind her.

"He's here again."

"Who? Jonas?"

"Yeah. What do you want to do? Shall I ask him to leave? He brought some plants. I thought that was sweet."

"He didn't call."

"No."

"Can you be near me?"

"Of course. The whole time."

Alice held the door open but I waited for her to go first.

Jonas was concave and self-conscious, out of place in the pastel living room. As I went down the last stair, he banged his knee on the coffee table but ignored the pain, holding his hands stiffly by his sides. I looked at him steadily. I wasn't scared. I'd watched him in the wing mirror of Alice's car as he'd run along my old road. Coincidence, I'd told myself. But no, the first time he'd knocked confirmed it was me he was chasing. I hadn't told Alice, but it had flashed through my mind hundreds of times and twice into my dreams.

"You look well," he said.

I saw Alice shut the fridge quietly so she could hear everything but neither of us spoke. I sat down in one of the chairs with low wooden legs and a deep cushioned base. The arm rests were polished, the material pale blue to match the sofa but with darker blue spots scattered over it.

"How are you?" Jonas asked.

"Fine."

"You look well."

"You already said that."

Alice passed me a juice. The seconds seemed like minutes, the tension increasing the longer the silence lasted. Now chit chat would make it worse. Jonas cleared his throat. His eyes darted over the ceiling.

"I suppose you're wondering why I'm here?" I nodded as Alice nearly replied yes before sinking back into her chair. "It's awkward." He pushed his right thumb over the skin of his left hand, turning the skin red as he repeated the movement. "Marjorie and Sean are well. They miss you," he added.

I started to acknowledge his comment with a flick of my chin but stopped, horrified to be imitating one of Mother's mannerisms. He stood up.

"Are you alright?" Alice asked.

"I should go."

"No. I mean, if you want to you can but... did you have something to tell us, to tell Lara?"

He averted his eyes. Took a step to the side. A laugh

escaped. "It's complicated." Alice sat forward. Jonas took a shallow breath then looked at me.

"I think I knew your mother." Complexions turned pasty. "It was a long time ago. I thought you'd like to know."

"Why?" I asked.

"Excuse me?"

"Why would I want to know?"

"I don't know. I would. I did, when my parents died. I listened to other peoples' memories. It helped, sometimes."

"How did you know her?" asked Alice.

"I worked at the morgue. Her husband—"

"You met my father?"

"Yeah. No. I worked there when—"

"Did you meet Luella and I?"

"No."

"But you saw them together?" said Alice.

"Sort of—"

"Was she upset?"

"Upset?" He frowned, trying to re-capture the memory. "She was distraught. They were very in love, you could tell. She kept kissing his hand."

"I can't imagine it," said Alice.

"If you want to ask me anything—"

"No."

"Nothing?"

"No thank you."

"Right. There we are then." He went to the hallway.

"The school," Alice called after him. "Can we reach you through them? Or Marjorie?"

But he was out of the door as if he hadn't heard her and now he'd gone, I wanted to know more about my father, how he'd died and where Mother had met him.

~

As Alice drove us down the tarmac track to the gardener's lodgings, a car approached ours head on, veering onto the mud to avoid a collision when Alice didn't slow down. I could swear it was Miss Simpson, an angry Miss Simpson from the way she'd tooted her horn. I squirmed lower in my seat, nervous of what Jonas might tell me.

"We didn't call."

"No."

"Do you think he'll be in?"

"Soon find out."

She parked in the clearing, next to a wood-stack, and together we walked to the front door of the run-down cottage. Alice knocked on the wooden door.

"What now?" a man's voice shouted.

She pushed the latch down and it opened. Jonas was lying on a double bed, on a maroon bedspread, two grey pillows plumped up behind him. There were two chairs in front of it, by a fireplace, sitting on a faded maroon rug, and a sink with two kitchen cupboards below it and one to the upper side of it on our left.

"It's us," Alice said.

He looked dopey, like Luella used to after a hot chocolate. "You didn't call," he smirked.

"Funny. Are you alright?"

"I stood on some glass."

He pointed to his bandaged feet. The room was spotless. It smelt of disinfectant. I couldn't bear the smell, it was too much like the morgue in the hospital. I left the door wide open.

"Can I make some tea?" asked Alice.

"I've only got coffee."

"Coffee then. No, you stay there. I'll do it."

He stared at the floor, the door, Alice's back as she looked in the cupboards for mugs.

"How did you hurt yourself?" I asked.

His eyes were half closed, like he really needed to be asleep.

"Gardening."

"Is it sore? It looks painful."

"A bit."

"Are you off work?"

"I guess I'll have to be. How's your new school?"

"The gardens aren't as pretty as here."

He chuckled to himself.

"Okay, that's bubbling." Alice rubbed her nose and headed out the door. "I just need to get a tissue."

"I've decided to move on too, like you have," Jonas slurred. "Back to Byron Bay. Why not, eh? It's time to go home."

I'd never heard of where he came from. "Why did you want to see me?" I asked.

"What?"

"Twice, three times if you include my old house. I saw you in the mirror."

"You weren't pregnant then?"

"What?"

"You must miss Luella so much. It's such a tragedy. When's your birthday? What month's it in again?"

Stupid, polite conversation; stupid, strange man. What the hell was wrong with him?

"You're an idiot, you know that?" I slammed the door behind me and got in the car.

"What's happened?"

"Can we go? We shouldn't have bothered coming. He's all drugged up. There's no point when someone's like that."

"But—"

"Now. Please Alice."

She reversed and headed back through the woods. "Do you want to stop and get some lunch? We could pop in to see Marjorie."

"No." I twisted my neck to look at the road we'd just passed. "You should have turned left there." Alice didn't slow down. "You need to turn around."

"I will when I find somewhere."

"There's nothing coming."

"It's too fast a road. I can't do it here."

"Alice."

"What?"

"Turn the car around. Now."

She pulled to a stop in Bridge Street.

"You missed the turning on purpose."

"I could really do with a coffee."

"Not here. Please."

"You should see your old friends, keep in touch."

"That's rich coming from you." I stuck my nail into my thigh, trying to puncture the cotton on my baby blue, cropped trousers. Words latched onto the roof of my mouth. If I said them out loud Alice would think me evil, throw me out, wonder what had really happened that night even though the bits I'd told were true. I couldn't risk her doubting me. It would all go mad again. "Sorry. I—"

"That's okay. I'm sorry too. We'll stop on the way home. It'll break up the driving."

The Awakening

I leant my head out of the dining room window. A breeze would be welcome. The forecast had promised a storm to follow the stillness; empty promises of the cheerful weathermen. Pear ice lolly juice dribbled down my chin. As I wiped it away, the lolly scraped over my hair, making the ends of my growing locks sticky. Now I'd have to wash it. The phone rang.

"Can you get that?" Alice said, pouring boiling water over the rice and turning on the gas.

A man asked if Alice and I lived there.

"Yes."

Alice started mouthing, "Tell them I'll call back," but she was too late. The ice lolly reverberated in my shaking hand, its juice sprinkling over the floor. Alice put down the knife and mushroom she was chopping.

"I'm sorry. I have to go. Sorry."

It wasn't meant to happen, not now. We were alright here, the two of us, the two of us living in her pretty house, windows open, walls white, light shining through.

"What's happened?"

"It's Mother. She's woken up."

~

The black metal gates were open. Alice's car bumped over lines of tarmac, the noise of the wheels getting louder as more loose gravel crunched beneath them.

"What's the number again?"

"637."

Marjorie had told Alice the plot number. She couldn't believe we weren't at the funeral, couldn't get over that we hadn't been told, had apologised again and again and again: "I never thought, it happened so quickly, I should have called, I just assumed, it didn't cross my mind, I'm so sorry, I just assumed she'd have told you, that someone would have."

Small wooden signs pointed in different directions, the numbers rising the higher the car climbed.

"There."

She braked and turned off the engine. "I'll wait in the car, unless you want me to come with you?" Shadows sprouted from the graves as the sun rose. "I really need to pee. Sorry. Do you want to come down with me? We can grab a coffee then come back together."

There was a fresh mound of dirt nine headstones along, fresh dirt for the dank dead. "You go. I'll stay here."

"Are you sure? I can bring you straight back, have a coffee later. It's no bother."

When I opened the car door, the sun warmed my ankles. "I'll see you in a bit."

Alice turned the car around, the front tyres kissing the grass in her three point turn. I tried to remember how Luella used to smell, the sound of her laugh, the feel of her hands. Hazy, rough memories flittered through my fingertips but nothing deeper. The blocking had worked too well. I stood in front of the new grave.

'Luella Jeffreys
Aged 16.'

That was all the headstone told a passerby: no beloved niece, loving sister, adored daughter of. I'd hoped she'd be next to our father's grave but the names on either side meant nothing to me. The one time we'd asked Mother where he was buried she'd told us it was none of our business and didn't matter anyway as what use was a dead daddy, for Christ's sake child, stop annoying your mother.

Luella shouldn't have been buried. In life she was always opening her arms, spinning and twirling, looking at the sky, laughing because we were going to leave home and rent a place with enough space for eating and sleeping; that was all we needed.

Memories banged against my forehead. Damn sister demanding all the focus. Again. Always drawing attention to the both of us when I knew to be quiet. And now look. No happy ending. There was no such thing. The wrong person was dead. It had all gone horribly wrong. I stamped on the fresh dirt and mud slipped into the gap in my shoe where pale pink canvas didn't quite meet the flesh.

Had Luella's body started rotting? After all that time on the freezing cold shelf, was she now melting super-fast? She'd be suffocating beneath the weight of the soil, hating the feel of it. She never wanted that. She said, "Burn me on a pyre then throw my ashes from a cliff. Let me fly and be free." She'd detest being trapped underground.

I started scooping mud off the grave. Slowly, methodically, big sweeps with my hands until the ground was even and a ridge of soil lay between Luella's grave and the one beside it. I felt eyes upon me and turned my head quickly expecting Alice to be smiling sympathetically, but no-one was there. Three trees stood together behind me, their low thick branches covered in hundreds of leaves, trunks wide enough that mourners could kick, lean, fall against them. Goose bumps erupted over my bare arms. I started digging. The soil got caught under my nails and stuck to my skin. My upper arms began to ache.

"Need some help?"

The sun blinded the face but the voice was familiar. I moved my hands over my eyebrows. Mud fell on my nose making it itch, making me sneeze.

"Bless you," said Mr Jonas. "You weren't at the funeral so I figured you'd come here. I thought you would be at it, for your sister, but then I- What's so funny?"

"Why are you here?"

"What?"

"I said why are you here? You keep turning up. You need to go away. This is private."

"But—"

"This is my time with her. Go away. Now."

"But I—"

"Go away!" I screamed, throat hurting from the effort. I shoved him on the chest with both hands but he only went back one step.

"Hey. Easy child." I pushed him again. He was a crazy man, turning up at my sister's grave, his head obviously demented from too much sun. A figure was walking up the hill. The shape, the hair, the walking from the shoulders rather than the hips, a familiar gait. Alice said she'd be here, she'd promised, but there was no sign of her car. I stepped from left to right, warming up to run, to escape the crazy adults. Then the figure waved and called my name. I nearly cried with stupid relief but instead waved back enthusiastically. Alice sprinted up the last curve.

"I ate some cake. Decided to walk it off. Jesus," she gasped. "Are you okay?" She turned to Jonas. "What the hell are you doing here?"

"I need to speak with Lara."

"As always. Look, this is her time, private time and—"

"That's what I said to him."

"But I—"

"I, I, I! It's always 'I' with you. Christ. What about her?"

"It's her I'm thinking of."

I dug my thumb nails into my index fingers. Alice turned on Jonas and punched him on the arm. "Leave her alone. Messing with her mind, like she's not got enough to deal with."

"Susan told me to talk to her."

"What? When?"

"At her house. Yesterday. I don't—"

"We've got to go." I tugged at Alice's sleeve.

"We need to talk. Please." He stepped in front of me.

"You need to talk. I need to go."

"When are you moving back?"

"Never."

"She said you're moving back in with her, now she's better."

"No. No, that's not right. She can't make me. Alice, come on. Now."

"She nearly died," said Jonas. "Have you even seen her to see how she is?"

"Alice," I pleaded.

"She's your mother. You have to—"

"You know nothing. Don't you dare tell me what to do when you know nothing."

The Visit

Alice sat with her feet on the sofa, her back resting against its arm. "She wants to see you."

"No."

"I'll stay with you."

"I can't. Please. You don't understand." She passed me a mint green, cotton handkerchief.

"She had a hard time of it you know, when she was young."

"So."

"Our mother was poorly. Mean. A bit loop-di-loo." Alice's hands fluttered through the air as if mimicking a butterfly.

"You came out nice."

"I was luckier."

"Why?"

"She was more tolerant of me. I don't know why."

"What did she do?"

"Susan?"

"Your mother."

"Stuff. You know. She had a bit of a temper on her. And our father never stopped her. I never got that, why he didn't intervene. I tried once, or I was going to but he said it was best not to get involved." She blinked fast. "I wouldn't leave you alone with her, not even for a second."

"You don't get it. The thought of seeing her, knowing I'd be in the same room as her. I can't."

"But it'd be a one off, the last time ever, I promise. In and out, then done for life. And afterwards we could visit Jeffrey's grave. She said she'll tell us where he's buried, if you agree to meet with her. You want to see your father's grave don't you?"

~

Alice parked ten doors down from the house. A fist of fear bashed my insides. Mother grew twenty foot in height. Dread coated me as the child was enveloped by the cruel giant. I shrank further. Alice put her hand on my arm.

"Don't let her ruin things, not any more."

That was the best she could offer, not maybe you'll become friends, start again, no pretending that she's not as bad as you think she is. I knew the visit would be awful. Sally had known, months ago, walking down the road. She'd wanted her and Sean to go inside with me. If I'd let them, it would have helped. I was sure of it and had added it to the list of things that were my fault: I should have read the signs, not been so wrapped up in myself, not given cause for further trouble, then who knew where me and Luella would be today, her alive, alive and us together.

In the wing mirror I saw Jonas walking along the road. I nudged Alice. She looked where I was pointing.

"Not again." She got out of the car. I stood behind her. I'd never seen him in shorts before, and a red T-shirt rather than a tatty woollen jumper.

"What are you doing here?" she demanded.

"I could ask you the same." Jonas sucked hard on his cigarette, frowning.

"We've come to find out where Lara's father's grave is. She wants to visit him."

"Right." He threw his cigarette butt onto the road. "Your mother invited me here. Midday and don't be late."

"That's the same as us." I turned to Alice. "I told you not to trust her. I said, didn't I? I told you but you didn't believe me. What do you think she's planning?"

"I don't know."

I stepped from left to right, desperate to run, needing Alice to go with me.

"There's only one way to find out you know," said Jonas. "We can go in together. Strength in numbers and all that."

"Lara?" Alice asked. "Can you do that? Last time ever?"

~

Jonas gave the door three knocks. She'd had it painted red so it was brighter than the old blood on the terracotta.

"Lara," Mother smiled, holding out the hand that wasn't gripping the wooden walking stick. My stomach cramped like after I'd eaten the bad smelling ham when I was eleven.

"Susan," said Alice. "Do you mind?"

She gestured at her sister to get out of the way. Mother shuffled to the side and Alice led me by the arm, past Mother, keeping herself between us. Jonas followed, sitting opposite us as I concentrated on not running from the room, thinking of the smell of freesias, the feel of flip flops rather than brown lace up shoes, pear ice lollies, sometimes even two in one day, Alice didn't mind.

Mother exaggerated her limp as she joined us, easing herself into the chair closest to the gardener.

"Right," started Alice. "Lara wants to visit her father's grave so—"

"I'm afraid that's not possible," replied Mother.

"You promised."

"No."

"Yes you did. You know you did. Tell us where he's buried."

"Where Jeffrey's buried? What does she want to know that for? It's not like she needs to say goodbye. She never even knew him."

"That's up to her."

"All those years without; there's no need to go now."

"She said they asked you, when they were little, where he was and if they could visit. You refused to tell them."

"I don't remember that."

"They were seven, that's right isn't it Lara? You told them they couldn't have dinner that night as they were too impertinent."

"No," said Mother.

"You said they were to never ask you again."

"Nope."

"Stop laughing. Christ. You always laugh when you shouldn't. It's not funny."

Mother pretended to wipe tears of mirth from her eyes. I closed my eyes like Alice had told me to when things got stressful: breathe in the good, expel the bad, breathe in the good, breathe out bad thoughts of my mother.

"Tell us where he's buried."

"You really want to see your father?" Mother turned to face me.

"I told you she does," said Alice.

"I'm talking to her."

"And I'm talking to you. Tell me."

"No. And she'll do as I say. *I'm* her mother."

"No."

"Yes. And this is my house. You're not the one in charge here."

"Listen, you—"

"No. You're not the boss of me."

"Christ. Do you hear yourself? Tell us where he is and we'll leave."

"You've made me cross now. Lara. Look at me. Lara!"

"Please. Just tell us where the grave is," begged Alice.

"Enough's enough Susan," Jonas added.

Mother leant towards him and put a finger on his lips. He brushed it off. "Lara, Jonas and I have some news, happy news we think." She stroked her belly. "Oh my." She paused for cheap, dramatic effect. "I can't tell you where your father's grave is because he isn't buried, because he isn't dead, because he's here, because this is him, because, because, because, because, because," her voice crescendoed as she held the note and raised her hand out like the students when they did opera singing in assemblies. "This is your father Lara. Can you believe it? Your father is Mr Jonas, Calton Jonas, J for Jonas. I saw the blood on the sheet of paper, snooping were you?" She smiled. "Oh I'm sorry, is this a shock? Of course it is. You've turned so pale."

Calton. All these first names for the first time. Calton and Susan sitting in a tree, k-i-s-s-i-n-g.

"Stop it." Jonas pushed her hand off his thigh. "Why would you do this like this? Why now?" His face had a green tint to it. Why wasn't he denying?

"What else am I supposed to say? There's no easy way is there? You've still got your father's watch I see. Now when you die you can leave it to your daughter."

"How do you know she's mine? It was only once. And you were married."

"Widowed."

"You're crazy."

"I beg your pardon?" Mother sat as tall as she could.

"Where's he buried please?" I mumbled.

"You can't have a child, run out on them like you did, then waltz back in denying everything, then want to be half in half out like some goddamn Christ almighty failure of a handyman saviour. All those years I had to raise her by myself while you did whatever you pleased. You owe me."

"She's a loon," Jonas pleaded with me and Alice.

"I am not," she shrilled. "How dare you speak like that about the mother of your child?"

"Where's he buried?" demanded Alice.

"Who? Jeffrey? How would I know? They took him away, wouldn't even let me attend the funeral."

"Why not?"

"Because I was pregnant with another man's child, of course."

"You had two," said Jonas. "She had two. Two at the same time. How can only Lara be mine? Ha! You forgot about Luella." He raised his hands triumphantly in the air.

"Superfetation," said Mother. "I felt different after we did it, I know I did. I was already pregnant when you got me with that one and sure enough, when they were born she was smaller, much smaller, so she's yours. Even the doctors said so. They're the ones that told me, a whole seven weeks younger by the size of it."

No-one had ever muddled us up, not ever, not the form teacher, not Marjorie, not the children in school, no-one, not ever.

"Where's my thumb?"

"What?"

"My thumb. You kept Luella's. Where's mine?"

"How should I know?"

"You must. You took it. Why did you keep hers and not mine?"

"What are you on about? What? You think I liked her more? You're going too deep girl. Soon as I had you, I wished both of you had never been born."

"Susan!" said Alice.

There it was. She did not care. She'd never loved me. There was my freedom.

"I thought you'd die you know. I thought everything would be okay because you'd stay unconscious in the hospital then die. I really wanted you to, wished you had, always will do." I walked out of the house and waited by the car.

"She's barking," Alice said, unlocking the door. "Is there anything you need to tell me? A story we need to get straight?"

"What do you mean?" I sniffed hard, the snot catching in my throat.

"About that night, if you wanted her to die and—"

"No. Life would be better without her in it, that's all. There's nothing more to it."

"I know. I do. I get it."

"I can't live with her again."

"You don't have to."

"I'll be no bother at all, honestly. And I'll leave as soon as I'm eighteen, I promise."

"You can stay with me as long as you like. I thought you knew that."

"I'll get a job, pay rent—"

"Don't be silly. You're doing me a favour. I like the company." Rain started falling, turning our dark brown hair black. "Let's go home. Let's leave the liars."

But before we could, Jonas joined us. "Are you alright?"

"Why now? Why did you come forward now?"

"I didn't know before. I had no clue until I saw her at the school last summer, so I watched and—"

"You should have kept quiet, or stayed up in Byron. Is that where you live now? Why didn't you?"

"She'd seen me. She got my number from Marjorie and called saying she had stuff to tell me but it had to be in person, made out that I couldn't miss the funeral, that it would have been wrong. I don't know. You do what she says don't you? Everyone does. And I thought maybe it'd be better to hear what she had to say, then talk to you and—"

"Better for who? Look at the chaos you've caused."

"She caused, not me. I didn't do it. Anyway, secrets are no good."

"They can be. That one would have been."

"I don't think so."

"The reason you let her tell me was for you wasn't it? It had nothing to do with me, with how I'd feel, and you know what? That makes you someone I don't want anything to do with."

"But I can help now, help make your life better."

"Too little too late Mister Jonas. Alice, let's go."

The Living

"I have to go on a work conference. It'll be a really long day so I won't be back until late. Do you mind? I'd rather not leave you but it's tricky what with Elizabeth being off this week and me having had so much time off this year."

Rather not.

Out of love and worry like a carer should feel, rather than the distrust of what a day's freedom might offer me.

~

Beds needed weeding. I grabbed the trowel from the shed by the back gate and started turning the soil. Halfway down, Alice picked up the fork and joined in. We moved onto the longest bed, nearly fifty foot, running the whole length of her garden.

"We always had to do the weeding, Luella and I."

"You like gardening?"

"I said *had to*."

"Ah. You don't *have to* do this one."

"I don't mind. Now it's a choice." I lifted her silver, wire chicken sculpture onto the grass so I could turn the soil beneath it. "It was an accident. You've made out like it wasn't sometimes, but it was."

"Sorry."

"Why are you crying?"

I could not take her tears. I curled up like a snail. Alice sat crossed legged, breathing in for three, pause, out for four, in for three, pause, out for four.

"The sky's pretty today, all those little fluffy clouds. That's what I love about living here; I could watch it forever," she said.

"Do you think she'll turn up one day?"

"No."

"How come?"

Alice changed her position to kneeling. "I know things. From her past. She'll leave us be, I'm sure of it."

I wasn't ready to hear what else my mother had got up to. My lips curled down. I felt so tired as I rolled onto my side. "It would have been nice. I think sometimes, it would have been nice to have parents like other people had, ones who cared, or at least one who cared. It's not fair that Jeffrey died is it? I reckon he might have liked us."

"He'd have adored you. It's tragic he died so young." Alice laid her hand gently on my back and started stroking it. "I didn't go to a conference yesterday. Sorry. I went to see your mother, just to get some info, like she'd promised. It wasn't fair that she didn't tell us anything. And it was worth it. Turns out you've got a grandad, in Canberra." All I could see were images of Santa and God. What did a grandad even look like? "I got his address. I thought we could visit him, when you're ready, if you want to. He'll have photos and stuff. You could learn more about your father."

"Find you what really happened to him."

"What do you mean?"

"Do I look like him? The grandad?"

"I don't know. Probably." I could quite happily never open my eyes again, just let the clouds keep passing on over me. "They're not the be all and end all you know, parents. People get shitty ones. It happens. Don't let Susan destroy what's ahead of you though. It'll get better. I promise. You can have a good life."

"In an apartment with two rooms."

"If that's what you want, yeah."

I scratched the stump where the top of my thumb used to be. I wanted to know what they looked like, if Luella and I looked like the other Jeffreys. I sat up. I would live a little.

Acknowledgements

Thank you to my wonderful husband and daughters for your love and support, and your patience for all the times I'm just doing some writing.

Emma, Pippa, Dom, Alex, and Mike P. – thank you for being my readers – your positivity and faith in my stories means the world to me.

A big thanks to my brilliant proof reader and even more brilliant friend, Sue. And to Jennie Rawlings @HelloSerifim for creating a perfect cover, and Leigh Forbes @writeleighso for the excellent type-setting.

Finally, a huge thank you to all the people who are so generous in sharing their knowledge about writing and publishing, in person and online, especially Sarah Savitt at Virago who was such a lovely mentor, Lounge Marketing whose newsletters and website are so helpful, and Jericho Writers for their excellent Library section.

PAH

Calton Jonas, orphaned at eighteen,
runs away and gets a job at a morgue.
Jeffrey Jeffreys, having never been on a date,
suddenly gets married.
Susan Brown, baby in her belly,
is unexpectedly widowed.
A tragic accident, the town whispers.
But what do they know...

Coming 2020

For more information on Orla Owen and her books visit
her website at www.orlaowen.com or follow her on
Twitter @orlaowenwriting

Printed in Great Britain
by Amazon

35877421R00161